The Talk of the Beau Monde

*Three unconventional sisters for
three infamous lords*

As the daughters of a famous portrait artist, sisters
Faith, Hope and Charity Brookes are regular
features at the best balls and soirees—and in the
gossip columns!

Daring to follow their dreams of being an artist,
writer and singer means scandal is never far
away, especially when they each fall for titled—
and infamous—gentlemen who set
the *ton*'s tongues wagging!

Read Faith's story in
The Viscount's Unconventional Lady

Read Hope's story in
The Marquess Next Door

And Charity's story
How Not to Chaperon a Lady

All available now!

Author Note

The Brookes sisters have been part of my life for a year now, so I am sad to say goodbye to them as I release the final book of my The Talk of the Beau Monde trilogy into the wild.

I've had to research Regency portrait painting and European diplomacy for Faith and Piers's book (*The Viscount's Unconventional Lady*) and the nineteenth-century publishing industry and private lunatic asylums for Hope and Luke's (*The Marquess Next Door*). For this one, Charity and Griff's story, it has been the trials and tribulations of opera singing, regional theaters, steam engines and onion fairs.

Yes—you did just read that last sentence correctly, but I won't spoil the story by telling why anybody bothered to have an onion fair!

Charity Brookes has been a delight throughout the previous two installments. She's loud, extroverted, exuberant, mischievous and flirtatious. A real bundle of fun whose opera star began to rise in the first book and then shine in the second. Now we see her embark on a sold-out solo tour of the north, but with every Brookes busy, she gets the worst possible chaperon—her childhood nemesis, Gruff Griff the Fun Spoiler...

VIRGINIA HEATH

—

How Not to Chaperon a Lady

HARLEQUIN
HISTORICAL

Recycling programs
for this product may
not exist in your area.

ISBN-13: 978-1-335-40738-2

How Not to Chaperon a Lady

This edition published by arrangement with Harlequin Books S.A.

For questions and comments about the quality of this book,
please contact us at CustomerService@Harlequin.com.

Harlequin Enterprises ULC
22 Adelaide St. West, 40th Floor
Toronto, Ontario M5H 4E3, Canada
www.Harlequin.com

Printed in U.S.A.

When **Virginia Heath** was a little girl, it took her ages to fall asleep, so she made up stories in her head to help pass the time while she was staring at the ceiling. As she got older, the stories became more complicated—sometimes taking weeks to get to their happy ending. One day she decided to embrace her insomnia and start writing them down. Virginia lives in Essex, UK, with her wonderful husband and two teenagers. It still takes her forever to fall asleep...

Books by Virginia Heath

Harlequin Historical

His Mistletoe Wager
Redeeming the Reclusive Earl
The Scoundrel's Bartered Bride
Christmas Cinderellas
"Invitation to the Duke's Ball"

The Talk of the Beau Monde

The Viscount's Unconventional Lady
The Marquess Next Door
How Not to Chaperon a Lady

Secrets of a Victorian Household

Lilian and the Irresistible Duke

The King's Elite

The Mysterious Lord Millcroft
The Uncompromising Lord Flint
The Disgraceful Lord Gray
The Determined Lord Hadleigh

Visit the Author Profile page
at Harlequin.com for more titles.

For Rebecca Silverman

Soprano extraordinaire

Chapter One

As the magnificent masterpiece that is The Marriage of Figaro *enters its final week, I have it on the highest authority, Dear Reader, that its youngest and brightest star, Miss Charity Brookes, has already secured another lucrative singing engagement. As soon as the final curtain falls at Covent Garden, the vivacious young soprano will head north to delight the musically starved masses there...*

Whispers from Behind the Fan
—April 1815

'I am not saying he isn't a perfectly nice gentleman.' Charity patted her friend's arm in the hope it banished the wounded expression now etched in her face. 'Nor am I saying Captain Sinclair isn't a thoroughly decent sort either, as he is undeniably both of those things. But there are gentlemen and there are *gentlemen,* Dorothy, so granting him both waltzes simply because he was the first to ask for them tonight isn't sensible, as it sends a clear message to all the other gentlemen here that you are taken.'

'But he was waiting at the door...specifically for me.'

'Which is all rather lovely and hugely flattering, yet you still shouldn't have blithely allowed him both. The waltz is...' An incredibly significant dance as far as the three Brookes sisters were concerned, when she considered that both Faith and Hope had fallen head over heels in love after their first waltzes with their now besotted husbands. 'Well...it's special, that is all because a gentleman only asks a lady to waltz if he has designs on her. Everybody knows that. Giving one out makes a statement—but two! And to the same man, then you might as well give up all hope of anyone else asking you to dance ever again.'

'So I shouldn't dance with him at all?' Now Dorothy looked crestfallen after thoroughly misinterpreting all her friend's sensible advice, staring mournfully at the Captain across the ballroom as if the sun rose and set with him. 'Even though I desperately want to?'

'Of course, you should dance with him. He is both charming and handsome and you will look very striking together on the dance floor. But only once at any ball. Those are the rules and they aren't just my rules either, Dorothy. Everyone knows what two waltzes mean. Simply tell him that you made a mistake and that he can have the first waltz but that you had previously promised the second to another. That keeps him keen and your options open.' Which was the whole point of Charity's cautionary advice in the first place, as in the last month her friend had rather worryingly nailed her colours firmly to Captain Sinclair's mast. 'And it also gives Lord Tevitt the opportunity to ask you too. The poor man has been staring at you longingly since you arrived.'

'Dance with who *you* want to, Dottie.' Typically, at

that moment Griffith Philpot decided to stop ignoring them to interfere and purposely contradict her. 'If my brotherly opinion is worth anything, I much prefer Captain Sinclair over the chinless Lord Tevitt and always have. And so what if everyone makes assumptions about the pair of you? Particularly if those assumptions are correct.' As his sister smiled he shot Charity a withering glance before running more interference. 'Sinclair is a sensible man of substance.'

Such a typically Gruff Griff answer. Charity rolled her eyes. 'There is substance and *substance*. And while it is true that the good Captain is almost as eminently sensible as Griffith here...' she pulled a face to ensure that her best friend's reliably irritating elder brother knew she found him as dull as dishwater '...there are plenty of other sensible gentlemen here too and a great many of them also have other more attractive attributes to recommend them.' It was second nature to always pull him down a peg or two, especially for his lack of breeding. A petty retribution for his canny knack of always making her feel less than perfect.

'Like stately piles and ancient titles, I suppose?' As usual, he stared back at her as if she was talking utter rot, making her feel six years old again and doomed to never pass muster. 'You would have my sister compromise her future happiness to chase such shallow attributes, Charity?'

That was his stock-in-trade answer because he always thought her shallow, which of course meant that she had to prove she didn't give two figs for his lowly opinion. 'While a captain is better than a mere mister—' like *Mr* Griffith Philpot, for example '—a captain is no match for an earl, and whether you approve of that or not, Griff, even you cannot deny that such an elevation in station would inevitably give Dorothy a much better life in the long run than Captain Sinclair ever could.'

Both her sisters had flourished since marrying their lords—in their private lives and in their careers. Faith's portraits were now almost as sought after as their father's and Hope's first book had positively flown off the shelves and there was already huge anticipation of the second. And, of course, they were suddenly welcomed and lauded everywhere. Although in fairness to her sisters, their success would have likely happened irrespective of whom they had married but she wouldn't state that part in front of Griff because it would make him right even though she secretly agreed with him.

He shook his dark head with no attempt to disguise his blatant irritation. 'My sister is an heiress who can well afford that better life for herself, as you well know, and that irrefutable fact is at the root of Lord Tevitt's sudden attraction to her. Whereas Captain Sinclair was partial to her before he took his commission and long before my father decided to make her a target for fortune hunters last year by announcing to the world she came with fifty thousand pounds.' A decision which had caused much consternation in the normally harmonious Philpot family between father and son which they still locked horns over, and which had turned Griff into the most annoyingly overprotective brother on earth who had returned to town on the back of it. 'Therefore, not only is that *mere* Captain a sensible man of substance, but a genuine one to boot. One who has an honest affection for my sister. I would be remiss in my duty as her brother not to point that out.'

When he put it like that, drat him, there was no real arguing the point. A title was all well and good, but it was no substitute for character. There were good lords, like her sisters' husbands Luke and Piers, but there were twice as many bad ones. She didn't trust Lord Tevitt's motives either, so he had been a very poor example to use to illustrate her point.

If he hadn't been Griffith Philpot, the only man in the world who had never shown the slightest bit of interest in her and had been her disapproving tormentor since she had been six, then she would have conceded it. However, since his return to Bloomsbury last year, he tolerated her less now that she was a grown woman than he had when he had been ten, therefore hell would have to freeze over before she ever agreed with him on any subject when he was digging his supercilious heels in.

'As an heiress, Dorothy has the pick of the crop, Griff, and she deserves the chance to peruse the entire harvest before she makes a hasty decision which will affect the rest of her life and her future happiness. Captain Sinclair has only just returned after two years away, during which time even you must concede he failed to send her one single letter. Therefore, I am not as convinced of his honest affection as you seem to be and I would be remiss in my duty as her oldest and dearest friend if I did not point that out too.'

Griff scowled, which was a sure sign he didn't have an immediate answer to her hastily cobbled together argument, so she patted herself on the back for her quick thinking despite knowing it wasn't entirely true. Any fool with eyes could see that the painfully shy Captain Sinclair was hopelessly in love with Dorothy and always had been, the poor thing. It was that shyness which had prevented him from making a declaration before he went off to war in his dashing regimentals. More worryingly, and no doubt selfishly, Charity was becoming increasingly convinced her best friend now shared the sentiment. Which was likely one of the main reasons why she was trying to slow things down between them, because now that both her sisters were deliriously settled, if Dorothy sprinted headfirst into marriage any time soon she would be the only single lady left from their close-knit childhood circle.

That uncomfortable truth niggled.

Because of course she wanted her friend to be happy, just as she had wanted Faith and Hope to be happy, and as a hopeless romantic at heart, not to mention the product of two happily married parents, she really did want that to be with a man who adored Dorothy. But Charity had also dreamed of the same for herself, desperately wanting a happily ever after as perfect as her sisters had found. She wanted a spiritual connection with a man who gazed at her with the same mutual adoration as Piers looked at Faith and Luke looked at Hope. It really made no difference if that man were a peer or a pauper as long as she loved him and he loved her back. Unfortunately, that heady state continued to elude her as the prime candidate she had selected was proving to be terribly slow on the uptake and no closer to falling in love with her now than he had been a year ago when she had first singled him out.

Against her better judgement and as her friend scurried off to break the bad news to her Captain, she allowed her eyes to wander to where Lord Denby, the handsome and charming heir to the Duke of Loughton, laughed with his usual gang of cronies. Despite eleven months of determined flirting, coincidental encounters and the occasional stolen kiss, he still hadn't made any more of a public declaration of intent towards her than the occasional dance. Usually when she had chivvied him into it. In private, however, he was beyond keen and made no secret of his fervent desire for her. Which meant that she was starting to think she had nailed her colours to entirely the wrong mast herself as her future duke didn't seem the least bit inclined to properly court her and likely wouldn't even know she was here tonight unless she purposely bumped into him again.

Too late, she realised Griff was watching her. Not only was he watching her, the wretch had angled his big body to face Lord Denby, his fingers tapping his annoyingly square chin as if pondering a great mystery. 'I suppose he'd be an entirely acceptable candidate to bestow both waltzes on? Assuming, of course, that by your mercenary rhetoric a captain is better than a mere mister and an earl is no match for a future duke.' He huffed out an unconvincing sigh as he shrugged. 'If only you weren't largely invisible to him, Charity, no matter how hard you throw yourself at him.'

She smiled knowingly, not wanting Griff to realise he had read the depressing situation entirely correctly. 'If that is what everyone thinks, then we are clearly doing a very good job of hiding things.' Denby was all over her like a rash if they were alone, and while she had hoped granting him a few liberties might make him yearn for more, the only thing he seemed to yearn for was taking her to bed.

'Oh, so he's purposely ignoring you, is he?' He was amused now rather than convinced, forcing her to suppress the urge to knock the smug smile from his face as she used to do as a child when he riled her to breaking point and instead summon every bit of her acting prowess to remain suitably unperturbed. Let him think what he wanted, it would be a cold day in hell before she allowed him to see the truth. 'What restraint the besotted fellow has if he possesses the willpower to avoid even glancing your way after all the trysts you have engaged in.'

Sometimes Griff's intuitiveness really grated. 'You know what the gossip columns are like. Or at least you would know if you were interesting enough for them to want to write about you.'

'True.' He took an unoffended sip from the customary glass of champagne he had been nursing for at least the last half an hour to ensure he avoided having to dance with anyone. 'It's either that or my lack of effort at courting them which keeps my name blessedly out of the things. But then, I do not require the constant attention and admiration of the masses that some individuals do to feel content about myself.'

The barb stung, exactly as it was intended to, but she shrugged it off exactly as she always did, wishing she didn't care that he disapproved of her so when she had always craved his approval most of all. An unfortunate character trait which had only got worse in the year since he had returned, no matter how much she tried to fight against it. 'That is just as well, really, Griff, isn't it? Because you would feel disappointed for ever if you did.'

As the last bars of the dance played, she made a great show of consulting her full-to-the-brim card ensuring that he could see all of the names of the gentlemen who had clamoured to be on it and tried not to feel relieved to see her next, and decidedly lacklustre, titled partner cutting a swathe through the crowds to fetch her from the one man who always saw too much. 'But as scintillating as your company continues to be this evening, I fear you must excuse me.' She managed to time her about-turn perfectly to coincide with her partner's arrival and used every drop of her theatrical training to beam at him as she curtsied. 'Lord Rigsby—what perfect timing.' Because once again, Griff had left her feeling unsettled, uncertain and not quite good enough. The least impressive Brookes out of the supremely talented Brookes clan, not that she had ever admitted that to anyone, and the trailing third place in the three-person race that had always been her life.

It galled that he kept watching her.

Despite promising himself he would fully immerse himself in the company of others this time, Griff's uncompliant eyes continually drifted towards Charity of their own accord exactly as they always did. In fact, tonight they had been particularly wayward to such a ridiculous extent he could probably recite each one of her many dance partners from the lovelorn Lord Rigsby to the illustrious Lord Denby she put so much stock in and who was currently twirling her around the floor in a waltz. And by the dreamy look in her big, blue eyes, the blighter was thoroughly charming the minx in the process.

Griff loathed him with every fibre of his being. Denby was all flash and no substance. Overconfident, over-polished, wore over-tasselled Hessians, over-pomaded hair, over-the-top brocaded waistcoats and over-complicated cravat knots in which he constantly wore his ridiculous quail's-egg-sized emerald stickpin like a placard of his wealth and status. Yet he also understood that his intense hatred of the man was as futile as his misplaced jealousy was irrational and that Charity was at the root cause of all of it.

Miss Charity Grace Brookes.

The bane of his existence since childhood.

The undisputed belle of each and every ball. Fêted

and sought after wherever she went. Gifted with the sublime voice of an angel, the skill to light up a stage or a room and a face that would easily launch a thousand ships. Every man wanted her, and every woman wanted to be her.

Beautiful. Effervescent. Witty. Ambitious. Meddlesome. Valiant and vain. Indiscreet. Indomitable. Incomparable. Alluring and intoxicating. Certainly as dangerous a flirt as any woman he had ever encountered and yet the most loyal and tolerant of best friends to his flighty baby sister Dottie, who hung on her every word as if it were gospel and who the dangerous minx frequently led astray.

Charity was the infuriating fly in his ointment. The persistent pain in his neck. A complete conundrum of a woman who he still couldn't work out despite almost two decades of trying, and for some reason the most unfortunate be-all and end-all as far as his wayward eyes were concerned.

Fortunately, his eminently sensible head had always had her full measure, else he'd have been as doomed to the same terminal disappointment in himself as the hapless Rigsby was. Never quite good enough for the lofty heights she had set her determined sights on and not at all the sort of man she was destined to snare and make miserable.

Thank goodness!

At least that fool was a fully ordained member of the blue-blooded aristocracy, ergo he stood a smidgeon of a chance with her. Whereas Griff was no more aristocratic than she was, but unlike Charity, was quite content to stay so.

He was also perfectly content with the fact that she would never be his. Even without the reassuring barrier of their sibling-like relationship, the last thing he wanted in his life was a woman who was as much hard work as she would inevitably prove to be. Only a complete idiot would choose a wife who would run him a merry dance, flirt with all and sundry, kiss them behind his back, ruthlessly pursue her own ambition and never be content with her lot, and he wasn't a self-destructive idiot. Not that she would ever want him anyway, so it was a rather moot point which didn't deserve quite as much pondering as he was giving it.

When he did seek a wife, and one of these days he was determined he would go hunting for one, Griff wanted the sort of marriage his parents enjoyed. A blissful meeting of minds and shared goals. An oasis in the desert and a calm port in a storm. A haven of mutual trust, devoted fidelity and ordered serenity. Miss Charity Grace Brookes was capable of none of those things and never had been. She had been a crashing wave of disorganised and determined chaos since the first moment she had barrelled into his life and broken his favourite toy. No amount of glue and paper patches had ever made that damned kite fly again—a telling metaphor and a stark omen of warning if ever there was one, and one he had always heeded as if his life depended on it.

Charity was best avoided.

If only his unhealthy, lifelong obsession with her would pass as he had incessantly prayed for seventeen long years that it would. Well perhaps not an entire seventeen years. When he had left London to learn his father's business from the ground up, spending an idyllic four years in their main engine factory in Sheffield, he had hardly thought about her at all. She had crossed his mind a time or two, or ten. Possibly a couple of hundred times, maybe…daily.

'Not dancing again, Griff?' Faith, Charity's oldest sister and his oldest friend, came up beside him and saved him from further unhelpful contemplation. 'You do realise it is considered the height of rudeness for a gentleman not to dance when there is a glut of eligible young ladies stood around without partners?'

'I have always hated dancing, you know that.' Dancing involved making a spectacle of yourself while admitting to the ballroom you fancied someone enough to ask them, while he preferred to keep all his cards close to his chest. Especially because the only woman he currently fancied was the one he wouldn't and couldn't touch. 'Although I confess that nowadays I dislike eligible young ladies more.'

'No, you don't.' She gestured to a nearby gaggle of young ladies who were doing a very poor job of pretending not to stare at him. '*You* hate being considered eligible.'

There was no denying that. When his father had misguidedly strapped a target on Dorothy to lure an aristocratic son-in-law into the family with a dowry of fifty thousand pounds, he had also strapped a bigger one on Griff. Now the entire world and his wife were alerted to the fact that the Philpot & Son Manufacturing Company was worth a fortune and, as the son alluded to in the company's proud title, so was he.

'You do realise I hold you entirely responsible for that intolerable fact.' Griff huffed out a put-upon sigh to amuse her. 'If you hadn't gone and married a viscount and your mother hadn't gloated about that tremendous social coup to my mother, then dear Mama wouldn't have harboured such futile delusions of grandeur herself. Some friend you turned out to be. And I am still absolutely furious at Hope for rapidly following suit as it's only made things worse. This last year has been unbearable on the back of it. So unbearable, I wish I'd stayed in Sheffield.' For more reasons than one—even though that main reason had pulled him back in the first place.

'I am sorry.' But by her broad smile she clearly wasn't. 'And I am sure Hope is too. But look on the bright side, at least now the women are positively throwing themselves at you, you do not have to make any effort at all with the ladies. Most gentlemen would kill for such a scandalous predicament. Perhaps you should embrace your new popularity a bit and have some fun for a change. Have a few mad and passionate affairs before you inevitably get caught in the parson's mousetrap too. All work and no play makes Griff a very dull boy indeed.'

'That's the second time I have been called dull by a member of the Brookes clan in as many hours.' Of their own accord, his eyes wandered to where the youngest sister danced again before he ruthlessly tore them away. 'I am rapidly going off your family.' The Brookes and the Philpots were closely entwined, God help him. How the blazes could he avoid any of them, and one in particular, when their parents had always lived in one another's pockets?

'That is too bad as I was about to invite you to a party.'

'When you know full well I abhor them almost as much as I hate dancing.'

'It isn't that sort of party, you old curmudgeon. Just family and close friends so no airs nor graces. A private celebration at my house.'

'What are we celebrating?'

'Charity.' Of course they were. Of late, and with her glittering star rapidly rising, he couldn't seem to escape her no matter how much he tried. And he really, really tried. 'They are going to extend her run at Covent Garden through the entire summer. Isn't that marvellous?'

More success to go to her ridiculously pretty head. 'Indeed, it is.'

'We only found out this afternoon, so it's still a secret until all the contracts are signed, but they are so keen they are prepared to work around her tour of the north.' The newspapers had droned on about that ad nauseam in the last week too. Solo performances at the four biggest provincial theatres in the country. And all expenses and a king's ransom paid for the honour. Lincoln, Manchester, Leeds and York. Four blessed weeks and hundreds of miles of good road between them when he would be blissfully free of her again. 'So it doesn't spoil her and Dorothy's little adventure in the slightest.'

'Dorothy?'

'Your sister is accompanying her. It was all arranged last week. Didn't she tell you?'

'Not that I recall.' Of course she hadn't. Because Dottie knew it would be a cold day in hell before he ever allowed that potential disaster to happen on his watch.

Chapter Two

Rumours abound, Gentle Reader, that at Lady
Bulphan's soirée last night Miss C. from Blooms-
bury and Lord D. shared more than a moment to-
gether, in the same orangery where she allegedly
kissed that cavalry soldier last year...

Whispers from Behind the Fan
—April 1815

'But we have both Lily and Evan as chaperons!' Charity glared at her mother dumbfounded. 'Not only are they husband and wife, you and Papa trust them implicitly, so we certainly do not need another tagging along.' Particularly if the additional chaperon was Gruff Griff Philpot. The one person on the planet guaranteed to royally spoil all her fun and squeeze all the joy out of her achievements.

'I am afraid Mrs Philpot has insisted, dear, for propriety's sake, and she makes a valid case. There are some vile people out there who would take advantage of two young ladies alone and, as mothers, we have a solemn duty to protect our daughters' precious V-I-R-T-U-E. A family member will do that more diligently than a lady's maid and a coachman. As loyal as Lily and Evan are, they will likely not be allowed into most of the entertainments you are bound to be invited to, which will leave you both unchaperoned for huge swathes of time.'

Which was precisely why Charity had argued so vociferously for Lily and Evan in the first place. This was supposed to be an adventure. Her moment. The one time that the limelight was firmly on her and nobody else. And a taste of freedom she and Dorothy had hitherto not experienced as the two youngest daughters, free from the well-meant shackles of their over-protective families. No doubt the intuitive Griff had worked that part of her cunning plan out and then gone to work scaring his mother. The wretch had always been a spoilsport.

'But Griff, Mama? Of all the people significantly better suited to the role, surely there is someone more appropriate than him?' The man who had never found anything about her unique or impressive. The one who had always preferred both her sisters to her. Who she had positively worshipped as a child, who she had always irritated without trying and yet still couldn't fathom. Too handsome, too tall and too clever for his own good, and likely the most unreadable and vexing bachelor who ever walked God's earth.

Bachelor!

Out of the blue, an idea hit. 'Surely it is highly improper for a single gentleman to accompany two single ladies, one of whom he isn't the slightest bit related to? With all the enforced proximity of a month away, he might get inappropriate I-D-E-A-S about me, Mama.'

Instead of frowning while she considered that glaring impropriety, her mother threw her head back and laughed, clearly well aware that Griff had rarely ever looked at her once, let alone longingly. 'Sometimes you do say the funniest things, Charity! As if Griff would ever consider you in that way! Why, you are practically brother and sister and as such, he will protect you with the exact same diligence as he will protect Dorothy. Griff has always been the most sensible one out of the five of you and the most responsible. The perfect older brother.'

Their families often threw around that term— brother. It had always baffled her because there was nothing brotherly about her relationship with Griff. At best nowadays, it was distant, but usually it was fraught. They tolerated one another because they had to and since his return not so much. Instead of mellowing over time, after four years away his disapproval of her seemed to have increased in the last year. Disproportionately in her humble opinion as she had far more sense at twenty-three than she had had at eighteen when he had left, though he had made no secret of the fact he despaired of her then too. In Griff's rigid mind, the very things she had always enjoyed, like dancing, chatting, flirting and having fun, had always been the things he most took umbrage at.

'What if I ask Hope to come?' Hope owed her a huge favour because Charity had known all along that she and her now husband had shared adjoining balconies which they met upon in secret when her parents were fast asleep. She had known and selflessly kept it a secret so that her sensible sister could finally have some fun. Hope had also stolen her sister's moment in January and still felt guilty that her book had come out on the same day as Charity had made her debut as Susanna in *Figaro*. Therefore, she doubly owed her.

'Aside from the fact it's hardly fair to drag a pregnant

woman across the country, or that it is horribly short notice and she has another book coming out imminently, I cannot imagine Luke will allow it. Impending fatherhood has made him more overprotective than usual and before you suggest Faith in her stead, she is as swamped with commissions as your father is and already has her hands full with your new niece.' A niece who had decided to arrive the day after Charity's debut too, overshadowing the achievement she had worked diligently for years for yet again. As much as she adored little Raphaela and her big sister, she couldn't help but wish the pair of them had waited just a little while longer.

'I would come, but I had already committed to the concert in Bath before your offer came in and I wouldn't like to let them down.' Her mother hated to disappoint her fans. 'I suppose you could ask Dorothy's mother...' Which would be worse than having her own ridiculously famous and talented soprano mother on the tour because Mrs Philpot had eyes like a hawk—exactly like her dratted son. 'But as Griff already has urgent business to attend to in the north anyway, I dare say it makes little sense to have both of them accompany you.'

Urgent business that had doubtless become significantly more urgent when he had discovered his little sister was spending the entire month alone with her. Charity was sorely tempted to dig her heels in and rescind Dorothy's invitation simply to prevent Gruff Griff from tagging along and putting a heavy-footed dampener on everything.

At her despondent expression, her mother cupped her cheek, smiling in sympathy as she cruelly sealed her fate. 'While I appreciate why you are desperately unhappy to have your wings clipped in this way, we both know that you could do with a dose of sensible on this trip, my darling. I will sleep sounder knowing he will be there to temper your usual recklessness and you are bound to have a splendid time irrespective of Griff's presence because you always do. You have always been my most tenacious and driven daughter, the most like me, and not even Griff's guiding hand could temper that. Come, the carriage is waiting outside, and you don't want to be late for your own party.'

Charity was subdued for most of the journey to Faith's house in Grosvenor Square, until she decided that Gruff Griff the Fun Spoiler could go to hell. Her mother was right, she was tenacious and she was driven. She had always had things to prove to herself and the world, no doubt that came from being the youngest and by default the last of her siblings to do everything. But this was her time to shine and she had earned it!

He could try to curtail her as much as he wanted because she fully intended to do things her own way regardless, exactly as she always had. When she wasn't working, she fully intended to have fun irrespective of what he had to say on the subject. Woe betide him if he laid down a slew of unreasonable rules, because rules were meant to be broken and, he was well aware, she had always been a rebel at heart. And as for the entertainments she hoped to be invited to, she would jolly well dance every dance with myriad handsome gentlemen until the small hours to vex him and spend as little time with *him* as was humanly possible.

Then, and only when they reached Sheffield, would she tell him the absolute best bit.

That she had made other plans for her last week in the north that rendered Griff redundant. Secret plans which she hadn't yet shared with Dorothy that meant that she couldn't possibly stay at the Philpots' northern residence while he attended to his trumped-up urgent business there. Because she would be attending Lord Denby's house party at his estate twenty miles away instead.

The house party she had practically goaded Denby into having when he let slip, the other night in Lady Bulphan's orangery, that he hailed from the north. A house party which would be conveniently chaperoned by the host's eminent parents who lived there. The perfect setting, she had convincingly argued, for Lord Denby to celebrate the milestone of his thirtieth birthday with his family as he should, and the perfect opportunity to finally make him fall head over heels in love with her rather than only in lust and perhaps tease out a proposal to rub under Griff's nose too. What marvellous revenge it would be to outrank him!

Feeling much better, she pasted on a smile just for him as she burst through the door, letting him know in no uncertain terms she wasn't the least bit fazed by his unwelcome interference, then promptly ignored him. Knowing Griff, he would make it his mission to approach her and outline his petty and pointless rules for the trip. There had always been plenty of those. True to form, she didn't have to wait long because her oldest sister, in her warped wisdom, had seated him directly beside her at dinner.

'I suppose you are furious with me.'

She suppressed the urge to snap her napkin open. Or directly into his much too handsome face. 'More curious than furious actually, Griff, as I cannot fathom why you would want to traipse behind me from theatre to theatre like a lapdog when you loathe the opera and only ever attend if your mother drags you, and even then

it's patently obvious you are only there on sufferance.'
Even Charity's singing failed to impress him, and drat
it, if she could do nothing else well in his book, she was
undeniably brilliant at that.

'Somebody has to watch out for my sister.'

'Because obviously I will only lead her astray.'

'You do have form in that area, Charity, and you
know Dottie loses all common sense when she is around
you.'

'Does she? I think you need to corroborate that
sweeping statement with evidence, Griff, as I do not
know it at all.'

He paused to allow the footmen to serve the soup,
then lowered his deep voice to a whisper which created goose pimples on her skin. 'What about the time
you dragged her down the Dark Walk at Vauxhall so
that the pair of you could have a secret assignation with
Lord Denby?'

'As I recall that incident, if Dorothy and I were guilty
of anything it was wanting to see the fireworks properly
and everybody knows that the end of the Dark Walk
nearest the fireworks tower is the best place to see them.
We were also completely chaperoned the entire time by
Hope, Luke and your good self.'

'Only because you were forced to be.'

'Did we try to escape your overprotective clutches
once?' She was sorely tempted to whack him on his
thick head with her soup spoon. 'No. We didn't. Unlike
my sister and her now husband who had an entirely inappropriate assignation of their own that night, Dorothy and I remained with you the entire time and were
with you when we all happened to stumble upon Lord
Denby—who was clearly only there with his friends to
view the fireworks too.'

'As I recall it, you flirted with him shamelessly throughout the display, so it was a good job I was there.'

That hadn't been premeditated. She had barely known Lord Denby before that fateful night and had only shamelessly flirted with him in the first place because Griff had been such a disapproving stick in the mud who had expressly warned her to steer clear of the group of gentlemen the first moment they spied them. His erroneous but typically suspicious assumption of her motive to misbehave had been like a red rag to a bull— so she had. As she had on countless similar occasions before. Simply to vex him.

'I flirt with every man shamelessly as a point of principle.' Except him. She had never once tried to practice her wiles on Griff as he was so stiff and disapproving of her they probably wouldn't work and would likely backfire if she did. 'There is no harm in a bit of flirting now and then if it means nothing, and at that time I hardly knew Denby so it most definitely meant nothing...*then.*'

He would see straight through that blatant lie if she tried to embellish it because all her flirting with Denby still meant nothing as far as Denby was concerned— beyond the physical. He was so non-committal about anything else, even the promised house party hung in the balance, which was probably the real reason she had neglected to inform Dorothy of it in the first place. Her hand-picked future duke hadn't sounded that enthused by the suggestion, despite agreeing to it, albeit reluctantly after she had allowed him to kiss her again and much more passionately than she was comfortable with.

'But I digress... You have argued that it is Dorothy who lacks all common sense around me and who needs protecting, yet she never flirted with anyone at all that night, did she? You are punishing her for my apparent misdemeanours and that is hardly fair.'

'If I hadn't been there...'

'Oh, for pity's sake, Griff, if you hadn't been there, I'd have still shamelessly flirted while I watched the fireworks because I enjoy flirting. Everybody knows that.' She was good at flirting. So good that it made her stand out and she revelled in the attention whenever Griff was anywhere nearby—that was the pathetic truth. 'Then, your sister and I would have come straight back to the rest of the party exactly as we always do. What else would we have done? We are grown women, not idiots and we know perfectly well how to behave. We certainly managed well enough all those years you fiddled with your silly steam engines in dreary Sheffield.' While she pathetically counted the days until his next fleeting visit home. Not that they ever proved to be worth the wait because he was never pleased to see her anyway.

'Do you know how to behave? It was an ill-considered whim of yours which could have ruined Dorothy's reputation.'

Charity rolled her eyes. 'How? If she was doing nothing wrong and there was nobody around to see anyway?'

'But what if somebody *had* seen, Charity? What if her name had been plastered all over the gossip columns and there had been a scandal? Then what would have happened?'

'The gossip columns print rot and scandals pass.' She knew that from experience as there had been quite a few. But like her father, she was from the never complain and never explain school of thought, which helped her float well above all the nonsense until it passed.

Nonsense which, to her shame, usually had its roots in her own impulsive and reckless errors of judgement before it was embellished further in print, so she only really had herself to blame, exactly as Griff had said. Drat him.

'Perhaps for you they do, because you are so used to them or do not care about them or downright enjoy them, but Dorothy doesn't have the voice of an angel or an army of devoted opera fans who will turn a blind eye to her many transgressions.'

'And what is that supposed to mean?' Although she knew full well what he was alluding to, it stung regardless. As a lifelong friend to her family and her similarly maligned sisters, he should know better. Salacious gossip was a lot like brambles in a garden. It always started small but soon got out of hand, until the barbed fronds of entertainment choked out all the truth beneath them and all anyone could see were the tangled thorns.

Griff made no attempt to disguise his disdain. 'Because of what you do, society will always give you more leeway when you misbehave than they ever would if my sister did.'

The *when* and the *if* in that sentence said it all. In his judgemental mind, Charity always misbehaved and always had, whereas Dorothy would be incapable of it unless she wilfully corrupted her. 'You believe everything they've ever printed about me, don't you?' She had always suspected he had a low opinion of her, but it had never been explicitly said aloud.

His hesitation was a moment too long and then he decided to stare resolutely into his soup as he answered, 'Not everything. I do give you the benefit of the doubt occasionally.'

'Occasionally?'

'There is always a basis for every rumour, Charity—
especially around you. You forget, your legendary exploits with the gentlemen even managed to travel the
two-hundred-odd miles to dreary Sheffield. Assuming
only a quarter of what those stories say are true, that
still means you have kissed significantly more men than
a proper young lady ever should.'

She sat rigid as she absorbed the damning insult for
all of five seconds before deciding he could go to hell
with his holier-than-thou attitude and unflatteringly
low expectations. Then she calmly stood, channelled
every bit of her acting prowess to look unperturbed for
the rest of their party, pretended to catch her skirts on
the table leg and with a well-aimed tug to release them,
tipped the entire contents of his soup bowl into his lap.

Chapter Three

'Surely there is no more luggage?' Evan, the Brookes family's coachman shook his head as she handed him a huge hatbox. 'I think you officially now have twice as much as everyone else, Miss Charity.'

'Of course, I have twice as much as everyone else.' She shrugged, unrepentant, as he helped her into the carriage where Griff and his sister were patiently waiting and had been for the last twenty minutes while her maid redressed her hair. 'Nobody else here has to pack costumes or wigs or stage make-up.' She arranged herself next to Dorothy and grinned, looking effortlessly beautiful and full of life. 'Isn't this exciting, Dottie? Four weeks of unmitigated fun and adventure stretch before us.' Then the smile was significantly less sincere when she glanced at him. 'In the absence of anything fun to do, I suppose you have diligently planned our route? I have to be in Lincoln for rehearsals by the fifth, but I want to stop off at Cambridge on the way as it has such pretty streets and eclectic shops.' Clearly she intended to relegate him to some sort of assistant for the duration.

Not that he cared if it earned her compliance. He waved his neatly organised timetable at her, pointing to the perfectly drafted columns of dates, times and booked stopovers.

'As you can see, we shall overnight in Baldock, then head to Cambridge first thing tomorrow. If the weather holds, you will be there by luncheon, Charity, so will have plenty of time to shop for your fripperies. The following day, we shall eat luncheon in Stilton, the home of the famous cheese, then press on to Stamford, the home of one of my favourite inns. Then it's Grantham on Thursday night followed by a dawn start so that we arrive at the theatre in Lincoln as stipulated early on Friday.'

Griff was already counting the minutes till then. By that time he would have been encased in this carriage with her for four interminable days. At least in Lincoln he would have some respite. She had rehearsals both Friday and Saturday and would perform on the Saturday night, which he hoped would keep the minx busy enough to give him several blissful hours of peace to recuperate from the ordeal. As they were stuck there all day Sunday, awaiting her second performance on the Monday, and it was anybody's guess what mischief she was bound to get into during those unoccupied hours, he would need to have his wits about him.

'Everything's loaded so Evan and I are ready when you are.' Lily, Charity's maid, poked her head through the open window closely followed by Augustus and Roberta Brookes, her parents who had come outside to wave them off.

'Have a marvellous time, my darling!' Roberta Brookes fussed with her daughter's already perfect blonde curls before kissing her noisily. Then she tearfully squeezed both his and Dorothy's hands. 'Look after my precious baby.'

'We will.' Or at least he would. Dottie would likely be more a hindrance and an accomplice to Charity than a help to him.

'And write often. All of you. I want to hear everything you all get up to.'

'Let them go, woman.' Augustus Brookes practically peeled his wife's fingers from the window frame before smiling jovially. 'Have fun, darling, and do try to listen to Griff.' He shot him a pointed look, one which confirmed all Griff's worst fears about the very real risk of shenanigans. Then he shook his hand with all the impassioned firmness of a man who despaired of his youngest daughter but still hoped for the best.

'I am entrusting you to save my headstrong daughter from herself, Griff, and no doubt, I shall be indebted to you by the end of this debacle if you manage it. Good luck herding these two. I suspect you shall need it but if anyone can do it, I have faith that you can. You have always had such an old head on your young shoulders that sometimes I forget that I am twice your age.' An unflattering compliment if ever there was one. One that made him sound exactly like the fuddy-duddy Charity always accused him of being. Then Augustus Brookes wagged his finger at her which she typically ignored. 'Whatever happens, under all circumstances, I have appointed him to be in charge, so listen to him, Charity, as you would listen to me and do as you are told.' As if that had ever happened.

She didn't agree. Not that either of her parents noticed as the carriage lurched forward the second she rapped on the roof. *'Au revoir*, Papa! I miss you already, Mama!'

Griff left her and Dottie to chat excitedly while he watched out of the window as the city disappeared, allowing their conversation to waft over him and trying not to enjoy the sound of Charity's voice.

She was a natural raconteur who always managed to make even the most banal topics sound engaging. However, today's topic was anything but banal. It was an interesting, witty and self-effacing behind-the-scenes account of her final night in Covent Garden, the day after she had dumped hot tomato soup in his lap and ruined his favourite cream waistcoat in the process.

As self-absorbed as Charity could be, she was also remarkably self-aware, poking fun at her inability to do anything on time and blaming the latest catastrophic hair crisis for causing the poor stage manager to have to plead with her outside her dressing room door to take her place in the wings less than a minute before the curtain lifted. She had Dottie in stitches describing how she tried to avoid Figaro's bad breath in the first scene while still trying to convince the audience they were devoted young lovers who were about to be wed. But he had eaten an entire onion tart in the inn next door to the theatre beforehand for his dinner and she suspected not all of those noxious alliums had been thoroughly cooked. As soon as that scene was done, she had accosted a stagehand and sent him on a mission to find some fresh mint leaves Figaro could chew on before the script dictated she had to embrace him in the final act. When none could be found, she went onstage clutching one of the roses an admirer had sent her and inhaled that scent each time the fetid Figaro and his hellish halitosis came near.

Griff vividly remembered the scene.

Could picture it clearly and had thought at the time he had never seen her wield a rose before. The flower had been pink. He remembered that too for some reason, but she had used it so comically and seamlessly that night he had put the thought clear out of his head while he was swept away by her performance exactly as he always was. Not that he would admit that to Charity or his sister. Or anybody else for that matter. Some things were just too personal and uncomfortable to ever have to admit aloud.

Nobody knew that thanks to his unhealthy obsession he had intentionally watched *The Marriage of Figaro* at least once a week since it opened in January, or that each time he heard her sing 'Deh vieni, non tardar' she left him with tears in his eyes.

Nobody knew any of this because they all assumed he had to be dragged kicking and screaming to the theatre, and he fully intended to keep it that way. It was curiosity that drew him. The conundrum of her. He wanted to—no, needed to—finally work her out to understand the strange hold she had on him, that was all. He wasn't one of her devoted minions who hung on her every word.

Far from it.

That particular night when he had gone to see her sing, which he had done with alarming frequency since she had made her stage debut in the chorus of *Così fan Tutte* last summer, he took his preferred invisible and solitary seat in the gods where nobody could see him. It was always easier to watch her when he didn't have to worry about how the sound of her voice made him feel or how he powerlessly reacted to it.

There was something mesmerising and moving in the way Charity performed which always stole his breath and plucked at his heart strings, leaving him strangely overwhelmed and off kilter by the final curtain every single time. To begin with, he had stubbornly assumed it was the genius of Mozart which affected him so viscerally because the alternative explanation was as unthinkable as it was unpalatable. It wasn't Charity. It couldn't possibly be. He was much too sensible to become entranced by her. Yet after experiencing the same phenomenon at the perhaps twenty or thirty performances which his stubborn pride adamantly refused to count, he was forced to acknowledge it was all down to her and, exactly like every other man she encountered, she had thoroughly bewitched him with her talent, her beauty and her charm.

Which was all a depressing and thoroughly pathetic waste of his time because no matter how much he might think he wanted her, he really didn't want *her* and he certainly didn't want to keep thinking about wanting her either. That was the heart of the problem.

It was also a futile and vast conundrum which he would likely never solve, unlike the simpler one in his satchel which he most definitely would. As the built-up roads turned green and leafy, he fished it out of his bag and forced himself to focus on the diagram which was also responsible for keeping him up at night. He might never get to the bottom of the unfathomable mystery that was Charity, but he was damned if he would let the mechanics of the planned new Philpot power loom best him!

'Surely it is time we stopped?' Her voice snapped him away from the intricacies of the steam pipes he was rearranging and reluctantly back to the present. Beyond the window was nought but rolling fields now and Dottie was fast asleep. By the look of her, all mussed and softly snoring, his sister had been sleeping for a considerable amount of time too.

Griff took out his pocket watch, surprised to discover they had been on the road for a good two and a half hours. 'We should hit Hatfield by noon.'

'Noon!'

'It is only half an hour away, Charity. That is no great hardship.'

'For you maybe, but then you seem perfectly comfortable all spread out.' She gestured to his legs which, to be fair to her, had taken over all the available space between them, and the small gap they hadn't was filled with the spilling contents of his bulky satchel. 'This isn't your personal study, Griff.'

'Sorry.' He hastily gathered up his things and deposited them on the bench beside him. 'I completely forgot where I was.'

'And clearly also completely forgot that you possess the most ridiculously long legs on the planet and that there are two other people in this carriage reluctantly sharing it with you.'

'I usually travel alone.' Which sounded as pathetic as

Augustus Brookes considering them middle-aged contemporaries. 'When I am on business, that is.'

She huffed, then dropped down the window. 'Evan— can you pull in at the next inn, please?'

'Consider it done, miss.'

Griff shook his head. 'The Greyhound in Hatfield are expecting us for lunch. I've reserved a private dining room.'

'I need to stretch my legs and we can eat at any inn just as well as we can at your precious Greyhound.'

'But it is a decent and respectable place which I always stop at when I travel this route for exactly that reason. Not every inn along the Great North Road is decent, Charity, so stopping randomly at one is never sensible. What if it's awful? You'll be the one griping all the way to Baldock if the food disagrees with you.'

She rolled her eyes. 'Must you always be so rigid and unbending? I swear you get older every year.'

'Everyone gets older every year, Charity. That's the whole point of birthdays.'

'I wasn't referring to your physical age, Griff, but this one.' She tapped her temple. 'There is barely four years between us, but it might as well be twenty in our outlooks. Since you've come back, you have become so…crusty in your dotage. Live a little. Embrace the unpredictable for a change, unencumbered by your meticulous charts and lists and diagrams and risk eating lunch somewhere new. I *dare* you.'

'I would prefer we stopped at Hatfield as planned where I know the service and the food are exemplary.' Even to his own ears that sounded crusty and he blamed Charity entirely for turning him into a parent at the ripe old age of twenty-seven as he knew already that was what being her chaperon was doomed to feel like.

'Yet I would prefer we stopped *now,* Griff. I need
to stretch my legs—among other things—and as this
is my trip that you have invited yourself on to and my
father's carriage, I would prefer it if you could muster a little compassion and learn to compromise.' Before he could argue, the carriage slowed and began to
turn, and a charming and busy thatched inn suddenly
loomed before them. 'Now...doesn't that look lovely?'
She nudged Dottie as if it were a fait accompli. 'Wake
up, sleepy head, it's time to eat.'

He was reluctantly, but solicitously helping Charity
out of the carriage when the militia arrived and, to his
utter dismay, was forced to watch at least fifty randy
uniformed young bucks all smile wolfishly at her in
unison while she beamed coquettishly back.

Chapter Four

Charity had thought Griff would have an apoplexy when the soldiers arrived, and he certainly almost had one when the flustered innkeeper informed him that both the private dining rooms were already taken and that they would have to eat in the taproom instead. While he continued to argue, and before he got all dictatorial and insisted they leave forthwith, she quietly told Evan to unhitch the horses and feed them, then quickly settled herself and her friend at a cosy table by the window and ordered some tea. Miraculously, it came straight away, so by the time Griff returned, all windswept and furious, they were happily drinking it. She gestured to the empty chair opposite with a jerk of her head. A chair she had chosen for him specifically so he had his back to all the delightful soldiers and would have to watch her flirt with them with her eyes throughout the meal as penance for being Griff.

'I've ordered us all the game pie, which I am told by one of the regular patrons, is delicious.'

'With this crowd, we'll be lucky if they serve it by supper time.' He had a knack for looking particularly handsome and brooding when riled. 'We should go now and cut our losses, then we'll still make the Greyhound in time to eat there.'

With the most perfect timing, a barmaid strode towards them holding the steaming pie aloft on a tray like the head of John the Baptist. 'Your game pie and all the trimmings, miss.'

Griff's imperious square jaw hung slack and Charity grinned. She couldn't help it. Clearly today, all the planets were aligned, and fate was completely on her side for once and most definitely not on his. 'What exemplary service!'

'The proof of the pudding is in the eating.'

He deserved the theatrical groan she responded with and the laughter which bubbled out of Dorothy's mouth at her purposely comical and exasperated expression. 'Oh, do sit down, Griff, you *old* curmudgeon. Preferably at another table as I don't want your sour mood spoiling my digestion.'

He was blessedly quiet throughout most of the excellent meal, speaking only when directly spoken to, and obviously irritated at being so thoroughly thwarted. Once their desserts were done, and purely because he kept checking his pocket watch as he was clearly in a hurry to get back on the road, she ordered more tea then took her own sweet time drinking it.

'How does this place measure up to the Greyhound, Griff?'

'I prefer it.' Enjoying her overbearing brother's disgruntled behaviour almost as much as Charity, and with far more experience of the journey north than she, Dorothy charged in like the cavalry before he could answer. 'It's less stuffy than the Greyhound. The food was nicer too. Wasn't that pie delicious, Griff?'

'It was all right.' He was sat with his arms folded and one leg crossed over the other, his booted foot tapping impatiently and causing the soft kerseymere of his breeches to pull taut over his thigh muscles. Since he had filled out at around the age of twenty, Griff had always worn his breeches well. And his coats. More so since his extended stint of apparently manual labour at the family factory in Sheffield. As much as he annoyed her, Charity could never help but admire his broad shoulders. They were particularly impressive.

'It was more than all right, Brother, as you had second helpings.' Her friend suddenly nudged her beneath the table with her knee, wrenching Charity's eyes from their perusal of his manly shoulders to the dashing young soldier approaching behind him. Although, up close and against Griff, and despite his smart regimentals, the poor thing looked more drab than dashing.

'Excuse the interruption.' The young man inclined his head politely, failing to notice her chaperon's instant and fierce expression of warning. 'But aren't you Miss Charity Brookes the famous soprano?'

She beamed at the gentleman and enjoyed Griff's incensed reaction as he beamed soppily back. 'I am indeed, sir.'

'I thought as much…' He glanced behind him, nodding once to a large group of his comrades who had gathered at the bar, watching their exchange intently. 'I was lucky enough to see you sing last month when I was in town visiting my parents. I hope you do not mind me saying that I thought you were magnificent… Better than magnificent actually. You were…quite breathtaking, Miss Brookes.'

'Why, thank you.'

'I was just telling my comrades how I had never

heard anything quite like it. You really do have the voice of an angel exactly as everyone says. You completely stole the show and had me utterly mesmerised from start to finish that I barely noticed poor Figaro and the rest of the cast even existed.'

Seeing that Griff's mouth had flattened into a disapproving line, she decided to vex him further and coax a little more gushing praise out of her new and clearly devoted fan. 'Which part of *Figaro* was your favourite…' she glanced quickly at the stripes on his uniform '… Lieutenant…?'

'Lawrence. Lieutenant Peter Lawrence. I should have introduced myself from the outset, Miss Brookes, but I was a little overwhelmed.' He smiled awkwardly, his eyes never once leaving hers while Griff glared. He reminded her a bit of a puppy—a ball of eager fluff stood next to a snarling wolf. 'But to answer your question— "Deh vieni, non tardar". That was truly awe inspiring.'

Like sheep, his comrades had all followed and now ringed their table as they hung on every word of the conversation. Instinctively, she offered them the beguiling smile she had ruthlessly practised in the mirror at the age of fifteen when suitors had first begun to call upon her eldest sister. The smile which she knew turned most men to putty, but which was guaranteed to make Griff frown. 'I was trying to explain the magic of your exquisite performance of that aria to my friends here, but as they have never had the pleasure of hearing you sing, I sincerely doubt my humble words did your sublime voice the justice it deserves.'

'You are too kind, Lieutenant.'

'I don't suppose you would sing for us, would you, Miss Brookes?' Another young officer stepped forward, his bold gaze earning him a stern glare from Griff.

'Only we are on our way to the Continent, you see. Off to join Wellington and round up that rascal Napoleon and a song from you would be the greatest parting gift. There's a pianoforte over there.' He pointed hopefully to the battered instrument in the corner. 'And I am sure among all these people, we can find somebody who can play it for you. I dare say the innkeeper will not mind.'

'Sadly, we must leave. Immediately.' Griff stood, pulling himself ruthlessly to his full height to intimidate her puppies and taking command. He then held out his hand to her as if he owned her, expecting her to take it. 'Miss Brookes needs to be in Cambridge by the morning.'

She ignored both his hand and him as a point of principle. 'I am sure I can spare the time to give these brave men one song.' Being a magnanimous friend, she directed all the attention over to Dorothy. 'Miss Philpot will play. She plays divinely and has the brilliant capacity to remember most of my repertoire without the need for any sheet music.'

As the soldiers cheered, Dorothy blushed prettily, completely oblivious to her brother's now narrowed eyes. 'I should be delighted to play for you all.' Although whether or not the ancient pianoforte was up to the challenge of being played was yet to be determined.

Within minutes, the inn was completely transformed. With the delighted innkeeper's help, the soldiers and other patrons moved all the tables and chairs to create a circle in the centre into which the battle-scarred and stained piano was dragged. Dorothy was helped on to the stool by a very handsome blond captain who kissed her hand and made her blush some more. A kiss which also had the added bonus of turning Gruff Griff near purple. Like the dull engines he was so obsessed with, she sincerely hoped his ears would vent steam too to make her happiness complete. After a brief confab with her friend and with Griff looking gruffer than usual as he watched from a disapproving distance, Charity grabbed Lieutenant Lawrence by the lapels and started to sing.

In typical Charity fashion, she started with a crowd pleaser. Not from *Figaro*, not even from the opera, but with a rousing and flirtatious rendition of 'Soldier, Soldier, Won't You Marry Me?', in which she dragged the besotted Lieutenant Lawrence into the circle to duet with her. The consummate entertainer, she acted it out too, making the crowd roar with laughter as she shamelessly stole items of clothing from gentlemen in the audience to dress her suitor with until he was left straining under the mountain of garments and she was theatrically disgruntled and huffing prettily to hear that he already had a wife.

It was an entertaining performance, he had to give her that, and one Griff would have appreciated in a theatre. Alone. However, in this intimate and unfamiliar inn, surrounded by strangers, most of whom were young, gallingly male and riddled with lust, it was hard to concentrate on it.

Despite promising them just the one song and doubtless to teach him a lesson, she delighted them all with 'Der Hölle Rache' from *The Magic Flute*. The one Mozart aria which was guaranteed to showcase a great soprano's impressive range and which everyone associated with her mother who had played the Queen of the Night at Drury Lane more times than he could remember. However, in his humble opinion and with no disrespect at all to Roberta Brookes's undisputed brilliance as a soprano, Charity had always sung it better and by the heartfelt *oohs* and *ahs* coming from the audience he was quite correct in that assumption.

She gifted the audience several more songs, making a point of smiling at him repeatedly as he kept pulling out his pocket watch to chivvy her along and then finally announced to the crowd that she had to go, knowing full well they would demand just one more, which of course the minx granted them. Then, clearly prearranged in advance with his traitorous sister and without missing a beat, she took a deep breath, centred herself and sang the one aria he was never ready to hear. 'Deh vieni, non tardar'.

Without an orchestra and stripped back to just the accompaniment of a solitary piano and the sultry sounds of her voice, the haunting melody of a woman hopelessly in love and yearning for her lover hit him in the heart like a battering ram. As he stood transfixed, powerless to do anything but let the sheer, wanton beauty of her voice consume him while his heart swelled in his chest, her eyes locked with his, and for one sublime, surreal and oddly significant moment, it was if she was singing those words to him.

For him.

Exactly as he had always yearned for.

The inn, the audience, the room full of lusty militia men all disappeared. All at once, all that heady, complicated and all-consuming emotion which only she elicited suddenly transformed and morphed, then mingled with a pain so fierce, so gut-wrenching it knocked all the wind out of him and left him reeling from the shock of it. Because he suddenly realised he wanted those words to be true!

Wanted her to say them and mean them!

Needed them as much as he needed air and water.

Needed her.

Wanted her.

Charity blasted Brookes!

The fly in his ointment since childhood. The one Brookes sister he had never thought of as a sister. The great conundrum and darndest dichotomy. The most wayward, selfish and vain flirt in all of Christendom and the one woman only the most masochistic of fools would want to possess. When he knew to his bones Charity couldn't be possessed. She couldn't be tamed. She couldn't even be trusted to behave respectably for five blasted minutes!

What the hell was he thinking?

Needing fresh air because he also suddenly wanted to punch every single hapless man present who was currently and very likely similarly yearning for her, Griff strode out of the inn and blindly into the yard towards their carriage, devastated by the knowledge that his feelings for her were more powerful than he realised. More lasting and much more resilient than he had ever given them credit for. This wasn't an unhealthy obsession or a transient infatuation. It was set in stone.

Cast in iron.

Written in blood.

It was love.

And, God help him, it always had been.

Chapter Five

It appears that Miss Charity Brookes has given several impromptu performances at every inn she has stopped at on her journey north. If my far-flung sources are to be believed, Dear Reader, a crowd of more than two hundred were gathered to greet her when she arrived at the Bell in Stilton. Where, I am told, she graciously sang to them all for an hour, and the only payment the generous soprano would accept for her trouble from the grateful innkeeper was a single wheel of cheese...

Whispers from Behind the Fan

—May 1815

The theatre in Lincoln was stuffed to the rafters. The hum from the audience's excited chatter permeated all the walls to her dressing room and turned the butterflies in her stomach into winged monsters which crashed against her insides.

She'd never had stage fright before. She'd thought it a myth. But now it crippled her and threatened to suf-

focate her. Icy tentacles of panic had wrapped themselves around her vocal chords and refused to release
their grip, no matter what warm-up exercise she tried
to use to banish them. In case those nerves showed
in her preparations, she had sent her intuitive maid to
find her husband and their seats. A hasty decision she
bitterly regretted now that she had nothing to take her
mind off the fear.

There was a rap on the door. 'Ten minutes, Miss
Brookes.'

'Thank you.' It came out as a croak as the light supper Lily had insisted she eat only an hour before threatened to make a second appearance. She stood to fetch
the glass of water she had left on the other side of her
surprisingly sumptuous dressing room and her head
started to spin as the floor tilted, and she realised she
was going to faint unless she got some air.

Ten minutes.

Ten minutes!

It was nowhere near enough time.

Choking, she slammed out of her dressing room, her
heart racing and her palms sweating, using the walls
of the narrow corridor in the bowels of the theatre to
support her as she staggered towards the stage door.
This close to curtain up, there was no one there to assist her. They were all already waiting in the wings or
doing their last checks to ensure everything ran like
clockwork. Charity couldn't decide if that was a good
or a bad thing. Her stubborn pride meant she would
rather die than allow anyone to see her like this—all
panicked and petrified—not when she was the star of
the show. The only performer in fact and this theatre
had paid good money for her because their expecta-

tions were so high. They had sold every seat. All five hundred of them.

Five hundred people had paid to see her!

Five hundred people who had likely never seen her sing a note before tonight but had spent their hard-earned wages on tickets anyway. And all based on the stupid things which had been said about her voice in the newspapers.

Her reputation and her mother's preceded her. Mama had performed here every year since this theatre had opened. The people of Lincoln loved her and were expecting great things from her daughter. Roberta Brookes certainly would never let an audience down. Her mother was always prepared. Always focussed. Always magnificent.

But Charity wasn't her mother.

For months she had fooled herself that she could be, that she might be just as good, but that had been in *The Marriage of Figaro*. An ensemble piece with other singers to share the huge responsibility of entertaining the masses. But tonight's show was just her.

All her.

And she bitterly regretted accepting it.

The backstage door loomed like a beacon. An escape. As tears stained her cheeks and spoiled her make-up, she quickened her pace to get to it.

If only she could escape. From all of it. Go home. Lock all the doors. But she was committed. People were relying on her. Every fibre of her being, all her training and the legacy of her brilliant mother all demanded that the show must go on.

She had to bury the fear. Put on a brave face. Hide the wretched truth at all costs.

Over the hum of the audience came the screech of

a violin. A cello. A flute. The orchestra were warming up their instruments ready for the off. Each note like a death knell sealing her fate while feeding the creature in her gut. It flailed against the walls of her stomach, jarring her ribs and robbing her of breath, eating her from the inside until there would be nothing left to escape with.

Or perhaps she could escape? There was still time. Not ten minutes any more, but at least eight. Enough for her to flee down the alley and out into the night. Evan wouldn't be there waiting but it wasn't that far away to the inn. Surely?

As her clumsy fingers finally wrestled with the door latch, she knew she was past the point of no return. She couldn't do this.

She couldn't! It was all too much.

She hadn't spent the money yet, so it could all be returned. And Griff would fix it. He was so good at organising everything, she would tell him to make it all right then take her back home where she belonged.

Her reputation and her career in tatters.

A fallen star before it had fully risen.

The lock finally gave and she flung herself out the door, then bent double to retch uncontrollably as she sobbed. Wishing she was more. Wishing she was…

'Charity?' His boots thundered on the cobbles as he dashed towards her. 'Oh, my God, Charity, what's wrong?' Strong arms supported her as she lost her supper. A gentle hand held back the ringlets poor Lily had wasted an hour creating. Wiped her face.

'I can't do it, Griff! I can't do it!' She collapsed against him, grateful that he was there. 'Take me home. Please.'

'Shh, love, it's all right.' He held her close and rocked her. 'It's just nerves, that's all.'

'It isn't. I can't do this. *I can't!*'

'You don't have to.'

'Will you fix it for me?'

He stroked her hair. 'Of course I will… If that is what you want. But we should probably get you cleaned up first, don't you think?'

She nodded. It took every ounce of her strength, but as he tried to help her back inside, her knees gave way. Quick as a shot, Griff effortlessly scooped her up, and as she clung to him for dear life, he carried her back to her dressing room, then carefully lowered her on to the sofa.

'Sit still. Breathe.' He cupped her cheek tenderly. 'Everything is going to be all right, I promise. I'll be back in a minute.'

Charity closed her eyes to stop the room spinning but still struggled to breathe despite feeling calmer. The orchestra were still warming up, the noise from the audience was still deafening, yet despite all that she felt better just knowing Griff was in control.

True to his words, he was back in a flash and pressed a glass into her hand as he sat beside her and guided it to her lips. Instantly she winced as the liquid burned her throat. 'What's this?'

'Dutch courage… Brandy actually. Not very good brandy to be fair but the best I could find in a hurry. It'll help to calm you down. Try to breathe deeply between sips.'

'I can't breathe. That's the problem.'

'I'm not surprised.' Then he slanted her a knowing glance as she tried and failed to sit comfortably. 'How tight are those stays?'

The heavy silk brocade costume was an homage to

Mozart, made especially for Charity from her own design which borrowed a great deal from the era of Marie Antoinette. A fashion which she had always thought romantic and theatrically glamorous, with fluted three-quarter sleeves, padded hip panniers and acres of underskirts. It also had a long, painfully stiff conical bodice which she had had Lily lace her into within an inch of her life to give her the tragic French queen's exaggerated silhouette. The long whale bones now dug into her hips and constricted her ribs. 'Perhaps a little too tight.'

He stood and helped her up, turned her briskly by the shoulders, and to her complete surprise began to unlace the back of her gown. 'What on earth do you think you are doing, Griffith Philpot?'

'I am saving you from yourself, Charity Brookes, before you pass out.' Which she had to concede was still a very real possibility. 'So hold still, you daft minx. You're trussed up like a ham. It's a wonder you're not purple.'

Within seconds, his clever fingers had loosened it all, allowing her to fill her lungs properly for the first time since she had put the garment on. Then, tugging her this way and that, he did it all up again, only this time there was a good inch of breathing space between the rigid bodice and her ribs. To be certain, he briefly slipped his hand down the back of the dress between the laces and her bare skin and created a wave of goose pimples which spontaneously erupted down her spine in the process. 'Now isn't that much better?'

She nodded dumbly, too flustered by the strange effect he was having on her to speak.

He helped her sit back down and ordered her to sip the brandy while he poured water into the wash bowl, dunked in one of the soft muslin cloths that she used to removed her stage make-up and then ruthlessly wrung it out. However, instead of handing it to her to allow her to remove it all herself, he knelt before her and gently dabbed her skin in specific places, almost as if he were repairing rather than eradicating all the paint. As the cloth came away with the dark smudge of kohl which had obviously run from her eyes and her racing pulse finally slowed, she suddenly noticed the noises from the theatre were unchanged.

'Why isn't everyone leaving?'

'Because I told the stage manager you were having a catastrophic ringlet crisis and would be ten minutes late. As usual.'

She slapped the washcloth away. 'You are supposed to be taking me home, Griff!'

'I am *supposed* to be looking after you as I promised your father faithfully I would.' His hands covered her shoulders and he gave them a friendly shake. 'You don't want to go home, Charity, not really, and to be frank, I am not going to allow it as I know you'll never forgive yourself if you did.' He sat back on his heels and smiled.

'There are five hundred people out there waiting patiently to hear you sing. They will happily wait all night if they need to because they know it will be worth it and you mustn't succumb to an uncharacteristic moment of panic and disappoint them. You can do this, Charity.' He shook her shoulders again, staring deep into her eyes, his face so close to hers she could count every jet-black eyelash that ringed them. Notice the flecks of copper and gold in his dark eyes.

'You've wanted this since you were a little girl. A stage all to yourself so you can show the world what you're made of. I know you are scared. I know too that you are currently a bit overwhelmed with the sheer magnitude of it all, but you *can* do this, Charity. You were born to do it. And I would never forgive myself if I allowed a silly moment of panic to ruin all of your dreams.'

'I am not a solo performer. Trying to follow in my mother's footsteps was stupid.' Because his brown eyes seemed to see right into her soul, she stared into the brandy instead, ashamed to be so exposed and so helpless yet unable to hide it. 'I can sing well enough—but I am no Roberta Brookes.'

'That's true. You are no Roberta Brookes.' His finger tilted up her chin and forced her to look at him. 'You are better. When she sings it leaves me breathless. When you do… I am left entirely undone.'

It was the first compliment he had ever given her, and it left her entirely undone too. 'For a man so stingy with his praise, that was rather pretty, Griff.'

'I have my moments.' He grinned. It suited him. It made those dark eyes sparkle and her pulse step up a notch further. 'Now go patch up your makeup and fix your hair, woman. That's an order and one your father stipulated you had to obey, remember?'

'There are five hundred people out there.'

'Twice as many as you sang to in Stilton, and three times as many as you performed to in Cambridge and you left them all in raptures exactly as you will here.'

'But what if…?' His finger touched her lips and they instantly tingled with awareness.

'You are the indomitable, intrepid, incomparable, infuriating and invincible Miss Charity Grace Brookes. When you walk on to that stage, any what, buts or ifs will become moot because you will own it. Exactly as you always do.' He tugged her up as he stood and pushed her towards the mirror. 'You have five minutes.'

He watched over her, arms crossed and foot tapping impatiently as she patted on powder and applied fresh kohl. As soon as the last bit of rouge was reapplied to her lips he grabbed her hand and marched her out of her dressing room and, without pausing, directly to the wings. Then with a nod to the stage manager he spun her to face him, his hands holding hers, his thumbs idly caressing her palms and playing havoc with her pulse.

'I'll be right here if you need me—right here, I promise—but you won't.' Then he tugged her close and kissed her mouth.

Brief, unexpected and potent.

So brief and swift Charity supposed she shouldn't read anything into it, but nowhere near brief enough to be brotherly and much too potent to be meaningless. 'Now go. Blow them away, my darling. Leave them breathless.'

And with a firm push, she found herself walking on to the stage at the exact same moment as the curtains parted and the audience erupted with applause, her fingertips touching her lips where the taste of his still lingered and every nerve ending suddenly alive as they had never been before.

Chapter Six

He shouldn't have kissed her.

It had been a reckless, impulsive and foolhardy thing to do but at the time he had been powerless to stop it. Griff had never seen Charity vulnerable before. Not once in all their seventeen-year relationship. She had always oozed confidence. Too much, truth be told, even as a child. Even then she had been the risk-taker of the five of them. The adventurous and forward one who would stride into any situation as bold as brass and deftly turn it to her advantage. But seeing her like that somehow made her more human and like a knight of old, and her sworn knight errant he'd had to protect her. Both for her sake and for his. It had felt natural to do so. To step in, keep her safe and see her right. And perhaps he had been doing exactly that since his return too? After another sleepless night of soul searching, made so much worse by the after-effects of that kiss, he was coming to realise he had been inadvertently wandering down this path for quite some time.

If he was being completely honest with himself, which he was because he was of the firm belief he had to understand his feelings to be fully able to conquer them, he had only gone to Sheffield to try to forget her. She had been eighteen then to his two and twenty, and finally old enough to attend all the same social functions. In true Charity fashion, she had burst into society from the outset, effervescent, beautiful and charming, and the men had fallen at her feet. Because of the close family connection, he couldn't and morally wouldn't be one of them, so seeing her flirt and dance with all those other men had sent him spiralling into irrational rage at every turn. He knew now that was mostly jealousy, tinged with a large dose of possessiveness which was completely unreasonable, and all of which he'd had to bottle inside.

Except he hadn't bottled it all inside because those chaotic emotions had been too powerful to contain completely and he had taken them out on her. He'd been judgemental, critical, argumentative and disapproving, and their previous teasing, sparring, playful relationship had deteriorated. And that had killed him. Sheffield had given him a reprieve from all those draining, confusing and toxic emotions and while he had never managed to relegate her completely to out of sight and out of mind, the powerless feelings of anger and misplaced jealousy had subsided.

Since his return, they too had returned with a vengeance and had coloured his relationship with her all over again. In fact, he'd been worse this time around. He could see that now. He could also see that it was unreasonable to be irrationally furious at a woman who was ultimately just being herself and who had no idea that she affected him so.

'Working again, Griff?' His head snapped up at the sound of her voice and instantly his breath caught in his throat. 'Why didn't you visit the cathedral with the others? Isn't Sunday supposed to be a day of rest?'

His sister was attending the morning service at the cathedral and was using that as an excuse to explore the soaring Norman edifice which dominated the city after the sermon was done. He had dispatched Lily and Evan as her chaperons the moment he had learned Charity was staying in bed instead, and set up camp in their private dining room, laying out all his work on the table more as a prop than an intention in case anyone saw fit to challenge his motives.

'I thought I would take advantage of the quiet to finally get to grips with these diagrams.' A blatant lie when he was standing guard over her again. She had been visibly exhausted beneath the exhilaration of last night's successful performance, and that too had come as a shock. He hadn't realised how hard she worked to put on such a show and had never considered the mental and physical toll two hours of keeping the audience in the palm of her hand took. From the stalls and from up in the gods, he had only ever seen the polished final product, but from the wings he could see the work which went into every perfect note and he had watched her smile drop and her shoulders slump as the curtain fell during the interval. Beneath the make-up, he could see the fatigue and the sweat as Lily had bustled on to the stage to assist her off it, taking the weight of the heavy skirts so that the tired Charity could walk off.

Then, while the masses laughed, drank and refreshed themselves awaiting the second half, the performer was redressed and repaired at such speed there was barely time for her to gulp down some water before she was thrust on to the stage again. By the end, she was dead on her feet and surprisingly subdued on the short carriage journey back to their inn, more relieved the ordeal was over than basking in the glory of it as he had expected. She had been pale, drawn and obviously spent.

Vulnerable again and that tugged ruthlessly at his heart strings.

Thanks to the whole morning's extra sleep, none of that was visible on her lovely face, and without Lily's ministrations, her golden hair was pinned loose in a simple bun which allowed him to see that without the artful ringlets she usually sported, it naturally fell in soft waves which he decided there and then he much preferred.

'No practising this morning?' Every morning without fail on this trip he had heard her ethereal voice drifting down the hallway of whichever inn they happened to be staying in. Strange breathing exercises and noises were always followed by twenty minutes of scales before she sang at least one whole song all the way through and he had wrongly assumed she would have done the same today so he could mentally prepare himself for seeing her.

'I never practise on a Sunday. Nor does my mother. Signor Fauci is adamant that a voice must be rested at least one day a week—even in the midst of a run of performances. He would kill me if he knew I had defied him.'

'Who the blazes is Signor Fauci?'

'Our singing teacher.'

'You sing brilliantly already and your mother has been doing it for ever, so why on earth do the pair of you still have a singing teacher?'

'For technique. Essential critique. To correct any mistakes or bad habits and to continually improve. An operatic performance must appear effortless. Every note has to sound seamless no matter how long you have to hold it or how much that hurts. The very last thing a singer wants is to show any exposed cracks in that façade. The audience must be completely convinced by the performance, not what goes on behind the curtains—both literally…and figuratively.' Her eyes clouded despite her smile and they both knew that she wasn't just referring to operatic technique. Last night, he had seen a little of the Charity who hid behind the curtain and she was supremely uncomfortable about that. 'And, of course, practice makes perfect, after all.'

To his ears and eyes, she was already perfect, perhaps more so now that he understood her better. Not that he would mention last night unless she did, and even then he would brush it off to maintain the status quo. That was safer. 'Surely you can hear any mistakes you make for yourself?'

She covered her relief at his less personal, safer question with a pitying look. 'The first rule of singing well is to never trust your ears because if you are listening intently to yourself you aren't really singing at all. Signor Fauci insists that I feel the music as that is a much better gauge.' At his baffled expression she shrugged and lowered herself into the chair opposite his, far too close for comfort. 'You feel the sounds, Griff—the way they vibrate inside your head or against your teeth. The way they tug on a particular muscle in your body.'

'Like the diaphragm.' His smugness at knowing something about her craft soon disappeared when she shook her head as if he were an uneducated and uncultured idiot and the sanctuary of their status quo was restored.

'The diaphragm is a breathing muscle, Griff, not a singing muscle. The singing muscles are lower, buried in the pelvis.' He didn't want to think about her pelvis because it housed other things alongside her singing muscles and none of them he needed to think about. 'But I digress...' Thank God! 'A singer's body reacts to different sounds in different ways, so you need to recognise exactly what happens when you are singing at your best. For example, in the final cadenza in "Deh vieni, non tardar..."'

To his horror she sang it. Just a phrase with the minimum effort, yet it still punched him in the gut.

'If I do it properly, I feel the highest note here.' Her fingers brushed the skin on the side of her neck beneath her ear. 'Like goose pimples.'

More inappropriate images skittered through his mind and he realised he had to change the subject again or she would likely kill him. 'You missed breakfast.' By about four hours. 'You must be starving.'

'Ravenous.' She smiled, a little shyly, which was also unusual. The Charity he knew was never bashful or unsure about anything, yet as sublime as that confident version of her was, this one...perhaps the real one...did odd things to his heart. 'Is it too soon for luncheon, do you suppose?'

'I shall make sure that it isn't.' Griff stood, grateful for the excuse to escape her for a moment to compose himself while he ordered her a feast. Since their unplanned stop before Hatfield, and his unfortunate epiphany, he had been awkward around her and avoided her wherever possible for the sake of his own sanity. Hence he hadn't been in the theatre last night when she had dashed out of it but had been pacing outside in two minds whether to join his sister in the audience or use his work as an excuse to back out of it altogether. 'Go and relax and I'll come and find you when it's ready.'

And when he wasn't feeling quite so aware of her in every possible way or so devastated that he could never act upon it.

He hadn't expected her to still be in that cosy private dining room when he returned and was emotionally unprepared to see that she had moved to the chair next to his and was scrutinising his drawings. 'What is this?'

'A high-pressure steam engine. Hopefully one strong enough to run thirty power looms at speed simultaneously.'

'Hopefully?'

'There were a few flaws in the initial design which are proving to be annoyingly persistent to rectify.'

'What sort of flaws?'

'The boiler keeps exploding.'

'It explodes!' She looked horrified. 'That sounds dangerous.'

'Only if you're within fifty feet of the flying shrapnel or indoors of course, where I dare say it could blow the roof off and bury you under several feet of raining rubble.'

'Perhaps you need to cut your losses and go with a different design if that one isn't working?'

Griff shook his head. 'Can't. The designer is too stubborn.'

'Then maybe it is time for a different designer too? One better at his job and not quite so set in his ways.'

'Can't do that either.' Then he shrugged as he grinned, suddenly embarrassed. 'Because the designer is me.'

'Oh.' She frowned then stared back at the complicated diagram rolled out on the table. '*Oh*... I never knew you were an inventor, Griff.'

'I dabble here and there, usually where steam is involved.'

'Because you enjoy explosions?' She smiled, entirely without her usual artifice and he decided he preferred that smile too.

'Because of the endless possibilities steam power could provide. It's already revolutionised the mining and textile industries and they already power boats with it in America to great success. The possibilities are endless, and it isn't only factories which will improve with such mechanisation. Agriculture could be improved with machines bearing the brunt of ploughing, harvesting or bailing. Mark my words, it won't be long before steam replaces horses and allows us to travel faster too with locomotives travelling the length and breadth of the country on rails in a matter of hours instead of days.' He was babbling and likely boring her senseless in the process.

'Locomotives? Like the one at that ridiculous Steam Circus which came to Bloomsbury a few years ago? The one you dragged us all to the day before it flew off its rails and smashed to smithereens? It was a miracle nobody died that day! I cannot imagine any sane person choosing to travel on those filthy things over the safety and comfort of a well-sprung carriage.'

'Even a well-sprung carriage will tip over if you drive it at full pelt around and around in a small circle.' He was still annoyed at Richard Trevithick for showing off that way and dragging their cause of progress backwards. 'There are other locomotives in use nowadays—for proper work rather than idle pleasure. A fellow called Stephenson built one last year which can shift thirty tons of coal from pit to canal in one go. And it's been doing it day after day since last summer in Tyneside without incident.' Perhaps it was her supreme skill at acting, but she seemed interested. 'If they can carry coal safely, they can carry people. It's the future, Charity, and one Philpot & Son Manufacturing will be spearheading if I have any say over it. Although to be fair to my father, who was sceptical at first, he is a convert now that we've seen sales of our steam-adapted machinery outsell the others two to one in the last couple of years.'

'All your doing, I suppose?'

He shrugged, not wanting to sound like a braggart. 'It is important to move with the times. People were sceptical of steam-powered looms a few years ago, and now, since they have evolved all the northern mills are rapidly converting to them because they make sound financial sense. They weave faster, longer, more efficiently and more accurately than any human being could manage. Passenger locomotives will follow suit as soon as one bright spark designs one which doesn't derail at speed. I suspect that is down to the wheels and the rails, not the engine.'

'Don't tell me you are attempting to build one of those too?'

'I am sorely tempted.' And he might already have a few hundred preliminary drawings stashed in his study that he pulled out from time to time and which he would work on seriously once he had convinced his father of the benefits. 'But I need to build an actual locomotive before I can adapt it for passengers, and to do that, I need to find a businessman with deep pockets willing to take a punt on my designs because dear old Papa is still a draconian sceptic on that score. And I need to fix this power loom engine first, as all those designs hinge on that. But something is wrong with the layout of the pipes and valves, which I am damned if I can find—but I will. It's just a matter of stripping it back to the place where it all went wrong, then rebuilding it again properly.'

'If it's broken, aren't you tempted to just scrap it and start from scratch?'

'And admit defeat?' He shook his head in mock horror, making her laugh. 'Out of the question. Where would the world be if the Egyptians hadn't invented paper or the Romans hadn't developed roads? If Archimedes hadn't bothered with his screw or Gutenberg had given up on his printing press? You need to be tenacious in this game—even in the face of crushing failure— and remember that if the basic premise is sound, then no problem is unsolvable and no mistake unfixable.'

'I sincerely doubt that. I've certainly encountered several unfixable problems.'

'That's likely because you saw the thing as a whole, which is always overwhelming. But the devil is always in the detail and once you put aside the whole and break it down into the component parts, you eventually find the single tiny piece that prevents success and you work on that. It might need a light tweak, it might need a complete rethink and rebuild, but if you persevere you will solve the puzzle.'

'And how long do you persevere for?'

'As long as it takes.' He laughed at her perplexed expression, knowing that was an entirely unsatisfactory answer for someone who always lived life in a rush like Charity. 'You just have to keep believing and plodding away at it.'

'A stubborn dreamer and an inventor.' She shook her head as she stared at him, obviously impressed. 'You've kept that quiet, Griff. But then you have always been a closed book, haven't you?'

'Have I?' It was odd that she thought of him that way because that wasn't how he saw himself. 'How so?'

'Well, for a start, I have known you since I was six years old, and it is only today and at the ripe old age of three and twenty, that I discover you can draw such complicated schematics and that you while away your hours designing steam engines. We have been confined in a carriage together this last week, and all that time I assumed you were totting up dull accounts, not doing this.' She swept her hand over the piles of diagrams scattered across the tabletop.

'You could have asked what I was doing. I would have happily told you.' Or would he? He had always been self-conscious of his academic leanings around Charity, because they always seemed so staid up against her vivaciousness.

'But we don't do that, you and I, do we?' She stared at him unblinking. 'We never have.'

'That's likely my fault.' It was all his fault because he had no idea how to cope with his feelings for her beyond avoidance. 'I suppose I am a bit of a closed book.'

'A bit?' She laughed. 'Getting anything out of you is like getting blood out of a stone. Most of the time I never know what you are thinking or feeling. To be frank, I don't think anybody does.'

Under the circumstances, he should have found that admission a huge relief because he worked hard to mask his inappropriate emotions all of the time. But now, after seeing an aspect of her he had been unaware existed, he wished she knew a bit more of the real him too. 'I find discussing anything personal difficult. We men are expected to keep our emotions tightly in check and I suppose I practice that a little too literally.'

'Yet you do disdain so very well, Griff.' A dig he undoubtedly deserved because that was how his pent-up feelings for her always leaked out. 'And all those things aside, we have never enjoyed the easy friendship that you have with both my sisters. Why is that, do you suppose?'

His inappropriate feelings again and a veritable hornet's nest which was best left undisturbed. 'I suppose Faith and I are the same age and Hope is only a year younger. We naturally migrated towards one another when we first met as you did with Dottie.'

'I think, if you ask Dorothy, she will confirm that we see that distinction quite differently, as we forged our friendship not because we were the same age but because we were excluded from yours. We were the annoying baby sisters that none of you wanted around. Or at least *you* never wanted us around. I always got on with my siblings like a house on fire when the only boy—Gruff Griffith Philpot the Fun Spoiler—wasn't around.'

'Is that what you used to call me?'

'I still do. Sometimes. When you are being overbearing and vexatious.' Her lovely eyes danced with mischief. 'I suppose I shall have to re-evaluate that now I've finally discovered you are a hopeless dreamer with a decent side.' Then she avoided his gaze, her fingers smoothing a tiny fold on one of his papers. 'And on that score… I owe you a huge thank-you for last night, Griff. It would be remiss of me not to mention it no matter how much my stubborn pride might want to pretend it hadn't happened. You saved the day and very likely my career too. I still cannot fathom what came over me but I am truly horrified that you had to see it.'

It was odd. She might well be horrified that he had seen the cracks in her façade, but he felt privileged to have been allowed to. He also suspected few had ever seen that side of her. Perhaps not even his sister knew that the indomitable Charity Brookes harboured any doubts about anything. He was still reeling at the revelation. Humbled by the rare honour of witnessing it. 'You floundered for a moment, that is all, but rallied immediately.' There hadn't been a single visible crack when she had walked on to the stage a scant few minutes later, and the determination and strength of character that must have taken staggered him and made him ridiculously proud. He wanted to tell her as much but didn't.

'I blame that silly corset you strapped yourself into entirely.' The mere mention of that intimate garment reminded him of the sublime feel of her bare skin beneath his fingers and made his collar feel tight. 'Those laces were done up so tight I doubt they allowed any blood to flow to your head. No wonder you had a wobble.'

'And you are doing it again…being nice.' She feigned an irritation which belied the sudden confusion in her gaze. 'After seventeen years of being denied so much as the scraps from your table, Griff, it is most disconcerting. How am I supposed to thwart you at every juncture of this trip as I'd planned, if I finally start liking you?'

'Have I been that bad?'

'Do you remember that time we all went to Brighton? You had a brand-new kite…'

'Because you had broken the old one.'

Charity narrowed her eyes, smiling, but continued undaunted as he gingerly sat beside her. 'I had just turned seven, I think, and was desperate to impress you. Do you remember how you decreed that you would only grant a turn to us each to fly it if you were paid in advance with a splendid shell for the honour? Faith, Hope and Dorothy all got several turns and with the most lacklustre shells to boot, yet each time I brought you one you declared it not quite good enough and sent me packing to fetch a better one. I scoured that beach for hours trying to find the perfect specimen so that I could play too, but you found a flaw in all of them and you never relented. Not once that entire weekend.'

'In my defence, I was still scarred from the previous incident when I entrusted you with my precious old kite and you stomped on it in a fit of pique.'

'That was an accident which you have never forgiven me for.'

'An accident? Clearly your definition of the word and your memory of the event differs greatly from mine.'

Before she could respond, the innkeeper knocked on the door and carried in a huge tray of food. Much too much for one, as he had ordered, and with two plates. Before he left them to it, and before Griff could decline the meal, Charity piled ham and cheese on both, handed him the butter knife then sawed off some bread.

'Do you remember the plays Hope wrote which we put on for our parents each Christmas, Griff? Despite having no obvious theatrical talents, you always put yourself in charge of the productions because you used to say such a complex task was a man's job, then when you divvied out the roles, you always gave me the minor parts with the worst costumes—the old crone, the town crier, the beggarman—part of the crowd in the distance.' He had forgotten all that and her reminder did make him wince. 'One year, you made me a tree, issued me with a bunch of paper leaves to hold and told me I had to stand as still as a statue for the duration as there was absolutely no breeze in the scene.' She prodded him in the arm. 'That was downright mean, Griff, and you knew it.'

'Yes… I suppose it was.' He had done his level best to curtail her and the profound effect she had on him, and all to no avail. 'Yet as I recall it, you still stole the show anyway and had everyone in stitches with your ridiculous poses throughout my impassioned final soliloquy.'

'It turned out there was a breeze that day. A gale in fact…' She grinned, flashing her becoming dimples which his fingers suddenly itched to trace. 'I had to get my revenge on you somehow for spoiling my fun.' Then she popped a chunk of generously buttered bread into her mouth upon which she had balanced a perfectly cut cube of cheese, her blue eyes widening in pleasure at the taste because her zest for life and all its many wonders was never far from the surface.

'You always stole the show as I recall. No matter how small the part. I knew at the time I should have given you the lead but churlishly refused to do so because an annoying little scrap of a girl had no right to be more talented at everything than a proud young man who was four years older.' Had he already lost his heart to her then? Probably. And had likely behaved badly because of it as he would have reasoned that a wizened, mature and bookish ten-year-old had no place adoring a flamboyant baby of six.

'Yet all these years later and I still annoy you. Or am I condemned for ever to be that little scrap of a girl in your decrepit old eyes?'

If only.

Nowadays, those four years of difference seemed inconsequential and all his greedy, adult eyes saw was the seductive woman she had become. So he grinned and attempted humour, hoping those inappropriate and overwhelming feelings would soon go away for both their sakes and that he would continue to have the willpower not to act on them. 'Sadly, I suspect you are doomed to be that scrap for ever, Charity.'

'Then why did you kiss me, Griff?'

The question came out of nowhere and it took all his strength not to outwardly show how flustered it made him. Better to dismiss it. To deny it. 'I kissed you?'

'You know you did. Last night…before I went onstage.' Her index finger touched her lips, drawing his eyes there and reminding his body what it had felt like. 'You kissed me and called me darling.'

'If I did, then it was out of brotherly affection and concern for you in your hour of need.' He shoved a big piece of ham in his mouth to save him from elaborating and did his best to play the part of man unperturbed, concentrating on his food. Hoping to convey that it had meant nothing and that he had absolutely no recollection of it, when he had done nothing but contemplate it since. Because a simple, quick kiss shouldn't have such a profound effect and it certainly shouldn't wield such intense power that he still felt the after-effects of it even now. As a veil of awkwardness descended, all entirely of his making, he forced himself to change the subject.

'Do you remember the time you stitched the bottoms of each leg of all my breeches closed and before I realised it I fell over trying to wrench a pair on and cracked my head open on the bedstead?' He lifted his hair to remind her of the scar on his forehead. 'Three stitches as I recall and all completely unprovoked.'

She laughed and offered him a guilty shrug. 'Perhaps you weren't the only mean one?'

'There's no "perhaps" about it, Charity. Because you always gave as good as you got. It was never a one-sided war. Not how I recall it anyway.'

'But it was fun though, wasn't it?' Her smile was wistful. 'I wish we could be like that again.'

Chapter Seven

'This doesn't look like York.' Charity had only visited the city once several years ago and certainly had no recollection of the vast expanse of rolling hills and meadows. While it was nowhere near as urban as London, York had more buildings than this place did. Considerably more.

'How very perceptive of you.' Griff offered her one of his dry half-smiles as he opened the carriage door and jumped out. 'That is because it isn't.' He stretched, rolling his broad shoulders to alleviate some of the inevitable stiffness from the journey before holding out his hand to help her down. 'This is Appletreewick.'

'What a quaint name.' The second his fingers brushed hers all her nerve endings danced exactly as they had done with giddy abandon since Lincoln. If he experienced the same, he hid it well and no sooner had her feet touched the ground than he let go to assist his sister.

'It's a quaint place apparently. Scenic, quiet and well off the beaten track. And this inn has been recommended to me more than once which is always a good sign. The food is exceptional, or so I am told, and the accommodations charming. Exactly what you need for the next few days.'

'Few days?' She frowned, trying to recall which day it was and failing miserably. 'We're staying then…not just stopping for luncheon?'

'We are indeed.'

'But I have to be in York by the…' She frowned again, her addled brain not quite working despite the three cups of strong and bitter coffee she had forced down over breakfast and despite her deep loathing for the stuff.

'The twenty-ninth. Yes. I know.' His hand grazed the small of her back, sending more ripples of awareness down her spine as he gently manoeuvred her and Dorothy towards the extremely old and charmingly lopsided inn while their carriage lurched forward to follow the signalling young ostler, who appeared to be the only inhabitant of Appletreewick. 'Which means we do not have to get there for *four* days. Assuming we'll need one of those days to travel, that gives you three blissful days of peace to recuperate.'

'I don't need to recuperate.' Even though she felt dead on her feet despite it being only noon.

He shared a knowing look with Dorothy who grinned, then stared at her blandly. 'Forget the date. What day is it, Charity?'

'It's…um…' She had definitely played her fourth and final concert in Manchester on the Saturday before they had headed directly to Leeds. With another three there and one…no, two…dinner parties interspersed on the off days organised by the cities' dignitaries in her honour, both of which had been surprisingly dull affairs. 'Sunday?'

'Not even close. It's Thursday. Which if my maths

are correct, which they obviously are as I've always had a head for numbers, means you haven't stopped to breathe in exactly three weeks. It's been nonstop since Lincoln and with all the additional impromptu and unnecessary performances you have been adding...'

'They are hardly unnecessary if the places are full, Griff, and I don't want to leave anyone disappointed. You have seen the crowds.' The shoeless masses in those smoke choked industrial cities had broken her heart. People who could barely afford food let alone a ticket to the opera but who had come out to see her anyway, hoping she might reward them with a song which might make one day in their hard lives brighter. She had been raised with a social conscience so how could she refuse? When a couple of songs in a grotty inn, which cost her nothing but time, gave them so much pleasure.

His stern expression softened. 'You have a good heart, Charity, and it does you credit, but you also need a break from it all. You are running yourself ragged and it's starting to take its toll. If I took you to York now, you'd be singing for your supper twice a day and that's before the proper rehearsals even start. It is my job to save you from yourself, remember?'

She didn't argue. Not only did she not have the energy to do so, she was also rather touched by his concern. He had been her rock these past three weeks, not only shepherding her around, but looking out for her too. Since her 'wobble' in Lincoln, they had both made more of an effort to understand one another and be more tolerant of each other's quirks. And in turn that had made them appreciate one another more for the first time in years. He now knew she too worked hard to hone her craft and was more forgiving of her theatrical tendencies and her constant lateness and began to enjoy them rather than despair of them.

He had also made it his mission to look after her at the theatres both before and after a performance, taking her mind off her nerves at the outset and spiriting her rapidly back to the inn once she was spent. She had lost count of how many times he had saved her from having to politely humour the more determined members of the audience who used their influence or their wits to get them backstage, acting as an immovable barrier who demanded that she needed to rest at the exact times that she had absolutely nothing left to give.

Griff had also deviated substantially from his meticulous travelling plan, stopping shy of the prearranged inns to protect Charity from over-exerting herself at more of the impromptu free concerts she had taken to giving. What had started as a way to annoy him had swiftly become a huge inconvenience, as more and more crowds gathered outside those inns along the Great North Road awaiting her arrival, all expecting to be entertained and who grew quite petulant if she only sang a few songs and became quite forceful in their demands.

That had been all well and good when the only singing she had to do was for them, but since Lincoln and with theatres packed with patrons who had paid for the privilege, she couldn't risk straining her voice on all those additional performances indefinitely and he had realised that long before she had. Thanks to Griff, she hadn't sung to a soul on the Great North Road in over a fortnight because he had found them different inns a little way away from it. She also hadn't run Griff the merry dance she had promised herself either. Frankly, she hadn't had the time and certainly didn't have the energy to muster the enthusiasm. Right now, trailing after him into the inn with a slightly knitted brow was about as much rebellion as she was capable of.

''Ow do.' The no-nonsense innkeeper barely inclined his head as they entered the taproom and was as gnarly as the ancient oak beams supporting his haphazard ceiling. A ceiling so low, poor Griff had to hunch a little to stop his head from hitting it.

'Good day, sir. We have several rooms booked. You should have received my message yesterday.'

The innkeeper acknowledged this with one curt nod. 'Then I assume you must be Mr Philpot and these must be your sisters?'

'They are indeed. This is Miss Dorothy Philpot and this...' Griff shot her a warning glance which dared her to contradict him '...is Miss Charlotte Philpot.'

'And you only stipulated the one room for your two servants. Are they brother and sister too?'

'Husband and wife, sir.'

The innkeeper jabbed the air with his finger. 'They had better be for I don't tolerate any funny business under my roof!' Then he eyed the three of them suspiciously. 'We don't get many London sorts 'ere. What brings the three of you to Appletreewick?' The innkeeper flattened his palms on the bar and curled his lip in disgust. 'If you've come expecting the Onion Fair, you're two months early.'

'Oh, that is a shame.' Griff's fake sincerity in the face of such open hostility made her lips twitch. 'But I am sure we will find other diversions in its absence. We are travelling around Yorkshire, sir, and taking our time exploring the Dales, on our way to visit family in Northumberland.'

'We don't get many tourists here, either.' Then the

innkeeper shrugged and huffed as if their presence was all a great inconvenience before he attempted a hospitable smile which fell woefully short of the mark. 'But I suppose there are some fine walks hereabouts if walking is your thing. 'Appen there's some pretty views from Simon's Seat over yonder too, if you've the stamina for the climb...' Although his expression as he pointed out of the window to the huge hill in the distance said he sincerely doubted Griff did. 'And Troller's Gill is a sight to see and less of a slog—just make sure you well clear of the place afore dark in case the barguest gets you.' He then pulled a horrified face as if such a thing were a fate worse than death. 'But you and the lasses will be safe in t'daylight and he never wanders further than t'gill so you've nowt to worry about elsewhere.'

'What's a barguest?' Because it already sounded fascinating to Charity.

'A huge, snarling black devil dog.' The innkeeper shuddered, his gnarled face knotted. 'Who prowls there at night and who'll turn you to stone if you are unfortunate enough to look at 'im in those blood-red eyes of his.'

Charity grinned, she couldn't help it. Devil dogs and onion fairs were a far cry from Bloomsbury. Her amusement earned her an insulted frown from the innkeeper and a sharp nudge from Griff.

'We'll be sure to heed your advice, sir. In the meantime, we could all do with some refreshments. It has been a long journey.'

'We only do stew on a Thursday for both lunch and supper. If you want owt different then you'll have to go to Burnsall two miles yonder which welcomes tourists.' By the look on his face, he would much rather they went to Burnsall anyway and left him well alone.

'Then we'll take three of those please.'

'It won't be ready for a good hour.' The innkeeper belligerently folded his arms in case anyone had the audacity to argue. 'Food's always served at one here and we make no exceptions.'

Because something about Griff seemed to raise the surly innkeeper's hackles, Charity offered him her sunniest smile, the one which always cracked even the hardest nut. 'An hour will give us plenty of time to freshen up, sir, so perhaps you would be kind enough to show us to our rooms instead? For I confess, I am itching to see them.' She touched his arm for good measure before she greased the wheels further with some interested flattery.

'Your establishment came so highly recommended from some friends of ours who passed this way last year and it is so very pretty. I'd even go as far as saying it's the prettiest inn we've encountered and we've stopped at many. You must work very hard, sir, to keep it so nice when so many of the inns we have stayed at have fallen wide of the mark.'

For a moment his expression twitched, as if he was trying to ascertain which of the underused muscles in his cheeks he needed to chivvy to smile, until the ingrained frown eventually flattened and only the one side of his mouth curved upwards. 'Thank ye, lass. Me and the missus work hard to keep it that way. This inn's been in our family for nearly two hundred years.'

'You are a credit to your ancestors, sir.' Dorothy's well-timed compliment earned her an almost smile from the innkeeper too, but then he glared at Griff as he grabbed three keys from beneath the bar.

'Follow me.'

The innkeeper led the way upstairs and allocated

the three bedchambers on the oak-beamed landing according to whom he liked the best. Poor Griff, who he had instantly taken a dislike to for some reason, got the smallest with a narrow single bed, Dorothy got a bigger one next door to him and Charity was led to the largest of the three, with a delightful old four-poster bed and spectacular views of the Dales.

While she waited for her baggage, she happily stared at it, feeling lighter than she had in days. She sensed Griff behind her before he spoke.

'If you'd rather we stayed somewhere else…'

She shook her head. 'No, Griff, this is perfect.' And exactly what she needed. 'Unless you want to move elsewhere.' The wicked grin was spontaneous. 'You have been given the short straw with that tiny room.'

'I've slept in worse.' The boyish smile which accompanied his resigned shrug did odd things to her insides. 'It's clean and despite its diminutive size, the bed is surprisingly comfortable so I shall grin and bear it—unless you are feeling as charitable as your virtuous name suggests and want to swap.'

She pretended to ponder it before she shook her head. 'As I am still not fully over the Brighton kite incident, you deserve to suffer.'

His exasperated arm fold was spoiled by a smile he couldn't cover quick enough. 'And I will do so happily if you promise me that you will try to relax while we are here. You look so pale and tired—I am worried about you.' Then he seemed embarrassed to have admitted that. 'So is Dottie.'

'I shall only promise it on one condition.'

'Which is?'

'That in the absence of the Onion Fair, *you* promise to take me barguest hunting…in the dark.'

* * *

Three days in and the colour had returned to her cheeks and she was back to being Charity again. Mischievous, adventurous and unstoppable. And while Dorothy had started complaining halfway up the steep hike up to Simon's Seat, Charity had taken it all in her stride, exactly as she had their nocturnal but fruitless barguest hunt last night which she had, of course, instigated.

'Isn't it beautiful, Griff?' Fearless as always, she was stood on a rocky outcrop and smiling in wonder at the rolling, untamed countryside laid before them.

'It is.' Though nowhere near as beautiful as she was today, with her thin summer dress plastered to her lush figure by the warm hilltop breeze and her windswept golden curls tousled and shimmering in the sunshine.

'You forget how pretty England is when in its cities, don't you? Yet the air here is so fresh it almost makes you giddy.' She closed her eyes to inhale it deeply, which was just as well as the gesture inappropriately drew his eyes to her pert breasts as they rose and fell in time with her breathing before he tore them away. When she finally opened them again, she stared at Dorothy below and shouted over the wind, 'You are missing something wonderful, Dottie! The view is spectacular. Come on up and stop being a spoilsport.'

'I am scared of heights!' His sister pouted stubbornly. 'And I am happy on this blanket reading my book and guarding the picnic from the birds. Just looking at you on that rock is making me dizzy.'

Charity slanted him an exasperated glance, because they both knew his usually affable sister could be intransigent when she set her mind to it and she had never been one for the great outdoors or for testing her boundaries. Traits which had never hampered Charity. 'Then it is just you and me for the summit, Griff…unless you are another lily-livered Philpot too and would prefer the safety of the picnic blanket?'

Griff folded his arms, feigning offence. 'Do I look lily-livered? When have you ever known me to shy away from a challenge? I'll have you know I build exploding steam engines for a living, so this piffling little hill doesn't faze me.' If one could consider a fifteen-hundred-foot hill piffling.

She pretended to consider it, her eyes raking him from top to bottom and inadvertently reminding his body that it was male. 'But are you up to it, Griff? That's the question.'

He stared at the wall of giant boulders piled on top of each other, some significantly taller than him, and shrugged with feigned arrogance. 'That's more a bracing walk than a climb.'

She grinned, mischievous eyes twinkling and flashing her distracting dimples, completely unaware, for once, of how lovely she was. 'Then I'll race you to the top and the loser has to forfeit their dessert tonight.'

She was off before she finished the sentence, skirts hoisted to her knees and clambering up the towering pile of millstones for all she was worth, giggling like a child. When she reached one so high it defeated her, she shamelessly used him as a step, not caring one whit that her walking boots left dusty marks on his breeches or that she wasn't being the least bit ladylike in her determined quest to beat him or that she had left him no choice but to manhandle her up that last foot. As she disappeared over the flat expanse of rock above him, he was left to fend for himself, and by the time he had hauled himself up she was sat cross-legged in the middle of it, smiling at the view and apparently completely at one with the world. 'I believe your treacle sponge and custard is now mine, slow coach.'

'Only because you cheated.' Griff sat beside her and then immediately wished he hadn't because it suddenly felt too intimate. They were all alone and out of sight, just the pair of them, the cloudless blue sky and the wind, and she fair took his breath away.

'It's funny…' She didn't turn from the view. 'I never understood why my mother always insisted she had to take a few months off between performances even though people were still clamouring to see her and why, halfway through a run, she seemed to live for that respite. Even if you had asked me a few weeks ago, I would have said that her attitude baffled me because I have always believed you need to grasp such things with both hands and strike while the iron is hot in case the opportunities disappear. The only theory which made any sense was that leaving them wanting more guaranteed her more attention because absence, apparently, makes the heart grow fonder. But now that I've lived it, properly lived it, I realise my theory is nonsense and her logic makes perfect sense.'

'How so?'

'The strange life of the stage is all consuming and it is easy to lose yourself in it completely and forget what is important. If these past few days have taught me anything, they have reminded me of what is important.'

'And what is important?'

She shrugged as she smiled at him with uncharacteristic awkwardness and no hint of her usual bravado. 'Myself, I suppose. What I am…how I truly feel…what I want. Others are important too, Griff, obviously…' She nudged him playfully with her shoulder. 'Before you accuse me of complete self-absorption and shocking vanity, though I don't mean it that way and you know it.'

'Are you saying that you are not self-absorbed and vain?' He kept his tone light even though he sensed what she suddenly needed to say was important. 'As I have never known another who needs at least an hour to get her hair just so.' Although to be fair to her, she hadn't given two hoots about it since they had arrived here and he was coming to see that that vanity was more for the benefit of others than for herself. Charity liked to put on a show and never wanted to disappoint an audience, no matter how small it was or what the venue.

'Of course, I am…*sometimes*.' She took the teasing comment as it was meant. 'We all have traits which make us imperfect. You, for example, can be sanctimonious, overbearing and controlling…*sometimes*. And yet at others, as I am coming to realise, you are actually rather…tolerable.'

'Only tolerable?'

'Let's not get too carried away with the gushing praise nor forget that tolerable is a huge improvement on annoying, which you certainly were up until recently.' Her shoulder nudged him again, the gesture instantly enveloping him in the subtle scent of her perfume and awakening every nerve ending he possessed. 'What I mean is, I understand now that as much as I love to be the centre of attention, I also appreciate that the adoration I get from an audience isn't real and that it is good for my soul to step away from it from time to time. To be me and not have to pretend to be…anything.'

'Clearly the Dales have brought out your philosophical side if you can see that. And there I thought you loved all the adoration.'

'I do.' She exhaled and stared out at nothing. 'And

bizarrely, I don't. I love to entertain and I adore being welcomed with open arms, to feel valued and special but…' She sighed again and shook her head.

'But?' He was sorely tempted to wrap his arm around her and draw her close because he had seen first-hand the toll it had all taken on her—the real her behind her performer's façade. Hold her tight and kiss it all better. Or just kiss her and to hell with the consequences. Wanted to desperately but didn't dare.

How could he when there had always been a hard and decisive line in the sand between the Brookes and the Philpots which he couldn't cross? A demarcation forged by years of familiarity and a shared childhood. The solid border of a clearly defined relationship which he understood. Crossing it was unchartered, unthinkable and likely irreparable. If she didn't feel the same about him as he did her, Griff had no clue how they would co-exist in the same close-knit family circle after he had bared his hand—or even if that circle could still exist at all. If they ever came to light, his inappropriate feelings were bound to make it awkward for everyone.

'It comes at a cost I had no concept of before now.' She leaned back on her hands to allow the afternoon sun to warm her face, not caring that without the shield of the bonnet she had left discarded below it was rapidly tanning her skin. 'Aside from the physical toll months of constantly performing and practising take, I never expected how suffocating it would all become. How beholden I feel to all those people who come to see me and how draining their adoration could be when I've craved it for all my life.' Two golden eyebrows kissed in consternation. 'It feels like they own me, Griff, or at least the me they think I am, yet no matter how much of myself I give them it is never ever going to be enough.

Does that make sense?' She sighed slowly, basking in contentment at the respite and the sunshine. 'That's why I now completely understand my mother's persistent insistence on distance.'

Another newly discovered aspect of her character which tugged at his heart. 'Oh, good grief, please don't say you're a poet now too?'

She swiped him playfully on the arm before wrapping hers around it, unwittingly sending his senses further into turmoil with her innocent, affectionate touch. 'These last few days have genuinely been a balm to my soul. It's been wonderful not having to smile or be entertaining or available to all and sundry. Or even to look my best.' With a mock frown she grabbed a loose curl and tugged it in front of her face. 'As the state of my hair is a likely testament to.'

'Your hair looks lovely.' Just like her. 'Natural.' Untamed and inviting. The sort of hair which tempted him to run his fingers through as he slowly pulled out every pin. 'You should wear it like that more often.' Even though it would likely kill him to keep looking and not touching.

'And you should probably get yourself some spectacles if you consider a bird's nest lovely, but I shall vainly take the compliment anyway simply because I cannot muster the enthusiasm to care what a fright I look and I adore compliments. That said, it's liberating not caring what anyone thinks.'

'Perhaps you should try it more often?'

She nodded, her expression wistful. 'I will. As I said, it now makes perfect sense to me why my mother takes such long breaks from the theatre and ruthlessly turns work down. Those months away from the demands of a baying audience keep her sane and grounded. And happy. I realise that now too. I also realise that the same has been sadly lacking in my life for quite some time.'

'You are not happy, then?' That revelation surprised him because she always seemed so full of life and fun. In all the years he had known Charity, she smiled a hundred times more than she frowned and most of them were genuine. She might be tenacious, determined, ambitious and irrepressible, but she had never been prone to sour moods or fits of melancholy. Of the five of them, she had always been the eternal optimist and the reliable ray of sunshine.

'I am…but…' She sighed again. 'You said something the other day which struck a chord. You said that I hadn't stopped since Lincoln and that just isn't true. If I am being brutally honest with myself, I haven't stopped for over a year, Griff. Not since I got my first part in the chorus of *Così fan Tutte*. Since then, everything has been a whirlwind. Part of that is opportunity—*Figaro*, this tour of the north. My own ambition has also fuelled things further. As the youngest of all of us, I've always felt I had something to prove and I have been on a mission to make it all a success from the moment I could talk. But another part, the part I had no awareness of until now, was the one played by the huge expectations and demands of others who have kept me in the centre of that whirlwind and prevented me from seeing any way out.

'I never went on our planned trip to Bath last summer because I was needed for rehearsals. I haven't visited my grandparents in Whitstable in for ever, or spent much time with my friends. I worked through Christmas rehearsing furiously because people had bought tickets and I didn't want to let them down when the show opened. I've barely seen Hope or Faith since they married because there have been so many demands on my time. We pass like ships in the night—which is sad when we have always been so close. I have a new nephew whom I barely know and another on the way, and yet...'

'Nobody blames you for being busy, Charity. Your sisters know how much this means to you and how hard you have worked for it. They are delighted by your success, so you have nothing to feel guilty about in chasing your dreams. They did too, remember. They still do.'

'I know they understand.' She stared at the horizon again, her expression troubled. 'But since the new year, I now realise that all I have done is eat and sleep the theatre. And these past few weeks have been the most ridiculous of all as everybody seems to want a bit of me—and because I've now become a hopeless slave to the whirlwind, I've given in to it. Even to the detriment of myself, my health and my sanity. So I thank you, Gruff Griff the Kite-Hogging Fun-Spoiler...'

Her hand sought his on top of the cool rock and she laced her fingers tight in his. 'Thank you for being sanctimonious, overbearing and controlling, and seeing all that before I did and for bringing me here to recuperate. As much as I hate to make you right about anything, I needed this break from it all. So very much.'

Her hand felt perfect in his, as if it were meant to be there and without thinking he pulled her close despite his better judgement so that her head rested on his shoulder. It felt good. She felt better. 'I promised your father I would save you from yourself, remember?' A quest which was slowly killing him now that he knew he wanted more. He settled for a brief kiss on the top of her head and a subtle inhale of her scent. 'And as a man of honour, my word is my bond.'

'I don't believe you did this for him, Griff.' Her face lifted, too close to his for comfort. 'I suspect you did it for me.' As confident an accusation as that sounded, her lovely blue eyes were uncertain as they stared deep into his, as if she needed to see confirmation of that unfortunate truth. 'Is it possible that after all these years, you actually, finally...*care* about me?'

'Of course I care about you.' An understatement. 'I always have.'

'Only because you had to. You tolerated me then, but it feels like something has shifted all of a sudden and we are finally friends now too?'

'We are more than friends, Charity.' The words came out before he could censor them or temper them with an explanation because he had lost himself hopelessly in her eyes and her smile. As her gaze searched his face and flicked briefly to his mouth, he felt his dipping helplessly towards hers, remembering the way she tasted. How wonderful she felt in his arms.

How much he needed and wanted her.

Only, when their lips were barely an inch apart, the sheer gravity of what he was about to do slammed home and he immediately straightened, uttering the often-said words he had never, ever felt. 'We are brother and sister.'

Chapter Eight

'A canny businessman must move with the times, Lord Ackroyd. This is an age of innovation and revolution after all.' The Earl of Thirsk's handsome son and heir twirled her in a wide arc across his dance floor. 'The Killingworth Colliery have been using a steam locomotive to haul their coal from the pit to the plant successfully for several months now, and I am reliably informed their Blucher can tow eight wagons loaded with thirty tons of coal all in one go.' Or so Griff had told her. Since the dramatic thawing of relations between them after Lincoln, she was coming to understand what a clever and forward-thinking businessman her childhood nemesis had become. 'Saving hours of manpower as well as money. Why wouldn't you want Thirsk Mining to follow suit?'

'How can you say that a thing which costs a king's ransom saves money, Miss Brookes?' She could tell by his expression he wanted to be convinced, because exactly like Griff, he wouldn't be able to alter the course of the family business without his father's approval too. 'As it would run into a cost of thousands, wouldn't it?'

'I cannot deny, it is a huge initial investment, my

lord, but it will pay for itself tenfold in no time and put you well ahead of your rivals at every conceivable juncture. Just think of the possibilities…' The waltz ended and she curtsied, then threaded her arm though his, trying not to feel the weight of Griff's eyes on them as she did so, or to glance his way.

It was brotherly concern. Nothing more. He had been quite adamant in that.

And as much as she still might occasionally try to fool herself he harboured unbrotherly feelings towards her too, because she was certainly feeling some decidedly unsisterly ones for him of late, staring longingly at Griff was futile when she had no place looking at him like that at all and he certainly wouldn't welcome it. Not after the odd moment they had shared at the top of Simon's Seat when she had been convinced he was about to kiss her, had been thrilled and giddy at the prospect, and instead he had quite emphatically set her straight in the subtlest and politest of ways which allowed them both to save face. To him they were family, and all things considered, that was probably for the best when she forced herself to put her feelings to one side and contemplate it all rationally.

She had been a little overwhelmed of late, and clearly wasn't thinking straight if she was suddenly considering their near life-long and platonic relationship any differently. Thank goodness she hadn't acted on the wild impulse to drag him back and press her mouth to his when he had first pulled away, because that would have made the last week in his company awkward in the extreme. A foolhardy, spur of the moment and inappropriate kiss which would have swiftly ruined the new friendly camaraderie which now existed between them for evermore.

Despite willing them not to flick his way, her traitorous eyes sought his across the sea of people separating them anyway, and once again she was struck by just how much he stood out among them all. And it wasn't just his handsome features and tall, broad physique which made her pulse instantly quicken in a wholly inappropriate fashion, it was something about the man he was within which had always called to her soul and tempted her body to want. So much, that it took all her willpower to focus back to her partner and the delicate diplomatic task in hand.

'If your mines are bulging with coal, my lord, doesn't it make more commercial sense to find a way to increase its extraction?'

'That is exactly what my fiancée says, Miss Brookes. It is a shame she isn't here this evening as you'd get on famously. She thinks we should invest in expansion.'

'And she is right, my lord. At the moment, like so many owners, you are constrained by the practicalities and limitations of your workforce and have to rely on nought but man and horsepower to transport it all to where it needs to be. Men and horses tire, don't they? And flag in the heat or the cold of the elements or get sick or injured from the backbreaking work. But with a reliable locomotive taking that strain, you could easily double, even triple your yields by redirecting your workforce elsewhere.' Lord Ackroyd's pale brows knitted together as he considered this, clearly with interest, so she embellished further.

'Besides, it stands to reason that as more industries inevitably mechanise, the demand for coal is only going to grow after all, and in the north that demand could become exponential in just a few short years. If you produce more, you can price your product more competitively to give your company the edge. In fact, if you are one of the first to adopt what doubtless will soon become the norm, you are bound to reap a more sizeable chunk of the potential profits than any of your competitors as the Killingworth Colliery's unbridled recent success is testament to.'

She had learned a lot about the marvels of the steam engine recently. Mostly because she was interested and partly because she enjoyed listening to Griff passionately explain it all. He was particularly compelling when his eyes sparkled, and it was just the two of them chatting in the carriage whenever Dorothy nodded off. Something she did with predictable frequency.

'While your arguments hypothetically make perfect sense, and aside from the huge cost such an endeavour would undoubtedly take, Killingworth will have Stephenson all tied up in cast-iron contracts and they would never share those valuable patents with their competitors. Therefore, to emulate their success, we would need to start from scratch—but without the genius of a George Stephenson behind it. Good gracious it is loud in here...' So loud they were having to shout over the music and the crowds. 'Shall we continue this fascinating conversation outside?'

Glad that he was clearly enthused on the subject, she happily allowed Lord Ackroyd to manoeuvre her towards the French doors and out on to the terrace as the crowded ballroom was so stuffy. Away from the hubbub she would no longer need to strain her already overworked voice to converse above the noise.

After three performances in the last three days, Charity was mindful that too much now could be catastrophic when she still had one last day to do here in York, where she would sing to the packed theatre not once, but twice with only a few hours of respite in between.

'There are other designers out there as good, if not better than Stephenson, my lord. Men with as proven a track record in steam and mechanisation *and* with the skilled workforce and resources required to build a locomotive too.' She smiled coyly as if sharing a huge confidence to pique his interest. 'I happen to know one, actually. And he is quite brilliant. He even has extensive designs for such a system ready to put into production and more than the means to make it.' Lord Ackroyd's feet paused as one eyebrow raised in interest, but she pretended not to notice as she gazed out into the dark garden.

'And who is this brilliant individual?'

Unthinkingly, she beamed with pride. 'Griffith Philpot of the Philpot & Son Manufacturing Company. You might have heard of them as they do a lot of work at this end of the country? One of their biggest workshops is in Sheffield, a stone's throw away. I say a workshop, when really it is a dedicated factory. One which only produces the finest and most modern machinery.'

Lord Ackroyd nodded, quietly impressed. 'I know it well. They supplied all our pumps a few years back when I finally managed to convince my father to purchase some.'

She smiled at him, feigning surprise, pleased he had taken the bait so quickly. 'Then their reputation precedes them, and you know already the superior quality of their steam engines.' Griff had appraised her of the connection when Lord Thirsk had invited her to his ball as the guest of honour when they first arrived in York, so she knew full well that the introduction of the Philpot steam pumps, which had had to be specifically designed they were so complex, had allowed their host to significantly expand his mineshafts and, ergo, his fortune. The Philpots had also benefitted hugely from the association and, as a result, were now the biggest supplier of mining pumps in the north-east.

'Tell me, for I am curious, were those new-fangled steam pumps you fought so vociferously for a waste of good money as your father suspected—or did they transform your business and increase your fortunes as *I* and your very clever fiancée suspect they did?'

He chuckled, basking in her subtle flattery, clearly aware that he had just demolished his own flimsy counter-argument. 'They did indeed transform the business, Miss Brookes. Since their installation, we haven't looked back. In fact, our coal production has doubled.'

'Innovation and progress in action then, my lord.' She squeezed his arm and stared up at him coquettishly through her lashes, knowing a little harmless flirting would help grease the wheels further. 'What a clever man you are, Lord Ackroyd, to see the future and to prepare for it in advance. I have always had a soft spot for a gentleman of vision who refuses to fit into the traditional mould. Your fiancée is a very lucky woman.'

Typically, he puffed out his chest like a peacock. 'I like to think of myself as a visionary, Miss Brookes.'

'I got that sense from you immediately, my lord.' It was almost too easy. No challenge at all. She hadn't intended on selling him one of Griff's speculative and experimental designs, but when the opportunity presented itself out of the blue, as so often all the very best opportunities did, she decided to grab it by the horns. It might be precisely the push that was needed to allow the Philpot & Son Manufacturing Company to branch out in the way its brilliant son envisioned and give him the chance to build the sort of locomotive which made his dark eyes dance whenever he mentioned it.

'You have a certain gravitas, my lord, which is rare and sadly lacking in most of the aristocratic young men I encounter in London...' If he was already half sold on the back of a short chat over one dance, he would be eating out of her hand after a protracted and uninterrupted discussion while they took a slow turn around the garden. Because nothing was more appealing to a gentleman than a woman who found them fascinating. 'What other revolutionary ideas do you and your clever fiancée have for your business?'

Who knew she was a born saleswoman as well as a soprano?

Griff jumped on top of the stone bench to see if he could spot her and growled into the silence when he didn't. It was his own stupid fault she had gone missing. In trying to be magnanimous by giving her both the benefit of the doubt and a little more freedom seeing as they seemed to have reached a tentative accord, Charity had been gone, completely unchaperoned, for a good half an hour. As too had the besotted Ackroyd, which didn't bode well when one considered he was the heir to an earldom, and she had a particular penchant for handsome men with titles.

That would teach him to let his guard down and her out of his sight! There was no telling what mischief the pair of them had got into in thirty minutes. Out here. In the dark. All alone. And he had faithfully promised her parents he would look after her and had, up until now, been doing a splendid job of it too!

As much as he dreaded stumbling across her kissing another man, a kiss was the least of his worries after so long a time when a kiss could easily have already morphed into more now—or much more if they lost their heads and threw all propriety out of the window. The more which didn't bear thinking about, yet he did anyway. Torturing himself with the same erotic images of her which had peppered his dreams for weeks now. Only in these hideous scenarios, the scantily clad Charity was sighing in another man's arms and not his.

Limbs entwined.

Bodies joined.

Writhing in ecstasy.

He didn't fool himself she was a stranger to such sports either.

Despite his regrettable and overwhelming feelings for her which only seemed to get stronger the more time he spent with her, Griff had never harboured such rose-tinted illusions about the sort of woman Charity was. Only a few weeks ago, she had enjoyed a similar tryst in Lady Bulphan's orangery with Lord Denby and had emerged looking unrepentant as well as thoroughly ravished. He had seen that with his own furious eyes at the time and he had read about countless other indiscretions in the gossip columns over the years, which she had always featured in with far more frequency than her older sisters ever had. But then Charity enjoyed rebellion and actively courted it, whereas Faith and Hope did not.

Categoric proof, he supposed, not that proof was needed, that with Charity there rarely was smoke without fire and that his stupid heart had chosen the worst possible woman to fall head over heels in love with. She wasn't the sort to be constrained for all eternity to the rules of monogamy he would insist upon. Charity drew men like flies to a honey pot, had done since her first forays into society, and made no secret of the fact that she enjoyed their company. Expecting her to give all that up for him was as futile as contemplating them having a romantic relationship in the first place.

He wasn't her wronged lover; he was her chaperon. He apparently needed to chant that inescapable fact like a mantra in the hope it talked some sense into his outraged heart.

He stalked further into the garden following the path in the vain hope she would have avoided the grass to save her expensive silk slippers. The silly embroidered concoctions had matched her daring blue evening gown which, he couldn't help but notice, also brought out the deepest periwinkle in her eyes. He knew this because he had caught a flash of them alongside her shapely silk-covered ankle as he had helped her into the carriage to get here and just that had had the power to send every drop of blood he possessed flying to his groin.

How blasted typical that after seventeen long and confusing years he had to settle for her ankle when Ackroyd got to sample the rest of the tempting goods on offer after an acquaintance of less than two hours!

Also, and undeniably Griff's own blasted fault too, as in a fit of uncharacteristic and unbrotherly madness he had almost asked her for that waltz himself. Even though he knew, and she certainly knew, that a waltz was tantamount to a declaration of intent. He had been so close to claiming it, he had even grabbed her dance card. Yet instead of writing on it, which ironically might have prevented her wandering off with her handsome lord in the first place, he had pretended to scrutinise the worthiness of her partners like any good chaperon would before half-heartedly doing the same to his sister's.

What a blasted lovesick fool!

For the sake of his own sanity, all this nonsense needed to stop.

And it would! If he managed to survive these last two weeks before he deposited her back home and then ruthlessly washed his hands of it all before he combusted from unrequited lust.

As he turned to follow the gravel towards the dark silhouette of what appeared to be a sculpture garden, he heard her earthy giggle float upon the wind, confirming all of his worst fears. Like a man possessed he sprinted towards the sound bellowing her name.

'Charity!' As incensed and upset as he was by what his foolish heart refused to see as anything but her infidelity, he wasn't masochistic enough to want to encounter her completely *in flagrante delicto* either. That would be sheer unmitigated torture. It was one thing knowing she wasn't a stranger to passion, another entirely to have to see it enacted in graphic detail before his eyes. 'Charity—where are you?'

'I'm here.' She had the gall to sound amused at his concern. 'Alive and well and not the least bit dead, if that's what you are afraid of.' He skidded to a stop in a paved circle, braced to discover a scandal and instead found her sat primly on a bench opposite Lord Ackroyd. Aside from a few loose tendrils of golden hair which danced in the weak night air, she still appeared to be completely respectable.

Unless, of course, he had arrived too late and the misdeed was already done.

'Poor Griff has been appointed my chaperon on this trip, at the express insistence of my father, and takes his responsibilities much too seriously.' Then she smiled at him, an odd expression on her face as if she were trying to tell him something important.

Knowing her and her determination to rebel against him, that secret message was most probably *go away*.

'I was just telling His Lordship about your steam engines, Griff.' A likely story. 'And what a talented and innovative inventor you have become. He is thinking of further mechanising Thirsk Mining and is particularly interested in the feasibility of installing a locomotive to move his coal uphill from the pit to the barges on the Tyne.' It was obvious she was trying to distract him from the sordid truth by navigating the subject towards one he preferred. Not that he was the least bit convinced by such a contrived tactic.

'The carriage is outside waiting.' Griff wasn't in the mood to make small talk either. Not when it was as much as he could do to speak, albeit through extremely gritted teeth. 'You have an early rehearsal first thing and a big day tomorrow.'

'Evan won't mind waiting a few more minutes. Come. Sit.' She patted the space beside her on the bench. 'I am sure Lord Ackroyd would much prefer to hear about Philpot & Son's *revolutionary* ideas for transforming mining straight from the horse's mouth rather than mine.' She patted the bench again, her eyes imploring. 'You have draft plans for a locomotive and rail system, do you not?'

'I do.' That would teach him for boring her for hours with his work. 'But alas, I cannot spare the time tonight to explain all its myriad complexities.' Not when spending any more time in Ackroyd's company would likely result in Griff pummelling the opportunist seducer with his fists. 'And neither can you, Charity. Dorothy is already in the carriage waiting and it wouldn't be fair to delay Evan any longer and then expect him to be up again at the crack of dawn to get you to the theatre on time.'

He held out his hand, glaring, quite prepared to throw her over his shoulder and carry her back kicking and screaming like a marauding Viking if she refused to comply. 'It is long past time to go when we expressly *agreed* midnight.'

'But, Griff...'

'I am afraid I must insist, Charity. It is almost one and I promised your father I would look after you and that includes seeing that you get enough sleep.' He attempted a polite nod towards their host who was staring at Charity with obvious lust still in his eyes. 'Thank you for this evening, my lord, and please excuse my over-zealousness to get my charge home, it has nothing to do with your excellent hospitality and everything to do with Miss Brookes's final performance. In her wisdom and against my advice, she agreed at the last minute to do a matinee as well tomorrow, and she needs to rest in preparation.'

She gave him an odd look but took his hand, then turned to Lord Ackroyd. 'Walk with us... I am sure Griff won't mind imparting some of his wisdom while we are en route to the carriage. And do please forgive him for his current mood. For he is as overprotective as any brother could be.'

That pertinent and deliberate description of the parameters of their relationship really galled—as clear a sign as any that his foolish heart was still barking up the wrong tree and that his unhealthy feelings for her had to stop. They were eating him from the inside like a cancer, and as such, needed to be ruthlessly cut out.

'He does take his promise to my father a little *too* literally sometimes—but to be fair to him, I suppose he is right. Tomorrow is a big day, and today has been a long one too. I would be short-changing the good people of York if tiredness got the better of me tomorrow.' Then she pinched Griff hard on the arm as she threaded hers through it.

'Griff, dearest, if you wouldn't mind taking your chaperon's hat off for a moment and donning your usual engineer's cap instead, perhaps you could explain to Lord Ackroyd how long you estimate it would take to build a working locomotive from scratch...'

Chapter Nine

*Opera's rising new star, Miss Charity Brookes,
left audiences in York begging for more when she
finally waved goodbye to the north. She is rumoured to be expected back in Bloomsbury late
next week. This news will, of course, delight her
current crop of bewitched suitors, who will be eagerly awaiting their first glimpse of her in a month
and, Gentle Reader, no doubt praying—beneath
the sheer weight of their ostentatious welcoming
bouquets—that the vivacious but fickle soprano
remembers they ever existed at all...*

Whispers from Behind the Fan
—June 1815

Charity had no clue what had caused the change, only
that for some inexplicable reason, the camaraderie and
easiness she had enjoyed with Griff only a few days ago
was gone and she missed it. He was polite enough—she
couldn't fault him for that. And on the surface, to any
onlooker, things would seem much the same. He had
still been her rock for her final performance in York,

ensuring that she was looked after and that her nerves stayed under control.

He had guarded her against unwanted attention and ensured her comfort in the inns he had carefully chosen since. He had even been pleasant, if uncharacteristically quiet company last night when they had dined at their final stopover on the way to Sheffield, and Dorothy was oblivious of the subtle change in him. Charity knew that because she had explicitly asked her, and her friend had laughed and said that she was imagining things. Griff was just being Griff, that was all, exactly as he always was.

Yet change he had, at least towards her.

He was distant all of a sudden and that wasn't just her imagination. They no longer shared knowing looks or quiet moments, private confidences or even the open and teasing conversations which she had enjoyed so very much. Each time they found themselves alone, she could feel him retracting and sense his discomfort, until he found any excuse to extricate himself from the moment and from her. Even now, when Dorothy was plainly sleeping on the carriage bench beside her, he was doing his level best to pretend she didn't exist— which was most odd when those intimate, honest, whispered moments had become the most delightful parts of their journey. Just him and her, and no pretence.

What had shifted?

'Have you conquered the mysteries of your power loom?' They were the first words she had spoken in almost an hour and he reacted with an impatient frown before he stifled it.

'I think so.' Straight away, his eyes returned to his drawing, as if he was eager to be back with it and resented the interruption.

'Then if you have cracked it and it is no longer explosive, why does it still occupy you so?'

'Because I still need to check all the calculations to be certain.' And there it was again. That flash of annoyance which he couldn't fully disguise, as if their relationship had regressed back to the way it had been before this month away, when he found her an irritant and she had chafed against his irritation as a point of principle. However, this time there was one stark difference in that familiar status quo. Before this trip, his standoffishness merely bothered her, now it hurt.

'But you have some confidence the engine will not explode with your new modifications?'

He nodded curtly, his jaw clenched in irritation, not even bothering with the courtesy of as much as glancing her way. 'Nothing is unfixable.' Then he lapsed into silence again which continued for the next five minutes until she could stand it no more.

She wasn't imagining it. She was certain now because the atmosphere in the carriage was tense, as well as silent, and that was all his doing too.

'Are you going to tell me what I have done to infuriate you or am I doomed to spend the next week walking on eggshells and feeling uncomfortable in your presence?' It was a fair question because that was how his sudden curt withdrawal felt.

She knew he was about to lie when he carefully composed his features before he glanced up from his work. 'I have no idea what you are talking about, Charity.'

'Of course, you do!' The urge to snatch his precious diagram from him and tear it petulantly into confetti was overwhelming, but she wasn't a frustrated child any more and he no longer enjoyed the gravitas which came from being the eldest. 'You do this all the time and I am sick of it! For reasons best known to yourself, you have placed me in purgatory again, and we both know it. What egregious crime am I guilty of this time? For I know I haven't broken anything precious to you or attempted to rebel against Gruff Griff's pernickety rule of law. In fact, I will go one further and say that I have been the model travelling companion and exceedingly well behaved since Lincoln, so you cannot even level that charge against me.'

He huffed softly as he returned to his drawing. 'Perhaps in your mind you have been well behaved.'

'Ha!' She prodded his solid arm, forcing him to acknowledge her. 'I knew I was guilty of some minuscule and inconsequential misdemeanour! Because your customary disapproval and all-round stodginess since York has been palpable!'

'Keep your voice down, my sister is sleeping.'

If that dismissive statement hadn't been patronising enough, he rolled his eyes so sanctimoniously, she had to suppress the urge to kick him hard in the shin. Instead, she settled for stamping her foot and managed to wake up Dorothy in the process regardless. Her friend squinted at them, disgruntled and bleary eyed, sensed the traditional battle lines had been redrawn and winced.

'What's happened?'

'Your brother has developed some new and huge grudge against me, though heaven only knows what it is based upon this time as he prefers to fester in his own righteous indignation like a child rather than admit to it like an adult!' If he could patronise, so could she. 'He's in one of his legendary sulks again!'

'By that, Dottie, she means that she is having one of her legendary tantrums because I have had the audacity to be too busy with my job today to pay the great Charity Brookes, *soprano extraordinaire*, the uninterrupted, unadulterated attention she thinks she deserves!'

That accusation was petty and uncalled for. 'How dare you level that at me when I have never behaved like that to anyone in my life!'

'Griff!' Even his sister was horrified. 'That isn't the least bit true. Apologise to Charity at once.'

'Hasn't she?' Far from contrite, his dark eyes were stormy. 'Then I suppose this entire trip hasn't all been about you? That we haven't all been dragged from pillar to post and left standing about and twiddling our thumbs in every godforsaken city on the Great North Road because of you either?'

'If, by that, you are alluding to the inescapable fact that this entire trip has been organised around *my* tour of the north, then I suppose you are right. But as for you being dragged from pillar to post and being left to twiddle your thumbs while I do *my job*, then I would remind you that your presence here was at your own instigation, Griff, because I certainly never invited you! You forced yourself on this trip and appointed yourself my chaperon without my consent.'

'And I am sick to the back teeth of it and of you!'

If he had struck her, he couldn't have hurt her more. But she would rather die than let him see it, so instead squared her shoulders and stared at him down her nose. 'Then it is just as well this trip is almost at an end then, isn't it?'

'Believe me, I am counting the days. Your spoiled, self-absorbed, reckless and scandalous behaviour would try the patience of a saint!'

'Griff!' Dorothy swatted his knee with her hand. 'What on earth has got into you to be so horrid?'

'Oh, come on, Dorothy, even you must have despaired of all the primping and simpering so she can outshine every other woman in the room. And all the sycophants she courts because she simply *has* to be the centre of attention? All the contrived flirting? All the eyelash batting? Aren't you tired of always playing second fiddle to her? Because I certainly am. So tired and so very bored with the relentless superficiality of it all!'

'You go too far, Griff!' Dorothy was quaking with anger. It was such an unusual sight it distracted the siblings from Charity's quivering lip. 'I have never heard you sound so mean and spiteful! Poor Charity has done nothing wrong as far as I can see, and even if she had—which she most definitely *hasn't*—she does not deserve to be spoken to like you just spoke to her. If our parents could hear you, they would be horrified. They brought you up to be a gentleman, Griffith Philpot—not a brute!'

He opened his mouth to retaliate then clamped it shut as a rainbow of emotions skittered across his features, running the gamut from blind fury to appalled regret. When he finally did speak, his voice shook.

'I am sorry, Charity…my sister is quite correct. My outburst was uncalled for and I am horrified by it. I had no right to take my bad mood out on you, and please believe me, I meant none of it. I swear it.'

It made no difference. The damage was done. She had seen the stark truth in his eyes where it mattered the most. Despite everything, all the time they had spent getting to know one another, all the laughter and all the honesty, when push came to shove he still thought the worst of her and likely always would.

'Of course, you didn't mean it… I blame this carriage.' Ever the peacemaker, Dorothy tried to pour oil on troubled waters by filling the painful silence. 'We've all been cooped up in here for hours, and after all the excitement and bustle of the last few weeks, and all the strange beds, the crowds and the interminable journeys, we are all so tired it is no wonder that tempers have finally frayed. It is a miracle they haven't frayed sooner really, isn't it?' She reached out to squeeze both their hands simultaneously. 'And yet here we are, three grown adults, all behaving like squabbling children at the tiniest provocation.' She forced a smile, one which became brittle when nobody else attempted to reciprocate. 'It'll be a blessing when we finally reach Sheffield as I think we could all do with a week of hearth and home again to restore things to an even keel once more.'

Charity's gut clenched in horror at the prospect. Another week would be pure torture now that she knew how he felt. Pure, unmitigated torture. How on earth was she supposed to survive it intact when she had always thought the world of him and he had always thought the worst of her? To him she was nought but a vain, selfish, thoughtless flirt. As shallow as a puddle and a danger to his sister's morals.

Was that what everyone really thought?

No…surely not? If she forgot about the changeable and judgemental Griff for a moment, she had lots of friends. Eager suitors too. And piles of invitations. Invitations which wouldn't have been sent if she were as awful a person as he had claimed.

Her friend squeezed her paralysed fingers tighter. 'I, for one, cannot wait for the next week. We shall have such fun exploring Sheffield together. The surrounding countryside is very pretty and there are many fine estates close by that we can all visit.'

Somewhere from the deep recesses of her mind

Charity remembered Lord Denby's solemn promise of a house party at his estate and she grabbed it like driftwood after a shipwreck. It didn't matter that she hadn't spared him a thought in weeks, or hadn't remembered before now that she had practically bullied the man into hosting her or that she had no real enthusiasm for it any more after the month she had had, because that begrudging, forgotten invitation allowed her to escape Griff at this precise moment.

'I should have mentioned before—I shall only be staying the one night in Sheffield.' She allowed herself one tiny moment of triumph at his stunned expression at this bombshell. 'I have been invited to spend the week at the Duke and Duchess of Loughton's ancestral residence in Nether Padley, which I believe is only an hour's drive away.'

'Denby's place?' The anger instantly swirled again in Griff's eyes, hot and dangerous. 'Out of the question! That certainly wasn't agreed when I signed on for this debacle and I have far too much work to do at the factory to play chaperon again while you coo over your future duke and his magnificent emerald!'

'That is just as well—because you are not invited.' Even if the invitation included the rest of her party as it likely would for propriety's sake, it would be a cold day in hell before she passed that information on to him. 'Dorothy is, of course, and we will both be adequately chaperoned by Lord Denby's mother and his married sister for the duration.' Her friend blinked back at her warily, not at all pleased to have been tossed into the middle of the fight and being expected to pick sides. 'So even if Dorothy doesn't accompany me, I shall be well supervised, and you can get on with your precious work unencumbered with the chore of me.'

'Your father put me in charge and I absolutely forbid it.'

Charity scoffed, so disgusted by him she could barely stand to look at him. 'And how will you stop me, Griff? Because I can assure you, I am as done with you as you are with me, and with me being so spoiled, self-absorbed and reckless it will take more than manacles and a dungeon to keep me in Sheffield against my will if you are there too.'

They rode the final hour in brittle silence and when they arrived, Griff slammed out of the carriage and stormed towards the house without as much as a backwards glance.

'I really do not know what has come over him. My brother isn't usually one for unreasonable displays of temper. Or any other frail human emotions for that matter.' Dorothy frowned as he disappeared into the house. 'Once he has calmed down, I shall talk with him and I am certain I shall be able to convince him to allow us all to visit Lord Denby's together at some point this week. In the meantime, let us have some tea, shall we? It has been a dreadfully long and unnecessarily fraught day.'

Charity didn't have the strength to argue with her. She was still too stunned by Griff's poisonous vitriol to string together enough of a sentence to explain that she couldn't bear to be near him any longer. Couldn't even bear to look at him. It hurt too much.

However, until she was certain of the exact arrangements of the house party from Lord Denby, she was stuck here. For her friend's sake, she mustered the facsimile of a smile as she stared up at the house which would be her prison in the meantime. 'Tea would be lovely.'

Inside, the Sheffield house mirrored the Philpots' home in Bloomsbury, the expensive furnishings picked for comfort over style much like her own parents favoured, yet it lacked the homely touches of both. She supposed that was because this house wasn't a home. It was a place Griff and his father stayed when here on business, a place to wine and dine potential clients and the place where both men worked on their frequent trips away from London. Mrs Philpot and Dorothy rarely came here any more, so this house had clearly lost its heart and felt cold as a result. Or perhaps that was simply because she knew that he was in it somewhere and he had dragged the toxic atmosphere of the carriage in with him.

'We shall freshen up before we take tea, Mrs Jackson.' Dorothy smiled at the hovering housekeeper. 'And shall have an early dinner too...at nine, I think. What do you think, Charity?'

'As I am exhausted, an early dinner suits me perfectly as I dare say I shall be fast asleep by ten.' Or more likely staring at the ceiling, wondering why and where things had gone so spectacularly wrong when she had thought that she and Griff understood one another better than they ever had. 'Have there been any letters for me, Mrs Jackson?' Please God let there be one from Lord Denby as she had given him this precise address and he had promised to write confirming all the arrangements had been made.

The housekeeper acknowledged this with a curt nod but no hint of a smile. 'There have, Miss Brookes. I shall bring them into the drawing room with your tea.' As she felt her shoulders slump with relief at that welcome news, the housekeeper turned to Dorothy again. 'I have taken the liberty of putting Miss Brookes in the blue room rather than the green as instructed by your brother, as we found a wasp's nest in the eaves above it only this morning and I cannot guarantee all those angry, stinging devils are gone. I hope that is to your satisfaction, Miss Philpot?'

Because Dorothy looked to her to answer, Charity shrugged. 'It makes no difference to me where I sleep, Mrs Jackson. Thank you.'

'Very good, miss.' The po-faced woman bobbed a curtsy. 'I shall have your trunks unpacked in there at once.'

'Oh, there is no need to unpack them.' It wasn't as if she were staying. If she had her way, right now she would be back in the carriage already and leaving Sheffield and Griff well behind. And perhaps, if she could finally convince Lord Denby that she was indeed the woman of his dreams as well as his desires, she could mentally leave Griff and all the hurt he had inflicted behind too. An unmistakably desperate and pathetic hope, but something positive to cling to. 'Most of my trunks are filled with my stage costumes anyway, so please do not trouble yourself as my maid Lily will remove what I need.'

The housekeeper received that information with a disapproving frown. Although whether that was because she disapproved of the fact that Charity had arrived with her own maid in tow or because she pranced around in costumes on the stage, she couldn't say. If the woman was as judgemental as her horrid master, it was likely the latter. For some, having the audacity to perform in a theatre was akin to being devoid of all morals. 'As you wish, Miss Brookes, Miss Philpot.' Her small eyes were as steely as the grey under her austere cap. 'The tea will be awaiting you in the drawing room in precisely fifteen minutes.' Then she scowled. 'If you girls dally upstairs any longer than that it will be too stewed to enjoy and I abhor waste.'

'We shall be there in fifteen minutes, Mrs Jackson. I promise.' They watched her leave. Only once she had disappeared from sight did Dorothy dare speak again. 'Come on...let me show you your room'

The blue room was lovely, the only issue was it was on the complete opposite side of the galleried landing to Dorothy's bedchamber. With Lily's help, Charity changed out of her hopelessly crumpled travelling dress into a fresh, cool muslin, washed her face, tidied her hair as best as she could in the time given and then dabbed some oil of roses on to her cheeks and lips to give her drawn face a subtle glow in an attempt to banish the sadness in her expression. If she had learned one thing from her family, it was to stand tall and proud in the face of derision. Let him think what he wanted, she would try not to care—but she would be damned before she allowed him to see that he had crushed her. With a final deep breath, she dashed out of the door and, to her horror, smack into Griff coming out of the adjacent bedroom.

He reacted with a face like thunder as he brusquely held her at arm's length. 'What the hell are you doing in there?' He glared at her trunks piled beyond her bedroom door. 'I expressly told Mrs Jackson to put you in the green room next to Dottie.'

'Wasps.' As disgusted as she was with him, something odd and now wholly unwelcome still happened to her skin beneath his fingers. Uncovered, the exposed flesh on her upper arms seemed to tingle as her battered heart wept. 'A nest.'

She had also apparently lost the power to talk in sentences and she blamed the peculiar sensation of his big hands on her body for that too. That and the disconcerting knowledge that he would be sleeping next door to her. Annoyed at her own pathetic reaction, and the wounded tears which pricked ominously at her eyes, she stepped back, severing the contact and stared at him imperiously down her nose. 'They found it in the eaves this morning and so the green room is out of bounds until Mrs Jackson is convinced all of the wasps are gone.' Then, desperate to escape him and the odd effect he apparently still had on her despite his callous outburst, she spun on her heel. 'If you will excuse me, there is tea in the drawing room and an enormous pile of correspondence awaiting my attention—all from people who have miraculously found something about me to like.'

Thankfully, he didn't respond, nor did he follow her downstairs, which was just as well as she didn't trust herself not to explode like his stupid steam engine if he dared say another hateful word in her presence. Then it wouldn't be his silly kite she stomped on, it would be his wretched head!

She took several calming breaths before she entered the drawing room. There was no sign of Dorothy, but piled next to the promised tea, there was a month's worth of correspondence. Still shaken, Charity frantically sifted through them all like a woman possessed until she finally found one emblazoned with Lord Denby's elaborate sloping handwriting and then tore it open. While her eyes scanned the letter, the tears finally fell as all hope of any rescue died with each of his damning words.

Chapter Ten

'*Oh, my goodness, Griff!* Oh. My. Goodness!'

Dorothy's breath hitched as she read the front of a stray letter her brother had found in the midst of his own mountain of correspondence which had awaited him in his study. When he had discovered it over an hour ago, he had been sorely tempted to continue with his pathetic plan to skip dinner and give it to his sister in the morning, but knew his blatant cowardice was unfair when that particular letter was the one which would mean the world to Dorothy and he really did need to heal the rift he had created with Charity.

'It is from Captain Sinclair!'

Dorothy beamed at her friend across the dining table while the servants cleared away their finished soup bowls, her joy at receiving the missive outweighing the awful atmosphere hanging like choking smog in the room since he had ventured into it only moments ago. An awful atmosphere which, he was only too aware, was all of his making. 'I wonder what it says?'

'Well, you could sit here guessing till the cows come home or you could simply open it.' Charity's tone was brusque and she still refused to acknowledge he existed as Griff risked sitting in his chair at the head of the table, her posture more rigid and her bearing more frigid than he had ever seen it.

His fault again.

He thoroughly deserved her cold shoulder. He still couldn't quite believe how he had lashed out at her earlier. His mouth spewing acid because he was in utter turmoil, and in his irrational, jealous and frankly overwhelmed state he had blamed her for it. When being with her, gazing upon her or being incarcerated in a carriage opposite her, intoxicated by her perfume and her mere presence and knowing he could never have her had left him feeling wretched and wronged in equal measure.

His outburst had caught him as much by surprise as it had her and he was heartily ashamed of his complete lack of reason and self-control. After giving himself a stiff talking to, Griff had now reclaimed both, or at least enough reason and control that he could contain his emotions and behave like an adult. Yet he also knew not so far beneath the calm surface he was at great pains to project was a wounded animal. Heart bleeding and hopelessly filled with longing and regret which no amount of avoiding her was likely to change.

So much for weaning himself off her!

Since the night he had found her with Ackroyd he had been behaving like a man betrayed, when calm and reasoned Griff knew she hadn't done anything wrong except be her normal, alluring, flirty self.

However, something about that night had brought it all rampaging home and made him realise that the past few weeks of living cheek by jowl, of having her all to himself and savouring every single second of that closeness wasn't how things would always be between them. It was a unique and transient moment in time. Brief and bittersweet. A particular set of circumstances that they would likely never share again, and which was doomed to end the second he returned her to her parents and her life in town.

In the not so distant future he would have to watch her tread her own path, one that would wend itself in a completely different direction from his. From a distance he would have to watch her star soar, watch her fall in love. Marry. While his entire life would still stretch before him and it would be unbearable if he spent all those years anonymously hidden in the stalls, listening to her sing and still yearning, pathetically refusing to move on. That wouldn't be fair, to her or him. That couldn't be his curse. He shouldn't and wouldn't allow it.

That had been why he had tried to extricate himself from her hold sooner. To ease the transition and prepare himself for the loss.

Except it hadn't been easy, it had been torture. The grief of it left him furious with himself for being so foolish as to fall in love with her in the first place. When he knew—*knew!*—their destinies were too different. As a result, when she had called him on his bad mood which refused to shift, then bemoaned the fact that she hadn't broken anything precious to him, all that turbulent and futile anger had erupted like a volcano. Because she had inadvertently broken something precious.

She had broken his heart all over again.

And was completely oblivious of that tragic fact. A state of affairs he intended to maintain even as he begged for her forgiveness later tonight.

Later…

Even now he was being a coward when it would be better for everyone present if he got it over with now. He glanced warily at Charity who still adamantly refused to look his way and steeled himself for the unpleasant conversation. While he dithered, struggling to find the right words to say, his sister gave him a small reprieve.

'What if it is bad news?' Dorothy was now staring at her letter like a cobra as the servants deposited the covered dishes holding the main course on the table. 'What if Captain Sinclair has become engaged to someone else in my absence and this note is merely to appraise me of that fact in case I come home with false hope?'

'If he has, he wasn't worthy of you to begin with and good riddance to him.' Charity's curt reply seemed a tad callous and his sister's face fell. Not that she noticed. She was too busy stabbing a lamb chop with her fork and doubtless imagining it was his face. 'The last thing a woman needs is a fickle man whose affections change like the wind.' That barb was clearly aimed at him and it stung, because the affection he felt for her was a very different sort from the affection she had for him. Hers was resolutely platonic. His most definitely wasn't.

'And I've said all along you can do better than a mere captain, Dorothy, and I still stand by that.' And there was the cruellest blade of all and the stark reminder that she was deserting him for the peer of the realm she had had her beady eyes on since his return last year. A mister couldn't compete with a lord and an apparent *brother* certainly could never attempt to compete with a future duke. Not that he would be daft enough to try. He had already made things unbearable with his outburst, never mind fuelling those flames with an unwanted declaration of his unrequited love.

'Accepting the first man who asks, simply because he asked is ludicrous. If I'd have done that I'd have been shackled to that dashing but dim-witted Lieutenant Hopewell since I was seventeen.' Charity gave a theatrical shudder to punctuate her point. 'Can you imagine how awful that would have been? Or Lord Keswick— another dud who originally showed promise. Or that Italian count who turned out not to be a count at all.'

If she was trying to rub salt into his wounds by reminding him of the many lovesick men who had proposed to her over the years, she was doing a very good job. If she wasn't, the reminder merely highlighted the fact that she knew full well that she was a catch and had every reason to be choosy.

It was also quite an unnecessary dig at Dorothy who was yet to receive one proposal, let alone three.

'Open it.' Putting his own misery aside, Griff smiled and squeezed his sister's hand in reassurance, not wanting her friend's blunt and depressing warnings to spoil her moment. 'Because I sincerely doubt he would have wasted the cost of the postage to tell you something you could read just as easily for free in the announcements section of a newspaper.'

She nodded, buoyed by his words and his approval, then clumsily tore open the seal, holding herself as still as a statue, only her eyes moving across the text as she took it all in. Then, all she did was blink.

'Well?'

'He loves me.' Shock turned to awe as the beginnings of a smile played with the corners of her mouth. 'He loves me, Griff… Isn't that wonderful?' She clutched the letter to her heart and sighed. 'He said that the last month without me has been pure agony but he is glad for it because it has made him see that he should have declared his feelings sooner, and that he is kicking himself that he hadn't because he cannot bear to be without

me for this long ever again…and…and he has asked…'
She was beaming now, grinning from ear to ear, excited
little hiccups popping out of her mouth like champagne
bubbles. 'He asked my permission to speak to Papa the
second I return to request my hand in marriage. Isn't
that marvellous?'

Griff nodded, happy for her even though he was in
the bowels of hell himself. 'It is—if that is what you
want, Dottie.' For her benefit and to prevent Charity
from interfering further, he stared at her seriously. 'No
matter what anyone else has to say on the subject, this
is ultimately your decision to make and yours alone.
Is that what you want? Do you *want* to marry Captain
Sinclair?'

'I do not think any decision needs to be made on the
matter now!' Charity dug the serving spoon into the potatoes with more violence than the task warranted, then
glared defiant, her lovely face pinched and her golden
eyebrows raised in their twin shock at her abrupt tone.
'Or am I the only person present who believes that a
proposal should be delivered in person rather than via
the mail coach?'

'And no doubt he will, Charity, as soon as we get
home.' He tried to convey she was being churlish with
his eyes, which of course made him a complete hypo-
crite when he had done far worse to her only a few hours
ago and still hadn't made any amends for it. 'If Dottie is
happy with her letter in the interim, we should be too.'

It was obvious she was bristling at the chastisement
as she stared at her plate, closing her eyes briefly before
blowing out a controlled breath. 'I am sorry, Dorothy…
If that is what you want, then I am happy for you. Congratulations…he is a good man. I am sure you will be
very happy together.'

His sister beamed with relief. 'Thank you, Charity. We will be... I am sure of it.' Then she stared at her letter again. 'I suppose I now have a wedding to plan...' Completely oblivious of the tears swimming in her friend's eyes, Dottie got carried away on the excitement. 'A trousseau to buy, wedding clothes. Of course, you must be my bridesmaid, Charity, and perhaps you would sing for us too at the wedding breakfast...which will necessitate some musicians too. A string quartet perhaps and a harpist. I do love the romance of a harp and maybe some lovebirds too...'

Charity's chair screeched back as she tossed her napkin on the table. 'If you will excuse me... It has been a long day. I have a sudden headache and must retire early.'

Griff kicked himself as he watched her leave while poor Dottie blinked at the abruptness, convinced she was the cause. In not apologising straight from the outset before giving his sister her letter, he had now successfully ruined dinner and his sister's engagement all in one fell swoop. Yet as much as the bulk of that was, without question, his fault, Charity still had no right to steal his sister's thunder in quite the way she had. Especially when her grievance was entirely with him.

'I am sorry, Dottie.' More guilt weighed heavily on his shoulders. 'And I am sure Charity didn't mean to be so rude to you either.'

She nodded, pity in her eyes. 'She's hurting, Griff. I know she acts as though she is impervious and always gives as good as she gets, but all those things you said in the carriage today have cut her deeply. I've never seen her so distraught as she has been since. Or so quiet and withdrawn. She's hardly said a word to me all afternoon and seems lost in her own thoughts. It's like her light

went out and I have never seen her like that... Not once
in all the years I have known her.' And just when he
had thought he couldn't feel any worse, he had apparently killed Charity's ever-present sparkle.

'I'll talk to her before she goes to bed.'

'Don't just talk to her, Griff. Make it right. You did
a great deal of damage today. Senseless, cruel and selfish damage which I cannot, for the life of me, fathom.'
Although by the odd look in her eyes, it was obvious
she had an inkling. 'And while you are prone to the odd
sulk and always have been, it's not like you to behave
so irrationally. Unless there is something else at play
here that you are not telling me...or her. Is there something else at play here, big Brother?'

'I'll go talk to her this very instant.' He pushed his
chair from the table in case his own eyes gave him away.
'I was tired and I was grouchy and she caught me at a
bad time, that is all.' Lies, damn lies and he suspected
his canny sister knew it. 'But I'll fix it, Dottie. Right
this minute. I promise.'

Chapter Eleven

Charity sank on to her mattress and stared blankly at the walls. She hadn't admitted to Dorothy that Lord Denby wasn't hosting a house party at his country estate this week, because she couldn't bear to admit that the prior engagement which prevented him from doing so was the announcement of his own engagement back in town.

To an earl's daughter no less.

All prearranged long ago by his parents, of course, and timed to coincide with his thirtieth birthday. Because such things were expected from a gentleman of his rank and stature when they reached that momentous age, and heaven forbid such a man ever dared to contemplate choosing his own wife and marrying beneath him.

She supposed that explained his reluctance to court her and why he blatantly ignored all of the increasingly unsubtle hints she had dropped over the last year. He was happy to use her as a diversion, would have been delighted if she had agreed to one of his countless invitations to engage in more than a kiss, but she wasn't in any way, shape or form suitable marriage material and he had clearly never considered her as such. However, and this had been the part which had stung the most, his parting words before he signed off had put her firmly in her place and let her know, in no uncertain terms, exactly what he thought about her.

But do not fear, despite my marriage I am still eager to pick up our special relationship exactly from where we left off.

He had underlined the words exactly in case she failed to remember that the last time she had seen him had been in Lady Bulphan's orangery where he had made no secret of the fact he was there to lift her skirts.

She would have been furious at the unbelievable nerve of the man if she hadn't been so devastated by Griff's cruelty.

A whole year wasted flogging the dead horse which she had hoped would give her the same happiness as her sisters. But at least to herself she would be brutally honest. It hadn't only been her sisters' happiness which had unsettled her then, it had also been him. Griff's return and his heightened disapproval had shaken her too—and perhaps more—and she had been determined to prove once again that he was wrong about her. How better to do that than to snag a future duke under his disapproving nose?

It was funny, she had thought Denby's decisive rejection would hurt more than it did, which she also supposed said a great deal about the flimsy strength of her own feelings for the man beneath the title. However, Griff's rejection was like a body blow, and that too spoke volumes. It had never really been Denby that her foolish heart wanted. It had always been Griff.

But neither of those revelations detracted from the unfortunate fact that Denby's engagement now left her in a terrible predicament. With no house party to hide at, she was stuck here with Griff for the duration. She was feeling broken and rejected and not quite good enough again and she hated that he held that power still. The next seven days stretched before her like an ordeal—and one she no longer had the strength for.

Unless she lied outright and pretended there still was a house party and holed herself up at another quiet inn somewhere off the beaten track to lick her wounds in private. A gross falsehood which would require the deceitful co-operation of at least Lily and Evan to pull off.

She could ask them, she supposed. Confess as much of the situation as she could to garner their pity without humiliating herself completely with the whole painful truth. Lily and she had always been close, and her and Evan's loyalty was to her family and not the Philpots, no matter how much they might like them. If that failed, she could pull rank and remind them who paid their wages...which was about as fair as taking out her despair on poor Dorothy downstairs.

She wasn't proud of herself for that either. Pouring scorn and doubt on her friend's happiness simply because she had a man head over heels in love with her whom she wanted to marry and Charity didn't was a low blow. When Captain Sinclair looked at Dorothy as if the sun rose and set with her and her friend looked the same way back at him. It was both sad and pathetic that despite all her new fame and her abundance of suitors, she still hadn't found the same because her stupid heart had apparently made up its mind and steadfastly refused to be budged.

She sensed Griff outside before he knocked and instantly felt worse.

'Can we talk?'

'Go away.'

The door clicked open anyway, forcing her to twist so that he wouldn't see that she had been crying. 'I hate that we are fighting, and I hate more that I am the cause.'

Even with her back to him he still dominated the room because she could feel him everywhere, but desperately wished she couldn't. Of all the people to fall for, her silly heart had chosen Griff, and there was every chance it had gone and done so seventeen years ago. That would certainly explain why no man had ever been able to worm their way into that fickle organ since. Not even one as eligible and titled as Denby.

'I came to apologise properly for earlier. I was out of order, Charity. Crochety, unreasonable and in a temper so I said too many things that I didn't mean.'

He had meant them.

Everything he had said echoed what she had always suspected he felt. Opinions so deep rooted she would never change them, no matter how hard she tried. And good grief, how she had tried. She had spent a lifetime trying to impress him and had always, *always* failed. At best, Griff only ever gazed upon her in exasperation, not in the special and spiritual mutual adoration that she craved. What a hopeless fool she was.

She sighed at the futility of it all. 'Your apology is accepted.'

'Just like that? I don't believe you...' A floorboard creaked as he came closer. Not that she had needed that sound to confirm it, when the tiny hairs at the nape of her neck fidgeted at his proximity. 'We really should talk it out properly.'

'To what point and purpose, Griff?'

'To clear the air...' The door closed softly before his

footsteps moved towards her again. 'To get things between us back to normal.'

She stood before he was close enough to face her,
rushing to the window as an excuse to compose herself before she eventually turned. Her expression bland.
Arms tightly folded. Supremely grateful for all the theatre training which meant she could don the mantle of
someone else. The better version of Charity who wasn't
dying on the inside.

'Let us not continue with this pretence when we
are in private, Griff—because it is as false as it is ex-
hausting. You said exactly what you felt, what you have
always felt about me. You consider me spoiled, vain,
selfish. A seeker of attention with the morals of an alley
cat and a bad influence on Dorothy.' Perhaps saying it
aloud would be cathartic? Like lancing a boil to release
the poison, vocalising the true state of their relationship,
acknowledging it warts and all, might miraculously prevent his censure from hurting her in the future. 'You
believe all the gossip about me, and you are convinced
what they print isn't the half of it. What was it you said
a while back? That I had kissed significantly more men
than a proper young lady ever should. How many le-
gions of men do you believe I have dallied with?'

'Charity, I…'

She stopped him with her raised palm. 'Spare your
platitudes, Griff, for they are hollow. I have always been
a disappointment to you, and I am at one with it. After
seventeen years of trying to be your friend, trying to
gain your approval and trying not to care that I shall
never have either, I have decided to accept our relationship for exactly what it is. We are adults now, the both
of us, and if we couldn't get on as children, nor in all
the years since, and have absolutely nothing whatso-

ever in common, then it stands to reason that it wasn't meant to be.' She choked back the emotion, knowing her out-and-out bitterness at the truth would be a sign of weakness when she was determined give him one final, virtuosa performance of strength.

'Irrespective of our family's unbreakable connection, you are you, Griff, and I am me and I fear that never the twain shall meet. In a strange sort of way, it is actually quite liberating to be able to say that at last, as I feel as though I can finally close that interminable book which I have laboured over for too long and begin a fresh chapter in a new story where you are blessedly not one of the main characters.'

As off-the-cuff speeches went, she was rather proud of both the content and the delivery and by the stunned expression on his face, it had more than hit its mark. She stood proud as he now sank to her mattress, raking an agitated hand through his dark hair before he stared at her wounded.

'That sounds like a goodbye, Charity.'

'I suppose it is, of sorts.' She just wished it didn't hurt so much. Wished her stupid, misguided heart hadn't plighted its troth to him. Not that she would allow him to ever witness that particular window into her soul. Right now, for the sake of her own pride, all he would see was the woman who meant business. Who had come to a difficult decision but intended to stick to it and not the one he had the power to cut to the quick with only a few careless words.

'For the sake of our families, of course, and for Dorothy especially, I feel it is best if we keep this between us, Griff, and on the odd occasion we do collide, we should probably behave politely so as not to cause anyone else's discomfort.'

Setting out the rules and boundaries might make her feel more in control, the victor rather than the defeated. 'But in private, if ever it is just us again, I see no point in pretending things are otherwise as it clearly makes us both miserable and it is unsustainable at any rate, as today's nasty quarrel was testament. And on a purely personal note, after seventeen turbulent years, I am sick and tired of trying.'

He was silent. His dark brows furrowed and his posture limp as if she had delivered him a devastating blow. Then he shook his head, disbelieving and stood. 'You are angry... I do not blame you, for I deserve every bit of it. My uncharacteristic outburst was unseemly and grossly unfair, but I beg of you...' He came towards her, palms outstretched. 'Let the dust settle. We had an argument, Charity. Just an argument. We've had hundreds over the years. In a day or so you will be calmer, and we can discuss things properly...' As his hands sought hers and her traitorous nerve endings fizzed and bounced wildly at the contact, she snatched them away.

'Oh, for pity's sake! Stop treating everything I do or say as a silly, selfish whim! Irrespective of what you want, *my* mind is made up and I am leaving tomorrow, Griff!' She had to. The sooner the better. Although God only knew where she would go.

He shook his head again, attempting a conciliatory smile this time as if she were being melodramatic. 'Don't say that... I shall move things around so that we can all visit Denby's place if it means that much to you.' His fingers dared to brush her arm this time.

Before she could stop herself, she used her flattened palms in the middle of his chest to push him away as she growled, 'You are not invited to Denby's place!'

Even though he would learn the truth about that other

defeat soon enough, she couldn't admit it now. That non-existent house party was her only viable excuse to escape and it would be a cold day in hell before she gave him the ammunition to gloat at her failure. 'When is that going to permeate your thick skull?' She pushed him again. 'I am going alone!'

'Be reasonable, Charity...'

'Reasonable!' She wanted to scream. Slap him. Curl up into a ball. Beg him to like her. Respect her. Love her. To look at her as if the sun rose and set with her smile. 'I think it is perfectly reasonable to want to be somewhere that I am wanted rather than stay here with someone who has made it plain he thinks I am a narcissist whom he only tolerates on sufferance!'

'I don't think that! If anything, I've always...' He blinked, went to say something then paused. When he did speak his tone was different. Measured. Too controlled. All those unseemly emotions which he disapproved of so very much buried under layers of rock where he thought they belonged. 'Let us not fight about more nonsense now too.'

'Hurt isn't nonsense, Griff! Pain isn't nonsense. Nor is disappointment or disgust or anger when it is rightly deserved. They are honest emotions and I will own them! I am all done with you, Griff! All done with us.'

Something hot shimmered briefly in his eyes before he slowly blinked to extinguish it. 'You know I cannot, in all good conscience, allow you to go unchaperoned to the house of a bachelor. I promised your father...'

'I am not a child who needs reasoning with!'

'Then you must realise that I cannot sanction...'

'Sanction? You forget I am over the age of majority! What my father wants and what you want have no bearing on my decision.' She went to push him again and he caught her wrists, so she snarled into his face instead as she tugged them away. 'I am a grown woman, Griff—I have been for some time—and I will go to whomever *I want,* kiss whomever *I want* whenever *I want.* And right now, I want to go to someone who wants me back!'

'But why him?' Two suddenly furious dark eyes locked ruthlessly with hers as all his buried feelings suddenly leaked to the surface. 'Answer me that! Why do you constantly throw yourself lock, stock and barrel at Denby when I have never seen any overwhelming evidence of his partiality towards you?' A cruel truth much too close to home for her liking. 'Don't you want a man who loves you like Dottie or Faith or Hope have? Because he certainly doesn't. No matter how many trysts you entice him into and how many passionate kisses you bestow upon him, he cares more for his cravat knots and ostentatious stick pins than he ever has for you!'

That was too raw, too humiliating and too insightful. Damn him to hell for seeing what she hadn't and bearing witness to her shame. Oh, how he would congratulate himself when he next read those stupid gossip columns he put so much stock in! And then he would pity her or shake his head at her impetuousness, her reputation and her stupidity or, worse, tell her that he had told her so and remind her that she needed to behave with more decorum or no decent man would ever want her.

'I don't need to throw myself at anyone, Griff! Don't you read the gossip columns? I am a seductress! A siren! My dance card is always full. Men queue at my door. They all want me! Every one of them desires me and I could have any one of them with a click of my fingers.' She snapped them in his face, aware that she was being irrational and yet powerless to stop it. 'I could have any man I want, Griff! Any man! Do you hear me?' She pulled her hands from his grasp and pushed him again. 'Any stupid man I set my mind to!' Except the only one her foolish heart apparently wanted.

He blinked back, either stunned or disbelieving and something snapped. 'Even you, Griff!' Charity grabbed him by the lapels, and to prove her point emphatically, kissed him.

At just the taste of her lips he combusted. All his remaining reason evaporated as he hauled her into his arms and greedily kissed her back. It didn't matter that emotions were high and the distant mumble of common sense told him that this wasn't sensible—it was what his heart and body needed and he was powerless to stop it.

She looped her arms around his neck and matched him in his fervour, her lush body sprawled against his so close he could feel her heartbeat through his ribs. Griff didn't care that his instant desire was rampant and evident. Wasn't capable of tearing his mouth away and being the prudent one as usual, no matter what the whispered niggling voice in his head said. How could he stop when this was what he wanted, what he'd craved for ever, and Charity's fingers were in his hair, anchoring him in place and her tongue was tangling with his?

As the kiss burned hot and consumed them, his greedy palms smoothed over her waist and hips, exploring the curves which had tormented him for years. She sighed into his mouth, rewarding him for his boldness by running her own over his shoulders and his chest. He had a vague recollection of tumbling backwards on to the mattress, but not of who had instigated it. It might have been him. It might have been her. It might well have been the both of them. But as soon as they were horizontal it was she who took control, winding her leg between his as her fingers undid every button of his waistcoat.

What came next could only be described as a frenzy. Lips, teeth, tongues. Fevered, earthy moans and erratic breathing as passion overtook tempers and the world shrank to the confines of the bed. A disjointed, surreal and sublime fantasy then unravelled which far surpassed everything he could have possibly imagined and left him powerless to do anything beyond the realms of the carnal, except react like a man gratefully lost in the woman he adored.

Later he would only recall snippets of what happened next. Disjointed sensory fragments because the whole was so overwhelming to comprehend in one go. The hunger in her eyes as she wrestled him out of his coat while he simultaneously hunted and removed every hairpin from her head with scant finesse. The intoxicating scent of her skin beneath her perfume as his hungry lips nuzzled her neck. The flutter of her pulse beneath his tongue. The divine feel of her bare skin above the tops of her stockings. Her hands beneath his shirt. Her pebbled nipples beneath his thumbs.

Clothes flying in impatience then the awed wonder at her nakedness. Excitement at her wantonness. The sultry sound of her sigh when his fingertips stroked her. The exquisite sensations of pleasure as she returned the favour and explored his hardness. The way she trembled in his arms and murmured his name while she opened her body to him, the overpowering need to possess and the way the emotion choked him as she welcomed him inside.

So wet.

So soft.

So utterly perfect.

Until he encountered the barrier he wasn't expecting—and hesitated.

Long enough to register the enormous ramifications of what they were about to do but nowhere near long enough to consider them as he should have. Because she wrapped her legs around his hips and tilted her body as she dragged his down, until she was all his in every way possible at last, and nothing else existed beyond her.

Chapter Twelve

The first rays of the sunrise streaming through the windows disturbed her eyelids, but it was the heavy, alien weight of a male arm wrapped possessively around her middle which instantly woke her fully.

His warm, rhythmic breath on her neck. His big body spooning hers, and even deep in sleep she could feel the latent evidence of his desire against her naked bottom. Staggeringly male and shockingly sexual, but not the least bit unwelcome.

Her own body felt odd too. Riper. More sensual as she certainly couldn't recall ever waking and being immediately conscious of all the nerve endings which hid between her legs. Nerve endings which she hadn't fully realised even existed at all until he had awakened each and every one of them last night with just his kiss, before he inducted her into all the sinful, intoxicating things, which those hedonistic nerves craved until he had turned her into a mindless, passionate and needy creature she didn't recognise at all. One who had arched and writhed in shameless ecstasy on the tangled sheets, oblivious of anything else beyond the quest for her own pleasure and the man who could give it to her.

He murmured and snuggled closer, but while it was tempting to snuggle back Charity held herself still in case he woke too, nowhere near ready to face the consequences of their actions, or indeed what to make of them.

They had been intimate, for pity's sake!

As intimate as it was possible for a man and woman to be and considerably more than she had ever intended to be with any man before her wedding night. Not only had there been no wedding night, there hadn't been any tender words of love and affection either. In fact, it had all happened so quickly, she couldn't recall any words at all. One minute they were kissing and the next...

Griff went from being her supposed brother to her lover in one fell swoop.

She swallowed hard, trying not to move another muscle, while she fought for calm. What they had done was so much more than she had ever dared grant another man. So much more than the brief kisses she had indulged in previously and considerably more than she should have allowed, irrespective of her impassioned state last night. What had started as an irrational way to put him in his place and make herself feel better about his and Denby's rejection had rapidly got out of hand. But as much as she wished she could blame Griff for it, she couldn't. She had started it, and at the crucial moment when she should have put a stop to it, when he had hesitated, his dark eyes stunned and questioning as he began to withdraw, she had passed the point of no return, wanted it all and would accept nothing less.

And now, what was done couldn't be undone. Yet she had no clue what she should do next or how she felt about it. Would this change things for the better between them? Would everything fall into place the moment she gazed into his eyes? Would she finally see love there? That elusive spiritual connection her sisters had with their husbands, where a mere locking of eyes said more than a thousand flowery, poetic words ever could?

Would she see that? Or was she doomed to be disappointed for ever because her high opinion of him wasn't reciprocated? As much as she hoped for the former, she suspected the latter might be their reality. The gulf between them had never been properly bridged and there had always been something in the way, something invisible but tangible which kept them apart. Even in his arms she felt its looming presence still and feared it in equal measure. She had never been able to read Griff. His inner thoughts had been a mystery for seventeen long years. But in temper...

As his cruel words of yesterday seeped back to haunt her, pathetically, she considered gently easing herself from his embrace, grabbing some clothes, dashing from the room and then ruthlessly pretending nothing had happened at all. Float above it all until it all went away. For ever, if needs be. Because discussing it all would be mortifying as well as painful if that elusive temporal connection was still missing despite their physical joining—and when she was still rightly furious at him for everything he had said.

If nothing else, she reasoned as his body began to gently harden again against hers, sneaking out prevented her from having to have the inevitable awkward conversation stark naked. It made no difference that that horse had already bolted and that she had not only shown him every inch, she had moaned as he had kissed it and caressed it too. And now that it was morning, and because the fresh evidence of his desire was giving her body more inappropriate ideas which she knew already would take little encouragement to act on, staying in his arms was no longer an option.

She would feel less exposed beneath several layers of clothes and, in the absence of anything else, that would have to do. Being dressed also meant she could intercept Lily before her maid inadvertently discovered their crime or Mrs Jackson the housekeeper ventured in with some tea or, heaven forbid, Dorothy came to check up on her after her abrupt departure last night.

No indeed—the fewer people who knew of their indiscretion and her heartbreak, the better and the least said, the soonest mended.

Decision made, she carefully lifted his arm from her body and shuffled away, then stiffened again as he muttered something unintelligible and rearranged his position. Only when his breathing was deep and steady again did she risk sliding her feet out of the covers and gradually inching herself off the bed. As she did so, her eyes frantically scanned the carnage on the floor, trying to locate enough of her discarded clothes to constitute an acceptable outfit which saved her the unnecessary and noisy effort of rifling through her trunks. She had barely stood when his voice made her jump.

'Charity? Are you…all right?'

She hastily sat back down on the edge of the mattress and groped behind her for the covers before she dared turn around, gripping them against her like a shield as she looked at him over her shoulder. Griff had rolled on to his side, his concerned, rumpled dark head propped on one elbow, the crumpled sheet only barely covering his hips and the distracting but obvious bulge beneath them and looking as annoyingly handsome as she had ever seen him. 'You are not…in any pain or discomfort?'

'What about this situation isn't uncomfortable?' Because she was naked and he had been inside her and she had no earthly clue what that meant.

She searched his face but could see no discernible change. Still couldn't read the truth in his eyes. How typical that was and how galling. That even after they had been intimate, that she had given herself to him, he could still keep his feelings a secret from her.

He acknowledged her comment with an awkward nod. 'All of it, I suppose.' Then he reached out and traced his index finger tenderly down her arm, sending more unsettling ripples of awareness through her body. 'Did I hurt you?'

In more ways than he could possibly imagine but not at all in the way he meant. 'No.'

'I'm glad.' He smiled, relieved, then immediately frowned as he noticed the two tiny spots of blood in the centre of the mattress between them marring the pure white sheets like the mark of Cain. 'Are you sure? We were rather...um...passionate.'

She nodded curtly, not wanting to discuss something so intensely personal when she was practically rigid with embarrassment at just how passionate she had been. Griff had seen and heard her in the full, uninhibited throes of it, thrashing about and moaning her encouragement. So shameless in her naked wantonness, so unseemly in her emotions, she had left nothing of herself to his imagination. She had even allowed him to kiss her between her legs and those needy nerves thrummed at the memory. 'I feel perfectly well.'

'So do I. In fact... I am more than well.' His eyes darkened as they raked her bare back and then retraced that heated look with the flat of his palm, sending tingles down her spine. Too many tingles which would only lead to her shaming herself further if she allowed him to carry on, so she shuffled her bottom so that more of the blanket than her skin faced him, even though that meant showing him more of her face and her emotions than she wanted. More of the truth which was likely best left hidden.

Deprived of touching her flesh, his hand rested on the mattress as he smiled. 'It's funny…last night…' His eyes wandered to the blood again and he shook his head bemused as if baffled by the existence of that damning evidence. 'It never ever occurred to me that I would be your first…until it was too late, of course…and miraculously I was.'

The comment wounded, because of course it hadn't. He was too busy always thinking the worst of her to consider the inconceivable prospect that he might be wrong in his judgement.

'Somebody had to be.' It took every ounce of her bravado to shrug as if it was of no matter. 'Try not to let it go to your head.'

He wound one finger through a loose tendril of hair, his expression wholly male and triumphant. 'Too late. It already has.' Then his features softened and she saw his guilt as plain as day. Guilt—not love. 'But I never would have let things go so far if you had told me you were a virgin. I feel awful about that.' Which told her in no uncertain terms he considered it perfectly acceptable to bed a woman who had been repeatedly bedded before and he was staggered that she hadn't been. Especially after she had kissed significantly more men than a proper young lady ever should. 'And I certainly wouldn't have been in such a hurry if I had known it was your first time.'

'We both lost our heads.' To put it mildly. All her wits

had deserted her the second she had foolishly pressed her mouth to his. 'But what is done is done.' She flapped it away, ruthlessly burying her hurt, gathering the blanket around her properly, wishing she wasn't so disappointed that he had failed to admit to any affection for her yet again now that the perfect moment to do so had well and truly passed.

'It is—and now that the deed is well and truly done, we have to decide how we proceed…and how quickly we do so.'

'As the house is awaking, I think speed is of the essence and you should go before you are discovered, and I am thoroughly ruined.'

He traced his finger down her arm with a wolfish smile. 'As I recall it, your thorough ruination has already happened…but you know full well I wasn't talking about *now*, I was talking about the future. *Our* future, Charity.'

Shyly, she smiled back, her battered heart racing as it filled with hope. 'Our future, Griff?' Perhaps she had been hasty and he was about to make it all right. 'Do we have one?'

'Well obviously.' He sat up and took her hand, then stared at it for the longest time before he sighed. 'I took your virginity, so it goes without saying that I have to marry you.'

Have to. Not want to.

Her heart plummeted at the cruel distinction.

'You *have* to do nothing of the sort.' She snatched her hand away and forced herself to stare at him in complete disgust despite the choking tentacles of emotion coiling around her throat. 'And neither do I.' She would not cry in front of him. Would not give him that pleasure of seeing how those latest thoughtless words wounded.

'Now, for the love of God, go. Get dressed and get out… then let us never speak of this again.'

He had the gall to look hurt at his dismissal. 'Charity?'

'I said get out, Griff!' She stood, taking all the covers with her, needing to put distance between them and the mattress she had disgraced herself on. 'Before someone discovers you here! Because I can assure you, last night was my biggest mistake and I would rather die an old maid than spend eternity shackled to you on the back of it!'

He absorbed that like a body blow, his expression momentarily distraught until the distant sound of a servant moving around downstairs galvanised him into action and he reluctantly stood, oblivious of his own nudity and came towards her, placating. 'Let's not argue again now, Charity…not when things are all so fresh and unexpected and our emotions are so close to the surface.' His hands found her waist and tugged her closer, and like an idiot she gratefully went into his arms, revelling in the solid feel of his chest and the comfort of the closeness.

'I am not denying that it was a huge mistake and that it's made a dreadful mess—but we'll find a way to make the best of it, I promise.' He kissed the top of her head, blissfully unaware he had just stuck the knife in further before he twisted it. 'Give me the morning to rearrange things at the factory and then this afternoon we'll talk rationally. I know this isn't quite what either of us wanted or even envisaged for our futures… because never in my wildest dreams did I ever imagine I would end up with you…but a wedding doesn't have to mean the end of the world. We'll find a way to make it work.'

Surely that had to be one of the most depressing and begrudging marriage proposals ever offered?

He took her silence as compliance and quickly dressed, his reassuring smile false, clearly eager to be gone. She let him go without argument, turning her cheek as he went to kiss her mouth in case her greedy lips disgraced her when she wanted him gone too. Then, more alone than she had ever felt before, Charity diligently set herself and the room to rights as if removing all the evidence of her rash stupidity might erase the last nine hours.

It didn't and so she sat for the longest time on the window seat, staring out as the sun slowly rose above the horizon, digesting every subtle but cruel insult of the most damning ten minutes of her life.

It never occurred to me I would be your first.

Have to marry.

Huge mistake.

Dreadful mess.

Not what I wanted.

Never in my wildest dreams did I ever imagine I would end up with you.

Exactly how were they supposed to make a marriage work when he thought of her in those terms? And how was she supposed to bear it?

It was only when Lily bustled in cheerfully, looking rested and happy after a night sleeping beside her beloved husband Evan, that the tears finally fell.

'What on earth's the matter, Miss Charity?'

'I want to go home, Lily. Today… Will you and Evan take me?'

'But Mr Philpot has his work…'

'I can't stay here with him, Lily…please…'

'If you've argued again, I am sure it can be fixed.'

'No.' She shook her head, crumpling in her maid's arms, ashamed and broken and so very lost. 'This can't...not when he's made his feelings plain and...' Why did Griff's words hurt so much more than Denby's engagement? 'He loathes me, Lily. He always has.'

'He doesn't.' Her maid stroked her hair exactly as Griff had earlier. 'He adores you. In fact, if I might be so bold, Miss Charity, of late I've suspected you were both developing much deeper feelings for one another.' She had been developing deeper feelings. Griff had been politely masking his. 'And when that sort of affection complicates things...'

Charity shook her head violently, too wounded to discuss that incorrect theory any further. 'Please don't talk about it, Lily. Or him... Just take me home to my family. Right this minute... I beg of you. Please. I cannot stay here.'

Chapter Thirteen

*The Duke and Duchess of Loughton have spared
no expense for their only son's wedding ball...*
Whispers from Behind the Fan
—August 1815

Charity slowly sipped her peppermint tea and tried to pay attention to the conversation wafting around her and stay as still as a statue while Lily fussed with her hair.

'I have such fond memories of this dress.' Behind her in the mirror, Faith held the scarlet watered silk gown against her body and swayed with a dreamy expression on her face.

'As do I.' From the mattress, her raised legs and swollen ankles flat against the headboard, Hope too beamed as she idly rubbed her ridiculously protruding pregnant belly. 'And seeing as it is the gown in which we both first waltzed with our future husbands, and our baby sister knows the significance of that better than anyone, it does beggar the question as to why she is suddenly adamant she is wearing it tonight?' They both turned to stare at her intently, twin expressions of curiosity on their smiling faces. 'Have you met someone,

Charity? Has a worthy gentleman finally swept you off your feet?'

The chance or the inclination would be a fine thing.

After the trauma and heartbreak of Sheffield two months ago, she was right off men and in no hurry to set her cap at another one any time soon. If ever. The stunning and seductive red gown was a handy prop to get through tonight and nothing more. A defiant show of confidence to all and sundry that she wasn't the slightest bit bothered by Lord Denby's impending nuptials, no matter what the gossip columns said to the contrary. And to prove it, she would dance with a string of eligible and handsome men and flirt with them all outrageously while she did so to force them to print something different. Because thinking of Denby inevitably made her think of Griff and that horrific morning, and the pain of his words would cut her again. Not that she would admit any of that to anyone—even to her beloved sisters.

'When would I have the time to meet someone? With seven performances of *Figaro* a week, I barely have time to eat nowadays, let alone flirt, as Lily will no doubt attest.'

'You have the time, Miss Charity, and I certainly bring the food to you before you head to the theatre, but it is you who chooses not to eat it.' The maid's eyes locked with hers in the mirror, the concern in them evident. 'She barely eats enough to sustain a bird lately and I am worried about her. Just look at how pale she is.'

'Now that you mention it, she does look a little peaky, Lily.' Faith peered over her shoulder at her sister's reflection in the mirror. 'Have you lost weight too?'

'I am merely a little under the weather.'

'By that she means she ails from something but refuses point blank to admit it in case your mother makes her rest. Heaven forbid she disappoint an audience.'

'I am not ill.' She glared at Lily through the glass. 'I have contracted a minor summer cold which is proving to be a little stubborn to shift. That is all.' A shocking lie when some days she could barely get out of bed.

'Because she is burning the candle at both ends.' Lily had been nagging her for weeks to take some time off and she didn't know the half of it because she was her mother's maid first and foremost and dear Mama had been blessedly busy with her own work of late so they barely crossed paths. 'Endless rehearsals in the daytime and a performance nearly every night bar Sundays—and two additional matinees—she is pushing herself too hard.'

'But it is a nice problem to have.' Charity forced a smile she didn't feel for her sisters' benefits. 'The theatre has offered to extend the run again until the end of September, isn't that marvellous?' Burying herself in work numbed the pain, even if the relentless march of performances left her more exhausted than she had ever felt in her life and no less miserable.

'I hope you haven't accepted.' Faith was still scrutinising her reflection like a mother hen. 'You've been working non-stop for months now and Lily is right, you do need a break. Such a punishing pace isn't healthy and soon takes its toll. That is exactly why Mama never accepts a run of more than three months, and now that you have made a name for yourself, you should probably do the same.'

Charity brushed that away, instantly regretting the sudden movement as another wave of nausea washed over her. 'Mama has a quarter of a century on me and if it wasn't for this temporary malaise I would be as right as ninepence, exactly as I always am. This silly ailment will be fully gone in a matter of days and I already feel much better than I did yesterday.' She took another cautious sip of her tea to calm her roiling stomach. 'Anyway, it is only another month and the theatre are doubling my salary for the privilege. I had to sign— I'd have been an absolute fool to turn it down when things are going so well.'

Nobody looked convinced.

'Charity!' With perfect timing, their father's voice bellowed up the stairs again to chivvy her for the umpteenth time. 'The carriages are *still* waiting, and your menfolk are losing the will to live! Get yourself dressed this instant, girl, or I swear, as God is my witness, this time we'll all leave for Mayfair without you!'

'That's his third warning in ten minutes so you'd best put this on.' Faith held out the dress. 'And knowing you, and despite being under the weather, this will become you most of all. You've always been the prettiest of the three of us and in this you will look stunning and will undoubtedly break more hearts than usual.' Her big sister smiled, sudden sympathy in her eyes as if she sensed all was not well. Except, like Hope, they both assumed she wasn't ill but heartbroken over Denby too, exactly like the newspapers did. 'And you never know... as this gown clearly holds magical powers, maybe tonight you'll waltz with your future husband too and fall hopelessly in love just as we did.'

As she gingerly stood, Faith grabbed her hands and twirled her in a circle, and to Charity's mortification, her stomach's reaction was instantaneous.

While she retched, Lily rushed forward with the washbowl in the nick of time and they all watched in horror as the peppermint tea and the single slice of toast she had choked down only an hour before made a sudden and violent reappearance.

Griff didn't need to see her to know she had finally entered the ballroom. Every fibre of his being sensed her as the air instantly seemed to crackle around him.

'I told you that she would come.' Beside him, Dorothy waved at the Brookes family as they all filed in. 'Charity is not the least bit disappointed that Lord Denby is getting married in the morning. I knew he wasn't for her.' She slanted him a knowing glance which he did his best to ignore. 'Which leaves the field wide open, big Brother, for a better man to sweep her off her feet.'

He sipped his champagne to cover the shard of pain which sliced through him. 'Doubtless it will not take her long to find a worthy replacement.' One who reached her lofty ideals of what the perfect husband would be.

It certainly wasn't him.

She had made that quite plain in the letter she had left him two months ago on his nightstand the morning she had fled. It was short but not the least bit sweet as she had reiterated her assertion that their night together had been the biggest mistake of her life and one which she implored him to keep to himself in case it spoiled her chances elsewhere. If the harsh words in the letter weren't clear enough, then her refusal to even as much as see him when he had chased her back to London on horseback had been.

After he had patiently waited out of sight on the corner of Bedford Place for hours until her parents went out and she was alone, it had been Lily who came to the door and resolutely refused to let him past it. Then the maid had told him, kindly, but in no uncertain terms, that Charity's feelings had changed since Sheffield and that he needed to be gentleman enough to accept that and stop making a pest of himself.

As he absorbed that blow, he had felt her eyes on him. But when he had looked up to see Charity staring stonily out of the window, she had curled her lip in distaste and then regally walked away without as much as a backwards glance.

He hadn't seen hide nor hair of the minx since.

Largely because he had retreated back to Sheffield like a coward that same day with his tail between his legs and his heart bleeding, trying to be that gentleman and hoping the distance and the reliable conundrum of his steam engines might make all the pain of Charity's callous rejection disappear.

It hadn't, of course, and it ate away at him until the intense pull of her had lured him back this morning. Though to do what, he still had no earthly clue. Part of him needed the closure of a face-to-face conversation to accept that their relationship had ended, the greater part still wanted to change her mind.

As Dorothy and his parents rushed forward to greet their oldest and dearest friends, he stayed put and risked gazing at her, then immediately regretted it as the sight of her fair stole his breath away.

Typically, she had become separated from her parents, waylaid at the door by a horde of eager suitors who all wanted a coveted spot on her dance card. She beamed at them all as she divvied up the dances, her blue eyes sparkling and her golden curls shimmering beneath the crystal chandeliers, outshining every other woman present without trying.

The confident red gown she had picked was, of course, a triumph. The bold colour doing wonders for

her complexion and the simple cut doing sinful things
to her figure. It went without saying that it suited her
because everything suited Charity, but somehow it am-
plified her beauty and her effortless sensuality, drawing the eyes of almost every man in the room from
the youngest buck to the silver-haired patriarchs whose
bucking days were long over. Their advanced age made
no difference. Even those men could dream and by the
twinkle in every male eye which turned, they all were.
All trying to imagine what it would be like to have her
and hoping against hope that one day they just might.

Griff sympathised because he had been there, but
what he knew, and what none of them did, was that
the reality far surpassed any fantasy and that he likely
would be better off not knowing how smooth her skin
was beneath all that alluring red silk. Or how sensitive
her pert breasts were, especially when kissed. Or that
the curls between her legs were a shade darker than
those on top of her head. Or how her earthy, breathy
moans while her body pulsed and climaxed around his
were more bewitching than her ethereal singing voice
and that the reality that was Charity had ruined him for
any other woman. He was hers now for ever—heart,
body and soul—and there wasn't a damn thing he could
do about it.

As if she sensed him, she glanced up and her daz-
zling smile slipped momentarily before she ruthlessly
pasted it back on for the hordes. Then, and doubtless
to avoid him, she bestowed her gloved hand on one of
them and he led her to the dance floor, his chest puffed
with pride and his eyes hopelessly filled with lust.

'Hello, Griff.' He had been so transfixed, he hadn't
noticed her sister come to stand beside him. 'I haven't
seen you in ages. Months in fact.'

Ridiculously off-kilter, he smiled, turning his back on Charity in case his eyes gave him away before he kissed her cheek. 'Hope! How are you?'

'As fat as a house, thank you very much, and thoroughly fed up about it.'

'It'll be over soon.' He glanced at her belly in sympathy. 'Or at least according to my mother it will be, and you know she views herself as the world's greatest expert on childbirth. She's plumped for next week in the Philpot sweepstake and is so confident of it she's wagered ten guineas.'

'Next week…' She absorbed this news as if it were bad. 'That's an eternity.'

He shrugged in sympathy. 'It's only seven days, Hope…and that's assuming it takes all seven for Baby Thundersley to appear. You do look about to burst at any moment.'

'Easy for you to say when I haven't seen my feet since June and cannot get out of a chair any more unless someone hoists me out of it.' She idly rubbed her bump. 'Enough about my misery, how are you? All recovered from your jaunt up north with our annoying baby sisters? You got the short straw there, you poor thing. I have no doubt Charity ran you ragged as penance for curtailing her freedoms. Was it as awful as I suspect it was?'

Not a subject he wanted to be drawn on. 'It had its moments.'

Hope stared at the dance floor and smiled with affection. 'I can imagine. And I can also imagine you managed to thwart her more times than not, which also explains why she looks like she is sucking a lemon each time your name comes up in conversation.' A depressing discovery which didn't bode well for his cause. 'Clearly she still isn't over whatever tiff you had before she high-tailed it home.'

Yet another uncomfortable subject he would not be drawn on. 'Your father put me in charge.' And he'd likely never be able to look Augustus in the eye again after the liberties Griff had taken with his youngest daughter's naked body. 'Therefore, there was only so much of me that she could stomach before it all became too much.'

Her sister grinned. 'Don't feel badly for it—none of us blame you for her rebellion. It was always going to end badly. My sister is a force of nature.'

'She is indeed.'

'But fair play to you for managing to keep her on the straight and narrow all the way through her tour though. Despite all the trials and tribulations she has undoubtedly put you through, I am glad that part went well and that her career is finally taking off. She deserves every bit of her success as nobody I know works harder or pushes herself more than Charity does.'

'She does indeed.' Her work ethic had been only one of many staggering revelations about the most vexing of the three Brookes sisters. Before their ill-fated trip, Griff had stupidly assumed singing wasn't a job at all and that all Charity had to do was stand on a stage and open her mouth for the magic to emerge effortlessly from it.

After a month glued to her side, he now understood what a challenge it all was. The hours of daily vocal exercises she did diligently each morning as soon as she arose, the endless rehearsals to get the sound of the music just right, the supreme talent of reading the audience to keep them entertained and the physical toll of performing for an hour straight without a break had made him realise that being a soprano wasn't an easy thing at all. No matter how effortless she made it seem. Of their own accord, his eyes wandered to the dance floor and drank in the sight of her moving gracefully while he tried his best to ignore the other man she was dancing with. 'She pays for every good review she receives with her blood, sweat and tears.'

'Until she has no blood, sweat or tears left and she makes herself ill—as she has now.'

His eyes snapped back to Hope concerned. 'She's ill?'

'Been under the weather for weeks according to Lily. Exhaustion we suspect... Not that Charity will acknowledge it, of course. She denies there is anything wrong. But then she'd battle through pneumonia with nought but a tisane and a handkerchief rather than admit defeat. She is such a consummate and accomplished performer, her entire world could have fallen apart and she'd rather die than let anyone see it. She has more stubborn pride than anyone I know. Faith and I are both worried about her—not that she'll listen to us either. Look at her... laughing and smiling as if she hasn't a single care.' Griff didn't need to be asked twice. He would happily stare at her for ever if he could get away with it. 'But doesn't she look pale to you?'

'Perhaps...' She looked beautiful. She always looked beautiful to him. Even crying or windswept or under the weather, the sight of her always made his heart stutter. 'If she is unwell and working too hard, someone needs to convince her to take some time off. They have to force her to rest or she won't do it.'

Hope threw her head back and laughed. 'Did you learn nothing about my sister during your month away?

She is too rebellious to be forced into anything and she certainly never rests.'

'She did for me—and for three days too without any rebellion at all.' Three idyllic days before he had ruined it all.

Hope's jaw hung slack, impressed. 'Then if you know a way to get her to do anything she doesn't want to, you must share it with us all at once, because she is as stubborn as a mule. Even if that stubbornness is to her detriment. So stubborn she makes me seem like the reasonable sister.'

As concerned as he was, he had to scoff at that comment. 'I wouldn't go that far, Hope. You've certainly mellowed since you married, that much I will concede, but you are still quite terrifying when you lose your temper. I wouldn't cross you.'

She chuckled. They knew each other too well for her to take offence at his summary. 'All right, I'll grant you her brand of stubbornness is less confrontational than mine and she rebels with more affable diplomacy, but seriously, Griff, if you do know a way to make her slow down, we'd all appreciate it. She has been like a woman possessed since she returned from the north and works all the hours God sends, and now that she's signed on to do another month of *Figaro*, I am scared she'll end up more than a little under the weather and she'll do herself real harm.'

'I could try talking to her.' A flimsy excuse to do so without raising undue suspicion, when he had come here tonight with that express intention anyway. 'Not that I'll expect she'll want to listen to me after our… er…tiff.' The necessary lie felt bitter on his tongue. 'I am not exactly her favourite person at the moment.' No indeed, he was her biggest mistake.

'But it is worth a try if she's listened to you in the past. She was so unwell before we came, Faith and I both cautioned her to stay at home. But you know Charity...' He did. Intimately. 'She's doubtless here to prove to the world that she doesn't give two figs about Denby's marriage, even though his engagement broke her heart.' More nails in the coffin of his futile dreams. 'Not that she would admit to that either—but I can see it in her eyes. She is still devastated by the rejection. Utterly crushed. I think she thought he was the one...'

'I'll go talk to her now.' If he refused to listen to the way she pined for Denby, then perhaps he could still pretend that he stood a cat's chance in hell of replacing Denby in her affections even though he lacked the aristocratic credentials.

And pigs might fly but he had to give it one last try.

Armed with his flimsy excuse and without a backwards glance in case he lost his nerve, Griff stalked towards the dance floor, his shoulders steeled for battle and his foolish, battered, yearning heart in his mouth.

Chapter Fourteen

All eyes tonight, Dear Reader, will doubtless be on Miss C. from Bloomsbury, who is rumoured to be still devastated at being thwarted from becoming a duchess and is apparently on the keen lookout for a suitable and immediate replacement for Lord D....

Whispers from Behind the Fan
—August 1815

'I believe this waltz is mine?'

Lord Cranham bowed, and Charity forced herself to nod as she dipped into a wobbly curtsy. She no longer felt queasy, thank goodness, but she did feel strange and that wasn't only because Griff was here. His sudden and unexpected reappearance, when Dorothy had assured her he intended to remain in Sheffield till Christmas had left her shaken, but the persistent stomach ailment she had picked up made her feel both weak and intermittently dizzy to boot.

She knew Lily and her sisters were right and that she did need some time off to convalesce because willing this horrid malaise away certainly wasn't working. If anything, in the last week it had only got worse and hiding the increasingly frequent bouts of vomiting from the eagle-eyed Lily was getting harder. As much as she had the maid's loyalty, Lily's fealty to her mother overruled everything else. While her mama might tolerate one of her daughters struggling valiantly though a mild cold with a stiff upper lip—because of course the show must always go on—she would order bed rest and physician for anything more.

And this was more.

Charity had never felt so ill in her life.

'Might I be so bold to tell you how lovely you look, Miss Charity?' Lord Cranham smiled as he took her hand and led her back to the floor, and that compliment buoyed her flagging confidence even though she had little interest in the young peer. That wasn't his fault. He was pleasant enough, polite enough and had a pleasing enough face, he was also wealthy and destined to be an earl one day, but she felt no attraction for him whatsoever. As he slid his arm around her waist and curled his fingers around hers, she experienced none of the heady frisson or sense of anticipation which had always been there with Griff.

Against her will, her gaze wandered to where he had been across the ballroom. But instead of laughing beside Hope, her sister now in deep conversation with Dorothy and her new fiancé Captain Sinclair, the elusive Griff was nowhere to be seen. Which was probably just as well as looking at him still hurt. Almost eight weeks to the day since that hideous morning in Sheffield and the pain of their last conversation was as raw tonight as it had been then. Of all the balls to turn up to out of the blue and like a bad penny, he had to pick this one—drat him. The one where she was at her most ill at ease, and just plain ill as well.

'I saw you in Covent Garden again last week...you were magnificent.' Her eager lord seemed determined that they should have a conversation while they danced and she forced a smile, knowing that her lack of enthusiasm was hardly fair to him.

'I am glad you enjoyed it.'

'I have seen you six times already.'

'You flatter me.'

'It isn't flattery. I am an *ardent* fan, Miss Charity.' To prove that, he decided to slide his hand from her waist to the small of her back as he tugged her closer.

Too close and that impudence galled.

Using the steps to aid her, she deftly manoeuvred her body to put some distance between them, but he immediately pulled her back. 'Take a walk on the terrace with me.'

'No, thank you.'

'It is a lovely summer's night, and the moon is full.' He tried to spin her from the edge of the floor in the direction of the open French doors, his assumption and impertinence grating.

'That is as maybe but I have no interest in visiting the garden.' She pushed against his lead, forcing him to alter their direction or stumble and he frowned as if greatly put out by her refusal.

'Perhaps later then?' She shook her head and was rewarded with outright petulance. 'If you are not interested in me then why did you agree to this waltz? When everyone knows a waltz is a declaration of intent.'

Because she had wanted to prove to Griff she was still sought after, that she didn't care one jot about his unflattering disapproval and because she had wanted to put off having to acknowledge his existence in this ballroom tonight for as long as possible. 'Then you must forgive me, my lord, as we are clearly at cross purposes as I assumed granting you this waltz was merely a declaration that I was willing to dance with you.'

Which, she now realised, had obviously been a mistake when Lord Cranham had quite a reputation for keeping a line of mistresses and by the looks of him, was clearly on the hunt for the next. And just like Griff and Lord Denby, he assumed because of the gossip columns' printed innuendo, she was the sort who was willing to be hunted. She stopped dead and severed the contact, quite done with the dance and not caring that several other couples were forced to quickly adjust their course to avoid colliding with them. She bobbed an insincere curtsy as a farewell without bothering to hide her annoyance because she was sick and tired of floating above all the insults and being treated with such flagrant disrespect. 'If you assumed it was any more than that, my lord, then I humbly apologise.'

'You have nothing to apologise for.' Out of nowhere Griff was suddenly behind her, his expression and stance threatening. 'But I think Lord Cranham certainly does as he appears to have forgotten his manners around a lady.'

Intimidated, the young peer nodded like a woodpecker. 'My humblest apologies if I have offended you, Miss Charity.'

Only slightly placated, Griff claimed her hand and before she or Cranham could argue otherwise, twirled her back into the swirling dancers until they were part of them. His big hand on her waist, his fingers laced with hers, his dark eyes boring into her soul like nobody else ever could.

'You might have asked for a dance like everyone else does.' She used the handy veil of imperiousness to mask her body's immediate reaction and tried to ignore how every nerve ending fizzed and came alive at his touch.

'If I had, you'd have only refused me and we really do need to talk.' His eyes were angry too, yet there was something else swirling in those unfathomable golden-flecked irises which she couldn't decipher. Uncertainty perhaps. Or maybe hurt. Which would be ironic when she was the one he had wounded. More likely, his judge-mental nose had been put out by her rejection of him, exactly like the presumptuous Lord Cranham, and he felt the urge to tear her off a strip or two for not yield-ing to his *superior* logic or thanking him for his lack-lustre proposal after she had misbehaved once again.

'I cannot think what about when I have said all I need to say.'

'Perhaps *you* have—but I have plenty more things to add to the discussion alongside the burning ques-tions that I came here specifically to ask. And I am quite determined to make a pest of myself until I get all the answers to them, Charity, because I confess I do not understand what is going on between us or why you ran away.' As she stiffened in his arms, his anger turned to concern while his voice dropped to a whis-per. 'Did I hurt you that night…? I know you said that I hadn't but…after you bolted the thought that I might have has played on my mind incessantly. I keep rack-ing my brains to remember if I did something which displeased you or if our…our…intimacy scared you. At the time, I was sure you enjoyed it but…'

'Oh, for goodness sake!' Even at a whisper, her im-passioned hiss turned a few heads, so she dropped her voice further. 'Did you come here tonight to confirm your extraordinary prowess as a lover, Griff? Because if you did, this public ballroom is hardly the place.'

'I came to find out why you left.' He spun her as they reached a corner and her stomach lurched worryingly again. 'And to see if there is any way to make you reconsider my proposal.'

'Why would you seek to do that when I have already relieved you from the odious chore?' A pathetic part of her willed him to banish away the hurt in a sentence. To say the words she craved. To show her that he cared. Wanted her and her alone. 'Anyone would think you feel obligated.'

'Of course I feel obligated!' Not at all what she wanted to hear. 'Your father entrusted me with your safekeeping, and I betrayed him. I took liberties with your person and I laid with you like a husband...' He dropped his voice an octave and pulled her closer so he could speak directly into her ear. 'I took your virginity, for pity's sake. That means something. A decent man doesn't walk away from such a responsibility.' He twirled her to avoid another couple and nausea swamped her. 'I know you were holding out for better... I appreciate you had set your sights higher...' his voice seemed to be coming from a distance as her head spun wildly '...but now that Denby and you are no more... I thought...' The floor tilted and all at once she found herself engulfed in his strength. 'Charity...are you all right?'

As speaking was currently impossible, she shook her head and clutched at his lapel to steady herself as he whisked her off the floor to an alcove then stared down at her concerned. 'You look grey.' His hand touched her face. 'And you're all clammy. Hope said you had been pushing yourself too hard again and now look—you've made yourself ill.' It was a gentle admonishment, one filled with more sympathy than irritation. 'You need to go home.' He searched around him for her family. 'You need to rest, Charity.'

'I just need to sit down for a moment…that's all.' Or perhaps dash to the retiring room so she could retch again before bribing a strange maid to dispose of the evidence like she had taken to doing every day at the theatre. 'Please don't cause a scene.' The absolute last thing she needed was to disgrace herself in the middle of Denby's wedding ball. 'Not here, Griff…' Her eyes flicked to the man in question. Another man who considered her unworthy. 'And not now. Please not now.'

He followed her gaze to where Lord Denby waltzed with his new fiancée and nodded, his expression instantly grim and disapproving. 'Very well. Not here and now. But only if you promise that you will meet me tomorrow so that we can discuss it properly. I shan't be swayed on that. And no more dancing! I mean it, Charity. Or so help me I'll put you in a carriage myself and drive you straight to the physician!'

Despite his palpable anger, he solicitously and subtly supported her back to the refreshment table where their families chatted amiably, guided her into a chair and stood over her like a sentry as she sipped the glass of water he pressed into her hand.

'It is definitely a girl, Hope.' Mrs Philpot's voice washed over her as Charity tried to use sheer willpower and deep breathing to settle her griping guts. Griping that wasn't helped by the pungent wafts of the trout laid out just inches away on the table. 'You are carrying too high for it to be a boy.' His mother tapped her chin as she openly apprised her sister's stomach. 'Tell me, do you crave sweet or salty things?'

'Definitely sweet,' answered Luke, Hope's husband. 'And trifle especially. I think she's eaten a ton of the stuff in the last few months and I'm quite sick of the sight of it.' The mere mention of food made Charity more bilious, the idea of trifle somehow now worse than the very real trout which taunted her.

'Then that is another sure sign it is a girl.'

'Ah—but she hasn't suffered from morning S-I-C-K-N-E-S-S at all,' said her mother blissfully unaware that even spelling the unsavoury word made Charity nauseous, 'and that is supposed to be a sure sign you are carrying a girl too.'

'I didn't suffer from it either though, Mama,' added Faith, enjoying playing devil's advocate. 'And while I am aware that I had a boy and that in itself may prove your theory correct, I would also remind you that neither did you and you had three girls.'

'That is very true, dear. We Brookes ladies have always blossomed during pregnancy.'

'Now you come to mention it,' said Mrs Philpot, 'I positively glowed with health and vitality when I was carrying Dorothy too. In fact, had never felt better in my life. But with Griff though…' She pulled an appalled face. 'Oh, my goodness, that was a truly horrendous time!'

'You had morning sickness with a boy?' Faith sounded smug to have been proved completely right. 'Well, that rather disproves my mother's theory too, doesn't it?'

'Oh, it wasn't just morning sickness, dear. With Griff it was near constant sickness—morning, noon and night. I was always dizzy, bone tired and barely kept anything down. Not that I had any appetite to begin with. My lifelong love of food disappeared the second I conceived. If I even looked at food in the first four months I had to lie down. Even the smell of it turned my stomach…'

Charity swallowed hard as an ominous chill skittered down her spine as Mrs Philpot rattled off a list of quite specific symptoms which worryingly mirrored her own.

Not that she could possibly be pregnant of course.

Aside from the not inconsequential fact that her scandalous night with Griff had been her first and only time, and everybody knew virgins rarely conceived unless they featured in a Bible story, Griff seemed to know what he was doing. He was annoyingly, but always eminently, sensible and would have taken steps to prevent planting a baby in her belly.

Surely?

As her panicked heart threatened to beat out of her chest, she frantically searched her mind for the last memory of her courses—the courses which had always been so reliably predictable she could practically set the clock by them.

The courses she hadn't given any thought to recently because she had been so preoccupied with everything else that was wrong with her life.

The courses that would immediately put her racing mind at rest.

She counted backwards, trying to pinpoint her last grace days from the theatre which excused her from performing as was her right, and couldn't recall one at all in August.

Or July for that matter.

Until she came to the earth-shattering conclusion that she couldn't actually recall being visited by her monthly curse in quite some time. And worse, if indeed her predicament could now be any worse, if she had to put her finger on the exact date of the last one, Charity hadn't seen hide nor hair of the wretched things since Appletreewick.

Well over two months and a half ago.

Chapter Fifteen

The first Griff had known of his impending fatherhood was when a furious Augustus Brookes had turned up at his front door first thing the next morning and punched him squarely on the nose.

Since then, the last week had been a bit of a blur. If indeed a week filled with rage, accusations, bitter recriminations, crushing guilt and family feuding, all wrapped up in an enormous and looming bow of scandal could be constituted as a blur. To say tempers were high was an understatement. Even now, sat on opposite sides of St George's Church in Bloomsbury, you could cut the atmosphere between his family and hers with a knife.

They all felt betrayed and they all blamed him, and he supposed that was no less than he deserved, all things considered. Even Dottie, who didn't have a mean bone in her body, couldn't look at him without shaking her head in disgust. Overnight, he had gone from being the sensible and decent Griff the Reliable Fun Spoiler to Griff the Despicable Despoiling Scoundrel and there wasn't a damn thing he could do about it.

His mother kept weeping. His father kept glaring.

Her sisters refused to speak to him, and her parents wanted his blood. The only two people in the church with a modicum of pity for his predicament were Piers and Luke, perhaps because his soon-to-be brothers-in-law understood how hard it was to resist a Brookes woman when you had inadvertently helplessly fallen in love with one—no matter how hard you tried.

Except at least Faith and Hope had loved those two men back.

In the last week whenever they were forced to collide, Charity had veered between being blasé and matter of fact or, when that façade cracked, utterly grief stricken. As she plainly was now. By the look of her pinched and swollen features she'd been crying for hours.

Not the best start to a marriage.

'Griffith Alexander Philpot, wilt thou have this woman to thy wedded wife, to live together after God's ordinance in the holy estate of Matrimony? Wilt thou love her, comfort her, honour, and keep her in sickness and in health; and, forsaking all other, keep thee only unto her, so long as ye both shall live?'

'I will.' God help him.

'And Charity Grace Brookes, wilt thou have this man to thy wedded husband, to live together after God's ordinance in the holy estate of Matrimony? Wilt thou obey him, and serve him, love, honour, and keep him in sickness and in health; and, forsaking all other, keep thee only unto him, so long as ye both shall live?'

She hesitated for an eternity, which he supposed said it all. Then her voice shook. 'I will.' She didn't sound the least bit convinced by any of those vows or particularly committed to them.

Nor did she look at him as he slipped the ring on her

finger or as they left the church in a carriage. Or even as they travelled the short distance from the church to his house in Burton Crescent.

Under the fraught and difficult circumstances, neither family had felt it appropriate to immediately celebrate their enforced nuptials with a traditional wedding breakfast. Instead, they had decided to break bread over a quiet dinner tonight at the Brookes' residence in Bedford Place once the dust of the dreadful day had settled. A dinner which wasn't as much a celebration as an attempt to heal the rift between them after Griff had thoroughly ruined their special and close friendship by thoroughly ruining Charity.

They had been duty bound to invite him as the groom, but he harboured no illusions that any of them actually wanted him there—his new wife included. Similarly, and in case he foolishly harboured any traditional thoughts of carrying her over the threshold, Charity marched through the front door the moment his housekeeper opened it and then stopped dead in the hallway. Then blinked at her new home like a startled deer staring helplessly down the barrel of a gun.

'Would you like me to show you around?'

His question earned him a single, awkward nod.

'Splendid…then I suppose we should start with Mrs Gibbons.' He gestured to his hovering housekeeper. 'She runs the place and does a very good job of it too.'

Mrs Gibbons bobbed a curtsy. 'Welcome to your new home, Mrs Philpot.' It wasn't his imagination. She winced at the name before she covered it with a polite smile for the servant's benefit. 'It's long past time this house had a mistress.'

To fill the ensuing silence seeing as Charity clearly had no intention of replying, Griff tried to laugh. It sounded hollow in his hallway, and a tad manic. 'Mrs Gibbons despaired of my bachelorhood, didn't you, Mrs Gibbons?'

'I did indeed, sir. Such a lovely big house deserves the hubbub of a boisterous family within its fine walls and not the silence of a single man who is always holed up in his study working. There are rooms aplenty upstairs too, Mrs Philpot. Ten of them in fact and I cannot wait for them all to be filled with the laughter of your children...not that there's any need to rush into that yet, of course. Not when I can plainly see that you are young enough not to worry about making haste. Besides, you are only a newlywed once in your lifetime and you should enjoy it for it is such a special time.' She smiled knowingly, clearly recalling her own special time with Mr Gibbons many moons ago. 'You'll want time to discover how to be a wife first before you run headlong into motherhood.'

Griff cringed, wishing he'd had the wherewithal to have had the awkward conversation with his housekeeper that he clearly should have had before today. It wasn't as if they would be able to keep the reasons for their hasty marriage a secret for much longer and his nosy housekeeper was no fool. She had birthed five babies of her own before Mr Gibbons has turned up his toes and had another five grandchildren. 'Right this second, I think my...er...new wife and I would enjoy some tea, Mrs Gibbons, if that's not too much trouble.'

Wife.

How strange that felt on his lips.

'Of course, sir. You show your lovely bride around the place and I'll have it set up in the drawing room for when you're done.'

He waited till she was gone then pulled a face. 'Sorry

about that…she means well and, in her defence, I haven't told her anything yet.'

Charity offered him another curt nod, obviously content to continue to leave him to suffer for his sins in silence.

Wordlessly, she followed him from one room to the next, nodding at his explanations while her wide, darting eyes took it all in, still clutching her wedding bouquet like a pagan sacrifice, her pale expression stark and her blue eyes outraged. Back in the hallway, there was no putting off taking her upstairs any longer, which inevitably meant kicking the hornet's nest they had tacitly so far avoided. Unless he could think of something scintillating about the architecture which delayed the great unsaid a little longer.

'There are three floors in total, discounting the servants' quarters in the attic and the kitchen in the cellar.'

Although what had possessed him to purchase such a ridiculously huge house last year when he returned was beyond him now, as it would likely only serve as a space they could both rattle around in while they avoided one another.

But back then, imbued with hope for a bright future and with no desire to return to living with his family after so many years of independence, he had foolishly chosen a house he had hoped he would grow into as well as grow old in. He'd had lofty plans of meeting a new woman, falling head over heels in love with her and then raising a huge family here with her just as Mrs Gibbons had said. That was, however, when he had still optimistically believed he could exorcise Charity from his heart and start afresh. A pathetic hope which he had clung to until Sheffield. Now that they were married and she was carrying his child, he had no earthly clue if that would be their one and only or if she would consider more. At this rate, and with things so frosty between them, he had no earthly clue if they would ever exchange a civil word let alone share a bed again. That detail, like countless looming others, was yet to be decided.

Like a condemned man on the way to the gallows he climbed up the stairs while she trailed behind, then he paused outside his door. 'I tend to sleep in this bedchamber.'

What sort of namby-pamby non-committal sentence was that?

He didn't tend to sleep there—he slept there. He'd be delighted if she decided to sleep in there with him too but he'd be damned if he'd admit that aloud any time soon. Not when she was still clutching her bouquet like a shield and looked ready to jump on any excuse to turn it into a weapon.

'When I am in London, I mean, as opposed to Sheffield...' Why the blazes had he said that when the word Sheffield always conjured images of what they had done in Sheffield? 'That's when I tend to sleep in there.'

Good grief, that was even worse!

His toes curling inside his boots he flung open the door so she could look inside, which she chose to do rooted to the spot behind him showing absolutely no desire to venture in and explore the space further, staring at the big bed and swallowing hard. An omen if ever there was one about the state of their fledgling union.

'And there's a matching suite over here.' He marched stiffly across to the adjacent door and then through it simply to avoid the brittle air which enveloped them. 'I thought this could be your bedchamber...if it is to your liking, of course. If not, there are eight more.' All without the threat of an interconnecting door in the wall between them. Not that he felt inclined to mention that convenience yet in case she deemed such a marital familiarity as a gross inconvenience to her.

Good grief this was all so blasted awkward! His feeble smile felt like a grimace but he still held it in place. 'But this has the biggest bed...' he found himself swallowing as he pointed to it, his mind instantly picturing her lying rumpled and naked on the pristine white sheets '...a dressing room and a lovely view over the garden.' Which he gestured to through the window with an over-enthusiastic sweep of his arm. That done, he suddenly had no earthly clue what to do with his arms, so he clamped them behind his back and resisted the pathetic urge to rock on his heels while he awaited her judgement.

Gingerly she stepped inside to give it the once over and then offered him the single curt nod which seemed to be the only way they were now doomed to communicate.

'Splendid...then I'll have all your things unpacked in here as soon as they arrive later.'

Another nod, a martyred one, and after a week of bending over backwards to do the right thing by her as fast as was humanly possible, his last taut and frayed nerve finally snapped in despair.

'This isn't just *my* fault, Charity!' Griff exploded like a grenade, arms waving and expression incensed. Real emotion at last after a week of rigid stoicism. 'There were two of us in that bed that night and I don't recall you being a passive bystander during any of it! In fact, it was you...' he shook a quaking finger at her '...*you* who instigated it!' Then he started to pace, mimicking her voice and punctuating every word with his stupid, sanctimonious finger too. *'"I could have any man I want, Griff! Any man! Even you, Griff!"'*

'I know what I said!'

'She speaks! It's a miracle!'

Incensed, she threw her bouquet at his head and scowled when he dodged to avoid it and it hit the wall instead sending a shower of petals everywhere. 'Go to hell, Griffith Philpot!'

'You're too late, Charity *Philpot*—I am already there!'

Then he huffed out a sigh and closed his eyes momentarily, no doubt burying everything inside again where she couldn't see it. When he opened them, they were filled with such sadness that it undid her. It was strangely reassuring to know that he was hurting too. 'But at least I am trying to make the best of it and am not behaving like a spoiled and belligerent child! And I am the one everyone has blamed for what happened.'

That was also depressingly true.

Not once, not with her family, and his, all railing at him for his treachery, had he ever hinted at her part in what actually happened. Or reminded everyone that she was a famously shocking flirt or even alluded to all the many scandalous stories about her in the gossip columns. Which had allowed her to play the innocent victim in their Shakespearean tragedy while he was cast as the selfish seducer. The insidious villain of the piece.

For all his low opinions of her, that was extremely noble. If anything, he had been nothing but decent about the whole affair—right from the morning they had awoken in her bed and he had unreservedly offered to marry her despite his lack of enthusiasm for the chore. Charity didn't suppose there were many men who would allow another man to punch them in the face on their own doorstep either, and not punch them straight back. But Griff had taken his punishment from her father like a gentleman and his stoic magnanimity and willingness to stand by her side this past week shamed her.

'This wasn't what I wanted.' She wanted to curl up into a ball and weep but had to settle for gesturing limply to the room with gloomy despondence instead. 'It's not at all the wedding day I envisioned.'

'You don't say?' He laughed without humour, his tone laced with bitter sarcasm. 'You mean it wasn't your girlish romantic dream to be carelessly impregnated by Gruff Griff the Repressed Fun Spoiler after one misguided night of passion, then shackled to him for all eternity on the back of it?' He raked a hand through his dark hair and slumped to sit on the mattress, all the fight in him suddenly gone and his expression as wretched as she suspected hers was. 'I am well aware I am not the husband of your choosing, Charity, and that hardly fills me with confidence for our marriage either.'

She sat beside him, deciding to be honest. 'I wanted what Faith has with Piers and what Hope has with Luke.' The magical ingredients of love, mutual respect and happiness.

'Ah…well…' He reached for her hand and instantly the world felt a bit better. 'Maybe a miracle will happen. But in the meantime, how about we try not to murder one another while we work out how to rub along first?'

'Just rubbing along?' She stared at their interlaced fingers in case he witnessed the disappointment in her eyes. 'Is that the best we can hope for, do you think?'

He was quiet for the longest time before he sighed. 'Beneath my undoubtedly gruff, dull and sensible exterior beats the heart of an optimist and a dreamer and for a little while, not so long ago, we were good together, you and I.' Then he kissed her hand—soft, tender, potent again—before he used it to haul her up. 'Come on…let me show you the rest of the house and then we'll have some tea.'

'And then?'

He shrugged, smiling. 'Rome wasn't built in a day, they built it brick by brick, and we are both clever people so I'm sure we'll work it out.'

'Because nothing is unfixable?'

He nodded as he tugged her towards the door. 'As long as you keep believing you can fix it.'

Chapter Sixteen

Poor Griff was a social pariah at the tense celebration dinner later that night. At best, their families ignored him as they tried to pretend that the strong bonds between the Brookes and the Philpots would see them through the crisis, at worst they were all unbearable. Hers, unsurprisingly, were the absolute worst. Whatever the topic, either her mother or her father found a way to use it as an unsubtle dig at her new husband, yet to his credit he took each unfair blow on the chin.

'How was Torbay, Piers?' Luke filled the umpteenth awkward silence during the interminable main course with an innocuous question while Charity warily chewed a sliver of boiled potato.

'Ridiculous. The place was still swarming with people even as I left, all desperately trying to catch a glimpse of Napoleon even though he was long gone. Apparently, it's been like that for the last month. From the moment the public learned the Navy were holding him on the *Bellerophon* just off the coast, the town was inundated. There were so many boats in the water one day, the Captain threatened to turn his cannons on them.'

'Did you get to meet the man himself?'

Usually reluctant to discuss state secrets even when they were public, Piers seemed uncharacteristically happy to spill it all thanks to the stifled atmosphere around the table. 'I cannot say we had a conversation, but I was present when Captain Maitland gave him his marching orders. Yet even then he tried to argue against his exile to St Helena and continued to claim asylum here in England—and he expected it to come with a house grand enough for his station and big enough for all his battalions of staff. Staggering really...the nerve of the man is unbelievable. He was so adamant of his due it was as if invading half of Europe and starting a huge war was of no consequence.'

'But some men are like that, aren't they?' said her mother with a frigid glance towards Griff. 'Shameless L-I-B-E-R-T-I-N-E-S who cause mayhem and take what they want with scant regard for whether it is right or proper. But at least we expect nothing less from Old Boney who has never tried to hide his villainy. It is the W-O-L-F in sheep's clothing who is always the rottenest to their core. Who say one thing with the utmost piety and do quite another. Who garner people's trusts and use it to prey on innocents and take advantage—'

'Enough!' Charity's cutlery clattered to the plate. 'Stop taking this all out on Griff!'

'And who else shall we take it out on, Daughter?' Her father slammed his wine glass down with such force the stem shattered, sending red wine all over the expensive Irish linen tablecloth while everyone else around the table audibly held their breath. All except Mrs Philpot who buried her tearstained face in her handkerchief. 'I entrusted that scoundrel with your safekeeping, and he repaid me by seducing you!'

'He didn't seduce me.'

'*Charity...*' From his exiled seat at the furthest edge of the table, Griff shot her a warning look. 'Your parents have every right to be angry with me.'

'No, they don't, Griff.' It wasn't fair that he should take the fall alone. It wasn't as if anyone around this table was in any doubt that they had been intimate with one another—like Napoleon, that ship had already sailed a week ago when she had confessed to her sisters her predicament and within minutes they had unleashed hell. 'I will not sit here and allow your entire character to be assassinated. Not when it was I who seduced you.'

'What!' Her father surged to his feet, his eyes bulging with fury as he pointed at Griff. 'Has he put you up to this? Manipulated you into taking the blame like he manipulated you into his bed!'

In for a penny, in for a pound. 'Actually, it was *my* bed, Papa, and Griff was only in my bedchamber because he was trying to reason with me and talk me out of going to Lord Denby's house party unchaperoned as I intended—and as Dorothy will confirm.' As her wide-eyed best friend nodded, Charity glanced at her new husband down the table and shrugged at Griff's exasperated expression.

'We argued. As I am sure you can imagine, because Griff and I have always done that so well. I didn't take kindly to either his interference in my plans or his intuitiveness when he despaired at me continually throwing myself at a man who didn't show the slightest interest in me...' She might as well throw it all out in the open. No matter what the circumstances or his unflattering feelings, he had stepped up and she knew in her heart that that noble sacrifice deserved some acknowledgement. Confession was supposed to be good for the soul, after all, and if any air ever needed cleaning it was the toxic fumes choking this dining room. 'I took umbrage simply because he was right... Denby didn't want me and I already knew it by then.'

Griff's expression was now as shocked as everyone else's. 'Because unbeknownst to Griff, before our argument that fateful night, I had just read a letter from Lord Denby informing me there would be no house party on account of his engagement. And because hell apparently really does have no fury like a woman scorned, in my irrational state, I took it all out on Griff and kissed him.'

Which was as much of the truth as she was prepared to admit to for now.

Her father's fist banged the table. 'A kiss is a long way from a seduction!'

'In my experience, that all depends on the kiss.' Luke's comment earned him a sharp nudge from a very pained-looking Hope and a sympathetic nod from Piers.

'He could have walked away! He *should* have walked away!' Her father wasn't ready to be placated, but Charity shook her head defiantly. 'He could have done the decent thing—the only *gentlemanly* thing—and left my youngest daughter well alone!'

As the smell of the gravy was making her queasy, she pushed the plate away before she answered. 'Who is your most headstrong daughter, Papa? The one most determined to always get her way?'

Nobody needed to say it was her. The way they all stared intently at their plates was confirmation enough. The only person who met her eye was Griff, his expression a cross between mortified, bemused and, she hoped, impressed that she had stood up for him. She offered him a resigned smile and he sent her one back. Oddly, it meant the world. 'I am the most reckless and tenacious one. The one you most despair of, Papa, and I started it and was quite determined to finish it—hence we all find ourselves here today trying to come to terms with the aftermath.'

Her father finally sat, heavy like a broken man, and groped for her mother's hand. His disappointment made her feel awful, but she didn't regret telling him the truth. As horrible as the situation was, they were all in it together and she and Griff most of all. It wasn't right that he be pilloried any more than it was fair that the lifelong bonds between the Brookes family and the Philpots be shattered because they felt the need to choose sides in a battle that neither had started.

She had.

And all to prove a point.

'I treated him like a son...' Her father shook his head in disbelief as her mother nodded, and Charity rolled her eyes.

'But he isn't your son, Papa, nor is he my brother, so stop behaving as if we've committed some hideous cardinal sin above the obvious one, because we haven't. We share no blood connection whatsoever so have always been perfectly free to marry.' That was probably why there had always been friction between them. She had always wanted him in a way he hadn't wanted her. She might as well embrace that truth too while she was being honest.

'Griff proposed the next morning, by the way, long before either of us knew I was pregnant, so he did the decent thing unprompted in case you level that charge at him too, and I stubbornly refused him. I thought I could pretend it hadn't happened, and like my frequent scandals, I thought it would all eventually disappear and be forgotten about. That's why I ran away and came home…and when he followed me and tried to do the decent thing again, I refused to see him let alone discuss it. If you don't believe me, ask Lily, as she was the one I tasked with sending him packing because I was too much of a coward to do it myself.' He had deserved better than that. 'But despite that, when the worst happened, he was there beside me like a shot and not once in this wretched last week has he been anything less than a gentleman about it all. Which, all things considered, is rather admirable really—don't you think?'

For several fraught seconds, you could have heard a pin drop as everyone digested this. Until her sister yelped as her waters broke and the whole house descended into more chaos.

It was an hour or so before dawn when they finally returned home. After assisting in the birthing room, Charity was dead on her feet and had almost nodded off on the short five-minute carriage ride from Bedford Place to Burton Crescent, so Griff had sent her straight to bed. In view of the hour he did the same, but with his mind whirring, he didn't bother trying to sleep and instead stretched out on his mattress while he tried to examine everything to make some sense of the muddle. His life had been turned upside down, and at such speed he'd had little time to make head or tail of any of it, but now that time ominously stretched before him his organised and logical mind needed a forward plan seeing as a significant part of the old one had so spectacularly failed.

There was one new and enormous constant which couldn't be ignored.

He was married.

That he happened to be married to the woman of his

dreams was by the by, because the circumstances and the premise weren't right. Charity was only his on a technicality and a veritable ocean still flowed between them. That had to be fixed, although he had no idea how. All he did know, without a shadow of a doubt, was he couldn't live with the situation as it was and certainly not indefinitely. It was too painful and if it continued on in that same vein, it would destroy him. Reason told him he had three viable options after the baby was born.

One—they could agree to live completely separate lives as so many unhappy couples in the *ton* did.

Two—they could divorce. It would be a scandal, of course it would, but as Piers had proved it could be weathered and once a suitable amount of time had passed, he and Charity could move on. There was no doubt she would any more than there was no chance he would.

Or three—they could make the marriage work as a good marriage should.

As the first two options would likely destroy him, that only left three on the table. But the odds were undeniably stacked against him. If he were a betting man, at best it was a long shot and…

He thought he heard a distant sob and sat bolt upright. Then another. Definitely coming from next door. She was crying and it broke his heart.

On leaden feet, he ventured to the connecting door and pressed his ear against the wood, not wanting to intrude on her misery but needing to at the same time, the sounds beyond more ugly than tragic. Anger perhaps on top of the sadness? Despair? Horror?

Another sob, then a cough and a groan and he could stand it no more. Without knocking, Griff burst through the door to comfort her and then skidded to a stop at her upturned palm.

'Go away!' She was on all fours on the floor, leaning over the chamber pot. 'Don't look at me!' Then she retched and sobbed and groaned some more.

'Oh, my God!' In a panic, he hit the floor beside her, tried to support her shoulders and she flapped his hand away. 'Shall I fetch the physician?' It was quite the wrong time to ask her a question, but she managed to shake her head then answer between each violent spasm.

'No point... Morning sickness...please go away... give me some dignity...'

At a loss at what to do to help her and damned if he'd leave her to suffer all alone simply so she could pretend all was well when it plainly wasn't, Griff turned his back and waited until it all subsided. Then, riddled with guilt, he helped her to the bed and fetched her some water. As she drank it, he wrung out a clean flannel and handed it to her too. 'I am so sorry.'

'For what?'

'This.' He gestured to her ineffectually as she wiped her drawn face. 'For doing this to you. For making you so ill. I had no idea morning sickness was so bad.'

'To be fair to you neither did I.' She flopped back on her pillow, so pale she almost matched the milky shade of her ivory nightgown. 'And for the record, morning sickness is a misnomer, for it gives the sufferer false hope that it confines itself to the mornings when it plainly doesn't.' Then she managed a limp smile as she touched her belly. 'Whatever demon you planted in here, Griff, ensures I am sick morning, noon and night.'

A worrying thought. 'Surely that can't be right?'

'According to your mother it is. Don't you remember? She said that with you she was in an awful state for the first four months—which I suppose only reiterates that you *are* to blame for the state I am in.' She thwacked him playfully. 'Proof if proof were needed that you have always been ornery, Griffith Philpot, and even before you were born you managed to royally spoil someone's fun.' It staggered him that she could find amusement in the situation when he was so appalled by it all.

'There must be something we can do to make it better?'

'Our family physician said it would pass eventually.'

'Well that isn't good enough! You cannot spend another two months like this!'

'Did you hear that, little one?' She lifted her head so that she could talk to her stomach. 'Your papa is displeased with your behaviour and wants it to stop.'

She was being ironic, typically flippant, yet had no idea what a profound effect that simple jokey comment had upon him. Because up until that moment he hadn't fully understood the full implications of their situation. But those two simple repetitive syllables in 'papa' kindled something strange inside him which he hadn't realised was there. Something primal and protective and all-consuming. An emotion which slammed into him like a locomotive at full speed.

Fatherhood.

An enormous responsibility and another new constant which couldn't be ignored.

Unaware that she had left him entirely speechless and floundering, Charity grinned despite her nausea as he sat on the edge of her mattress. 'This baby won't listen, of course, because the half that isn't ornery like you will be rebellious exactly like me, and therefore will instinctively chafe against direct orders. What on earth was fate thinking to amalgamate two such troublesome personalities as ours? Unless it's clearly intent on punishing us both for being so troublesome in the first place.'

Or fate was pushing them together.

As stunned as he was by their new situation, Griff couldn't help but think there was also a sense of inevitability about it all too. A sense of rightness. That might be because he knew that if his heart had had to choose his wife, it would have chosen Charity—no contest. There would have been no other candidate as far as that fickle organ was concerned, no matter what his sensible head had to say on the subject.

'We might even have created a monster, Griff. Have you considered that?'

'Impossible.' He smiled trying to picture the character of their minute offspring, and of its own accord, his hand gently rested on her belly. That too felt right. 'In here is a brilliant inventor. So brilliant he's practically a genius like his impressive father, and he will invent steam engines so sophisticated they will fly.'

She laughed as she shook her head, her hands resting on top of his, unconsciously completing their unlikely family circle in a way which touched him profoundly. It felt like fate—his destiny—that with this woman was exactly where he was always meant to be. 'Obviously, *she's* a soprano—but I see no reasons why she shouldn't tinker with steam engines on the side if that happens to take her fancy too as she's bound to be a genius because she'll follow me more than you. I have decided to insist upon that.'

'The Philpot & Daughter Manufacturing Company...?' Griff let the idea marinate for a bit and decided he liked it. 'It has a nice ring to it.' His eyes drifted to the gold wedding band on her finger and decided he liked that there too. And behind it was another thought. The realisation that he had to fix the unfixable, no matter what it took, because his bursting heart told him that there really was no other option.

Chapter Seventeen

With all the many, many, many suitors Miss C. from Bloomsbury has accumulated over the years, alongside all the rife speculations that came with them, I have to confess, Gentle Reader, that not even I could have predicted yesterday's unlikely groom...

Whispers from Behind the Fan
—August 1815

They spent over an hour with the expensive Harley Street physician the next morning. Charity trying to take it all in and Griff asking numerous questions while making copious notes. Doctor Macdonald was much more verbose on the subject of pregnancy than the Brookes family physician, probably because Griff seemed to need to know the ins and outs of everything, and while most of what the physician said seemed straightforward, some of it was so daunting Charity wished she had remained ignorant of it all. Breech births, childbed fever, caesareans, forceps, stitches… complications that would likely give her nightmares for the next seven months. It was all so daunting her head was spinning by the time they got home. Not that this strange house in Burton Crescent felt anything like her home yet either.

Mrs Gibbons greeted them in the hallway. 'I sent the footman to the Minerva Lending Library as you requested, Mr Philpot, and the books are all in your study. I expect you and Mrs Philpot shall be wanting some tea after your busy morning...' She offered Charity a slightly awkward smile, one that told her that Griff had finally appraised his housekeeper of her predicament. 'Shall I bring it to the drawing room?'

He stepped forward to help Charity out of her light pelisse before the housekeeper could. 'The terrace, please, Mrs Gibbons...and could you also brew up some peppermint tea for my wife too.' As she scurried off to do his bidding, he took Charity's arm and gently wrapped it around his. 'It's a lovely day and Dr Macdonald did say that plenty of fresh air would help with the nausea.'

This time, when he led her through the house, she noticed more, and as if he knew she had been in too much of a state yesterday to pay much attention, he took his time leading her through it. 'I bought the house from a banker last year when I returned from Sheffield. After four years of living on my own, it didn't feel right moving back in with my parents. It was only built five years ago so I confess I haven't changed much about the place from the previous occupant beyond purchasing some furniture. Obviously, you'll want to change the decor and as I have no clue about such things I shall happily leave you to it.' Then he smiled, delightfully boyish and awkward as they paused in the centre of the spacious and airy drawing room. 'I want you to feel happy here, Charity. This is your house too...now.'

His thoughtfulness touched her. 'It's a lovely house, Griff.' And it was. There was no denying that. Dappled sunlight streamed through the open French doors, emphasising the pristine cream walls which cried out for some coloured wallpaper and a few of her father's and sister's paintings, and the highly polished parquet which would look magnificent against a silk Persian carpet. 'A blank canvas…' She spun a circle then ran her fingertips over the barren sideboard which cried out for a huge vase of flowers. 'Tell me—was the banker you purchased it from a bachelor too?'

'He was.' Griff chuckled, unoffended at her appraisal of the plain decor. 'But he painted the study where he doubtless spent the most time, and in a very odd shade too.' He pulled a face. 'That had to go.'

'Is that the only room you redecorated too?'

'It's the one I spend the most time in as well.' He took her elbow again. The lightest of touches yet she felt it everywhere. 'My mother planted some flowers in the garden though, because she despaired of the pathetic and empty rectangle of lawn and decided she couldn't bear the lack of colour everywhere.' As he manoeuvred her out of the doors, his hand grazed the small of her back. Brief and solicitous though it was, it was intimate enough to still make her pulse quicken. 'And there were already a few trees so I'm rather proud of the result even though I had no hand in it.'

'It's pretty.' Quite charming actually as it reminded her of her parents' garden and she needed the familiar. The paved terrace was raised and surrounded by a stout columned wall which barely reached her waist. Three wide steps led down to a rose-filled flowerbed which flanked a winding path that meandered down the lawn, the rectangular shape softened by dotted trees and clumps of summer flowers all in full bloom.

While they waited for the tea, she wandered down it while Griff watched from the terrace above. He was anxious, she could tell, and no doubt as unsure about everything exactly as she was, but he was trying and she was grateful for that. Since he had found her being ill this morning, he had barely left her side and, much to her surprise when one considered their stark differences, she had appreciated his attentiveness. Bizarrely, as mortified as she had been to be found throwing up into a chamber pot, Griff had taken it all in his stride and this somehow made her feel better, as if they were in it together. He had sat with her for ages afterwards, talking to her because he sensed she needed the distraction in order to settle, until the constant tiredness got the better of her and she drifted off. When she awoke, it was to find that he had covered her with a light blanket and left a fresh glass of water on her nightstand. She hadn't noticed he had left the connecting door open until he poked his head through it to check on her. Then he personally brought her some toast and tea and kept her company while she gingerly ate it.

It was funny. They had been with one another for hours since, chatting amiably about everything and nothing, but in all that time they had both tacitly avoided conversing about anything important. Yet there were so many things they still needed to discuss, and those things had hung over their heads like an ominous dark cloud all morning. She supposed there was no putting it off any longer.

He was already pouring the tea when she re-joined him, looking every bit as if he too knew that they had to have a serious conversation and was dreading it much the same. As she sat he slid the cup and saucer towards her across the small ironwork table and smiled his awkward smile. 'You have questions, don't you? I can hear the cogs of your mind whirring.'

'A few.' The most burning of which concerned her career. 'I am legally committed to the theatre till the end of September.' She had taken a few days of absence because of the wedding and her understudy was doing those performances, but the theatre expected her back tomorrow and she wanted to be there. As tired and ill as she was, she needed that thread of normality in this new, confused tapestry of upheaval.

'I know.' His eyes were kind. 'I do understand how a contract works, Charity. However, I cannot deny that I am worried about you fulfilling that commitment in your current state.'

'I shall be careful and rest as much as possible in between performances, exactly as Dr Macdonald said.' She chose her words and tone carefully, mindful that this was no time for one of their customary battles of will because, as a wife, she was now legally bound to obey him. No matter how much she might loathe that power and hope he would never use it, there was also no denying he could put a stop to it all instantly and there wasn't a damn thing she could do about it any more.

'Do the theatre know that you are with child?'

She shook her head. 'Nobody outside of our circle knows yet and it is much too soon to tell them.' Aside from the inevitable scandal, the doctor had cautioned that the chance of miscarrying was at its highest in the first three months.

'I agree.'

'Singing is everything to me, Griff, and I don't want to give it up.' She blurted out the truth and held her breath, but he tilted his head, bemused at the force of her outburst.

'I know that too. Did you honestly think I would try to prevent you from doing it?'

'Some men expect their wives to give up everything so that they can be at their husband's beck and call.'

'Some men might, but I'm not daft.' He shook his head and laughed as if the idea hadn't even crossed his mind. 'I meant what I said just now—I want you to be happy and I am well aware of the fact that I shall always have to share you with the stage. But your mother and sisters all manage to juggle family and their careers, so I dare say we'll do the same. Asking you to give up music would be as ridiculous as asking Faith to stop painting or Hope to never write another book again— or expecting me to stop tweaking machinery—because ultimately such a request would only make us both miserable. For better or for worse, we are shackled together for all eternity, remember?'

Shackled was such a depressing word, but probably the right one given the circumstances. It wasn't as if he'd had any more choice in the matter than she. Then again, he could have refused and abandoned her to have their child out of wedlock as so many lesser men did every day. That was food for thought too. 'We don't have to be…for ever, that is.' One good turn deserved another and as he had made a sacrifice, so could she. 'Once the baby is born you could divorce me.'

His cup froze midway to his lips, his expression suddenly unreadable. 'Is that what you want?'

'It is an option…if things become unbearable.' Although even contemplating it made her sad. 'You might want a different sort of marriage.' She took a sip of her own tea to mask her unease. 'A different sort of wife.'

'I won't.'

'You say that now, but let us not forget how much you despair of me...' His dark brows furrowed and before he could politely lecture her, she decided it was better to invite it. 'So, I can still perform and I can redecorate, but what do you expect from me in return? What are the rules of Mr Philpot's charming house?'

'Rules?' He laughed again, but it was tinged with something more than amusement. 'I am not your master, Charity. I have neither the time, the inclination nor patience to attempt to bend you to my will or curb your rebellious spirit.'

An enormous relief which unknotted some of the tight bands strangling her innards. 'But there must be some things you expect?'

'Requests perhaps—but not defined expectations.'

'And those are?'

'I would always request your honesty, no matter how painful or how much admitting it goes against your stubborn pride—or mine. This marriage has begun on enough of a back foot that it needs no lies to hamper it further.' As she nodded his eyes locked with hers, stormy and intense. 'And I would request you give our marriage a fair chance before you give up on it.'

'Or you give up on it, Griff. That door swings both ways.' He was hardly entering into their union wearing rose-tinted spectacles as far as she was concerned and, of course, he had form when it came to being changeable. They had gone from friends to enemies in a heartbeat after York and she still had no clue exactly why beyond the unpalatable fact that she had worn his patience too thin simply by being her.

'I shan't.' Her disbelief must have been obvious. 'You have my word on that.'

'Because your word is your bond?' It seemed appropriate to make light of it, but Griff wouldn't let her. He lifted her chin with his finger.

'Because I firmly believe nothing is unfixable—even us—and I fully intend to fix it, Charity, or I'll die trying.' His tone was fierce. His stare fiercer. 'We've made a child, and we owe that child a proper family. The sort we both grew up among.'

Which suggested a proper marriage in every sense, with laughter, intimacy and perhaps even love.

Didn't it?

In case it didn't and the hopeless romantic within her was trying to find some among the overwhelming sense of responsibility where none existed, she nodded again and sipped her tea. 'Then you have my word too that I shall persevere for as long as it takes. Any other requests?'

He shook his head. 'None.' Then he surprised her by taking her hand, his thumb lightly massaging her palm in the most distracting manner.

'No *wifely duties* you expect me to perform?' Like occasionally sharing his bed. They hadn't discussed that important detail either and it had played on her mind all night. She forced herself to stare at him boldly to ensure he got the innuendo, to be blasé about the prospect of more intimacy even though she wasn't. Their one foray into passion aside, if it came without the emotional connection and respect she craved, she sincerely doubted she would ever feel comfortable with that side of things again.

By the bland way he composed his features before he sipped his tea, he understood completely what she alluded to. 'Not that I can think of, no.'

She had no earthly idea if she was relieved by that or

disappointed. It certainly felt like a bit of both, but she nodded again, supremely conscious that his big hand was still caressing hers and it felt lovely.

'Splendid.' Clearly embarrassed to be discussing such personal things, he severed the contact to pick up his tea again. 'And what about you? What requests do you have for me?'

There was only one that she could think of off the top of her head. 'That you let me in.' She touched his forehead. 'That you allow me to see what is going on in here. That you entrust me with more of the real Griff— the one you keep so tightly locked up until all those un- seemly emotions you feel so uncomfortable with bubble out as anger like steam in an...'

He smiled. 'Engine?'

'I was going to say kettle, but I assume the princi- ple is the same. Will you try to open that book rather than blow hot and cold and always be completely hon- est with me too?'

He nodded. 'I will. I promise. What else?'

'Nothing else springs to mind.'

He took her hand and allowed her to see his awk- wardness and his hope. 'Then seeing as we have the rest of the day free, how about we do some shopping for *our* new nephew and then try to rebuild the bridge between our parents? If we are annoyingly persistent, I firmly believe they'll have to forgive us eventually. After all, they can't keep claiming that they are prac- tically a family, then bemoan the fact that we finally made the claim official.'

Chapter Eighteen

Charity settled back against her sister's pillows and watched fascinated as she fed her baby. Her usually caustic middle sibling was smiling at her newborn as he nursed, an uncharacteristic sereneness about her which Charity hadn't seen before which she assumed came from motherhood. That mystical, instantaneous state of complete love, devotion and selflessness which apparently miraculously occurred in a woman the second her baby arrived in the world. It had happened to both Faith and Hope in quick succession and she couldn't help but wonder if it would be the same for her, or if her selfish streak was just too strong and ingrained for her to ever be that good a mother herself.

All she knew for certain was that she didn't feel it now, but oddly, there was already something different about her feelings. The initial pangs of resentment had given way to curiosity and, as her hand instinctively went to her stomach, there was some excitement among all her worries for the future alongside an undeniable link between her actions and the needs of the child inside her which now controlled them.

'Does it feel odd to have something attached to your bosom like a limpet?'

Her sister smiled. 'I suppose it should—but it doesn't. It is what they are meant for, after all. And, of course, being the only one capable of feeding Radcliffe gives me an edge over his besotted father and I quite like that. It is the one thing that I can do that Luke cannot and it ensures he has to hand our son over at regular intervals or I swear he'd hog him completely.'

'He's a natural father. Piers is too.'

'Griff will be the same.'

Hope had held out an olive branch and asked Charity and Griff to be little Radcliffe's godparents and that had meant the world. The service this morning had been a small, private family ceremony followed by an informal al fresco lunch in the garden because her sister and her husband had little time for big social affairs and that had made things easier today too. A week after her wedding and she was still getting used to being Mrs Philpot in private. Being Mrs Philpot in public too was a daunting prospect, especially as it was plainly obvious to everyone that they were more awkward around one another than they ever were. There were moments where they seemed to get along well but just as many others where they had no earthly clue what to say or how to behave.

'Do you think?'

'Of course.' Her sister seemed surprised that she had any doubt. 'He's always had the patience of a saint and has a lovely gentle way about him. He'll make a fine father.'

'I suppose…' She couldn't deny he had a lovely, gentle way about him, but he had never had the patience of a saint around her. That might be because she really was as difficult a person as he had often lamented, or it might simply be because they had very different personalities which were always destined to grate against one another. 'I cannot say we really know one another well enough yet to be able to make a judgement.'

Hope laughed at that. 'You have known him most of your life!'

'I have...but I don't know him like you and Faith do. I was always the annoying little one who got in his way and got on his nerves.'

'You adored him as I recall and did some outrageous things to get his attention.'

'Initially perhaps...' Trust her sister to have seen her behaviour then for exactly what it was. 'But the bloom was soon off that rose and besting or thwarting one another quickly became the norm. We were always more rivals than friends and that never changed.' Although it had. Briefly. And it had been glorious. 'We are only married because we have to be.'

Hope's smile collapsed into sympathy. 'Are you very miserable?'

'Not very—we rub along well enough all things considered.' She forced a smile, not wanting to spoil such a joyous time in her sister's life with her woes. 'Griff seems determined to make the best of it and I, at the very least, owe him the courtesy of doing the same.'

Bizarrely, the best times this past week were when she was at her most ill which was usually in the middle of the night. Then he was a rock by her side and had the canny knack of making her feel all better afterwards when he tucked her back into bed and sat beside her on the mattress—stroking her hair while telling her in soothing, whispered tones about his day or something he had read in the newspapers or reminiscing about their shared childhood. When he sensed that she was settled again, he had taken to explaining in complicated detail the intricacies of one of the machines his factory built, using them as lullabies which never failed to send her softly back into the comforting arms of Morpheus.

But for some reason, the easiness they shared when it was dark outside seemed to evaporate when the sun was up and she had no idea why. It wasn't just Griff who became awkward, it was her too, and for the most part the rest of each day passed with cautious over-politeness and avoidance interspersed with snippets of the playful friendliness they had discovered during those brief halcyon weeks between Lincoln and York.

'Especially after I ruined his life.'

'He said that?'

Charity shook her head. 'Of course not. He's been annoyingly noble about it all—but I am not his favourite person and have no delusions on that score. He's never liked me much and before this happened…' she tapped her belly '…he called me spoiled, self-absorbed and superficial, accused me of kissing significantly more men than a proper young lady ever should and said he was sick of the sight of me. And now I have condemned him to look at me for ever.'

She attempted to force a smile, but a self-pitying tear fell regardless which she angrily swiped away. 'It's all a dreadful mess.' Griff's telling summation that broke her heart. 'Those *are* his words—although I echo the sentiment, yet I have no idea what to do about it.' Certainly, all the annoying self-pity wouldn't fix it and she was much too miserable to formulate a proper plan. The forced smile physically hurt but she maintained it regardless. 'I've made my bed, and now I must lie it in. Till death us do part.'

Hope put little Radcliffe in his cradle and came to wrap her arms around her. 'Oh, Charity... It doesn't have to be for ever if you don't want it to be. There are ways out of these things. Piers managed it and now he has found happiness. There is no reason you cannot do that too.'

'I offered him a divorce after the baby is born and he declined so I am stuck. He's convinced he can fix things.'

'Do you want him to?'

She shrugged, not wanting to admit that she hoped he could but feared it was futile.

'I want what you and Luke have and what Faith and Piers have. I want a husband who adores me, not one who suffers me because he has to. That plainly isn't Griff.'

'Perhaps it could be...if you give it time. As furious as I am at him, he has always been one of my favourite people.'

'Then maybe you should have married him.'

'I would have if any spark of attraction had simmered between us—he has an arsenal of good qualities and a girl could do much worse. There is clearly an attraction between the two of you however, else you wouldn't have indulged in a rampant night of unbridled passion.'

'That was a foolish mistake.' One she wished hourly she could take back to make the pain it had caused go away.

'A telling answer if ever there was one.'

She tapped her abdomen. 'Well, it *was* a mistake.'

Hope grinned. 'I was actually referring to what you didn't say rather than what you did, sister dearest, because it has not gone unnoticed that you made no effort to deny that *it was* a night of rampant and unbridled passion so clearly there is something there.'

Charity's cheeks combusted as she failed to stutter a convincing response. 'Stop putting words into my mouth.'

'I don't need to.' Hope licked the tip of her finger and pressed it against her face and made a sizzling noise. 'They are written all over your face.'

Because it was, she hid behind a pillow. 'I lost my head that night along with my virginity.'

'Rampant, unbridled passion will do that. There *is* a strong attraction there and it is clearly mutual. Maybe you can build on that?'

'Fleeting lust isn't love or adoration and one night of passion in a lifetime of disdain isn't a firm enough foundation to build anything upon.'

'One night? I take it you and he haven't repeated...'

'*No*...' Charity risked lowering the pillow. 'Not since York. It's all too awkward.'

Faith chose that moment to poke her head around the door and huffed. 'There you are, Charity! Thank goodness! We were about to send out a search party!'

'What's happened?'

'There's an expectant father downstairs in a flap, searching for you everywhere, convinced you are lying prostrate on the floor ill and probably dying and no amount of reason will convince him otherwise. He's beside himself with worry. You have to come and put him out of his misery this instant as I've never seen poor Griff in such a state.'

Hope's eyebrows raised knowingly. 'That sounds like adoration to me.'

Charity waved it away. 'He's just being overprotective because I've been so unwell and he feels responsible, that's all.'

Her middle sister pondered that for a moment and then frowned. 'Perhaps that explains *this* particular outburst of overprotectiveness—but it doesn't explain all the others.'

'What others?'

'Insisting on chaperoning you to the North, for a start, when I am sure he had better things to do.'

'He didn't want me leading Dorothy astray and told me so.'

'And then there was that night at Vauxhall when I am sure he thought Luke had designs on seducing you instead of me. He was rather proprietorial then, wasn't he?'

'That was to protect Dorothy too because he is convinced I am a bad influence on her.'

'Now that you mention it,' said Faith catching on to the thread quickly, 'I have noticed Griff watching you a lot since he returned. You specifically and not Dottie.'

'So have I!' Hope nodded. 'He couldn't take his eyes off you at Denby's ball. I put it down to the fact the pair of you had clearly fallen out in the north but perhaps it wasn't. And he did break with all tradition and waltz with you that night too, when Griff never dances. To be frank, I wasn't even aware that he could dance until I saw him twirling you!'

'And let us not forget you were wearing the infamous scarlet dress, Charity!' Faith was wide-eyed now as she pointed at her. 'Perhaps it has worked its magic again?' Then she sighed. 'Which is rather romantic actually…'

'He was merely rescuing me from an amorous suitor.' And proposing again. 'We danced for all of thirty seconds before I was ill.'

'But he danced, Charity!' Faith grabbed her by the shoulders. 'That is momentous! And I'm sure I saw him at the theatre in the spring, sat all the way up in the gods but Piers said I was imagining it.' Her gaze locked with Hope's suspiciously as her brows furrowed. 'Because why would a man with all of Griff's money sit in the cheap seats? But now I am thinking that perhaps I did see him. He is rather striking and difficult to miss.'

They were clutching at straws now. 'Griff loathes the opera.'

Hope nodded. 'Luke thought he saw him in the gods too once just after *Figaro* opened, but *I* dismissed it out of hand because Griff always makes such a big show of disliking the opera. Perhaps too much of a show now that I think upon it, because he never used to mind it when it was just Mama who performed…and it is certainly a strange coincidence that there have been two suspected sightings and both long *before* you seduced him into that rampant night of unbridled passion.'

'Will you stop saying that!' Each mention reminded Charity of just how unbridled it had been. How unbridled she had been. 'Mama might hear!'

But Hope was on a roll and wouldn't be silenced on the subject. 'And it makes no sense that a man who doesn't like you, who finds you superficial, spoiled and self-absorbed, and a man who is as sensible, measured, logical and guarded as Griff undoubtedly is, would be so readily seduced. He would have put an immediate stop to things before they got out of hand.'

'Unless he wanted to be seduced.' Faith wiggled her tawny eyebrows. 'And years of pent-up lust and longing all exploded in one go and all his sensible logic and guardedness went to hell in a handcart. That is rather romantic too…' She sighed again as she clutched her heart. 'There is no better sight than a man all undone. All fervent and desperate and only you will do.' Then she grinned wickedly. 'There has always been a frisson between the pair of you. Even as children you and he had a different relationship from the rest of us. You always gravitated towards one another and it seemed to affect everything, didn't it, Hope?'

'It did indeed and frisson is the perfect word for it. Their relationship was always different from ours. Exclusively so. They went out of their way to make mischief for one another. Why did we never notice it before?'

Charity stared at the ceiling, praying for strength, not wanting to be seduced into the tempting fantasy they were weaving. 'It was different because it was fraught, and it was fraught because I drive him mad, Faith. I've always driven him mad.'

'With lust,' said Faith winking. 'And possessiveness.'

'He was certainly in a hurry to interrupt that waltz.' Hope spoke directly to Faith as if Charity wasn't there this time. 'We were in the midst of an important conversation and he sprinted away from me that night as if his breeches were on fire the second I asked him to talk some sense into our headstrong baby sister.'

Even though she wanted to believe it, Charity couldn't. Not when she'd seen the truth in Griff's eyes and heard the disappointment and disgust in his voice. 'You are both romanticising a situation which isn't the least bit romantic and reading something into nothing to make a depressing situation sound more palatable.'

Hope shared another knowing look with Faith. 'Or perhaps we are finally reading it all correctly for the first time and there actually is more than a grain of attraction and love in it all somewhere? Perhaps he has romantic feelings for you, too?'

'This is ridiculous! Neither of us has feelings! Romantic or otherwise.'

They shot her twin disbelieving looks.

'I wouldn't be surprised. There has always been that palpable, charged atmosphere between them...' Clearly Faith had made up her mind. 'Which was bound to develop into more. Strong emotions like that cannot be denied for ever. Especially if they have been bubbling under the surface for almost two decades.'

'This is going from the sublime to the ridiculous.' Charity hauled herself off the mattress and stalked to the door. 'And your silly theories are now most definitely bordering on the ridiculous.

'You can deny it all that you want but it doesn't detract from the single most damning truth of all.' Hope folded her arms smugly.

'Which is?' Charity tried to hide her rising panic behind a mask of imperious and bored bravado not at all liking where this conversation was going but powerless to stop it—or to staunchly deny it.

'That despite undoubtedly kissing significantly more men than a proper young lady should, you, baby Sister, still chose to save the rest of yourself for Griff.'

Chapter Nineteen

Griff didn't particularly want to be in White's this close to midnight because he preferred to be home when Charity returned from the theatre. Somebody needed to check she hadn't overexerted herself and encourage her to eat something before she went to bed and she was too strong a character to listen to anyone else. But, as his two new brothers-in-law had suddenly invited him to dine with them here, and embrace him back into part of the family fold, he felt he had no choice. Instead, he had intended to beat a hasty retreat after the dessert was done. But that had been ages and far too many drinks ago.

'More champagne, I think,' said Luke as he grabbed the passing waiter.

Griff shook his woolly head. 'No more for me.' Thanks to pre-dinner champagne to toast his new nephew, the wine over dinner and the after-dinner port, then the brandy, he was starting to see double. Or perhaps treble. There was certainly a fuzzy, nondescript replica of Luke now poking out from the edges of the original.

'Nonsense, my good fellow!' Luke's large hand

slapped him on the back. 'We still have your nuptials to celebrate.' The *celebrate* came out slurred. 'Surely that deserves a toast?'

'We all know that there's nothing to celebrate there. We had to get married, remember?'

'But still...' His enormous bearded brother-in-law winked as he slapped him on the back again. 'You got yourself a beautiful bride that most of London would envy you for.'

'You have to give credit to Roberta and Augustus.' Piers held up one of the bubbling crystal flutes which seemed to have magically appeared on the table. 'Between them, they made some mighty fine daughters.' He grinned soppily. 'Obviously I snagged myself the most beautiful one but the other two aren't bad either so you both did well.'

'You're clearly blind as well as a blithering idiot,' said a slurring Luke clinking his glass to the other. 'Because my Hope outshines all of the Brookes girls by a country mile. She's prettier, cleverer and far and away the most talented.'

'Have you forgotten the way Faith paints?' Piers jabbed the air instead of Luke's shoulder. 'Now that's a talent. I'll have you know there's a two-year waiting list for one of her portraits.'

'But can she write a book?' Luke pressed the remaining flute into Griff's hand. 'Weave intricate plots and complicated, layered characters seamlessly? Of course, she can't. That takes *real* talent. Hope has bigger brains and better beauty. What say you, Griff? Seeing as we two are at loggerheads, you must have the casting vote. Who is the prettiest sister?'

'Charity.' Even three sheets to the wind, it was no contest as far as he was concerned. He drew a wonky spiral in the air with his finger. 'She has all those golden curls and those deep blue eyes and she shings...' He huffed out a sigh as he readjusted his tongue to cope with the difficult word. 'She *sings* like an angel. Much better than her mother can. And she's funny and charming and maddening...' He took a long glug of his champagne then subtly burped out some bubbles. 'And good hearted.'

Luke jabbed Piers with his elbow. 'I told you he loved her.'

'What good does that do me when she doesn't love me back?' A conundrum Griff had pondered long and hard this past week. 'She only married me because she had to...' He waved his glass around to punctuate that point. 'And she shtuck with me, the poor thing, when she could have had anyone and she's going to regret marrying me for the rest of her life and I just don't know how to fix that.'

More wine was sloshed in his glass and over the tablecloth by Piers. 'But she married you, old chap, so that has to count for something. A bird in the hand is worth...is it two or three in a tree?' He frowned trying to remember.

'It's defiantly two,' said Luke with great authority. 'In an oak. Or it might have been a birch. I'm not much of an arboriculturist.'

Piers frowned and leaned closer, squinting at his friend perplexed. 'How the blazes can you say arboriculturist perfectly, a word of six complicated syllables, when you can no longer pronounce celebrate which has only three?'

Luke shrugged, his expression confused. 'I have no idea...but I can.'

Piers toasted him impressed then thumped Griff on

the arm. 'Well, there you have it. Two birds are in your tree, Griff, so half the battle is already won. All you need to do now is get her to fall in love with you and everything in your garden will be rosy.'

A conclusion he had come to himself days ago without anybody's help. 'And how do you suggest I do that?' Because that was the crux of the problem. 'How do I get a woman like Charity to fall in love with a man like me?' Griff thumped his chest so hard he winded himself. 'When I am a dull scholar and she is a sparkling performer? I like diagrams and she likes arias. I quietly sulk while she throws loud tantrums. We have absolutely nothing in common at all.'

'Opposites attract.' Piers squinted at him now. 'Just look at me and Faith. She stands out and I blend into the panelling.'

'Then if that is the case, why do birds of a feather flock together?' Griff took another glug of his wine and shook his head. 'Not that it matters in our case anyway because she loves that bejewelled fob Denby. He is the one she wants.'

'Yet it was you whom she took to her bed.' Luke raised his eyebrows. 'Hope said that you were her first. That has to count for something.'

'Perhaps it might have if the basic premise wasn't all wrong to begin with.'

'What basic premise?' Luke poured the last dregs into Griff's glass.

'For Charity and me it's not just back to front—but wonky too.'

His companions stared at him befuddled until Piers shook his head. 'You lost me at basic premise, old boy.'

Griff grabbed the waiter himself and demanded some

paper and a pencil, then when it arrived began to explain it in the only way he knew how.

With a diagram.

'In the normal course of things, a workable marriage requires a specific set of processes to get it started—that forms the basic premise.' He drew six misshapen boxes and connected them with wobbly arrows. 'You find a girl you fancy, then you woo her with a courtship.' He tapped the third box pointedly with the pencil because that was the most important missing component in the puzzle. 'Both parties fall in love with each other rather than someone else. Then the chap proposes, they get engaged and finally, with much dizzying anticipation, they get married.'

Both men nodded their understanding as they huddled over the drawing, so Griff waggled his hand off into the distance as he scribbled another long arrow to run off the end of the page. 'All the other stuff like nights of passion and babies is supposed to come afterwards. But Charity and I did it backwards. We did the passion bit and made the baby first, then got married and missed all the rest of the steps. The fundamental steps which guarantee success.'

'Then simply reverse all those fundamental steps,' announced Piers as if he had just invented the wheel, 'and you'll inevitably end up with the same basic premise.'

'But you don't.' With great care, he drew the six boxes again the other way around and frowned when they inexplicably turned out messier than the first set. 'If the wedding happens without the dizzying anticipation of the engagement and there has been no wooing or courtship, then there cannot be any love either.' He tapped the all-important fourth box this time then drew a lopsided heart around it. 'Ergo, the basic premise is fatally flawed because there are vital processes missing and without those essential fundamentals we are doomed for it all to remain unfixable for ever.'

'But hang on a minute...' Luke slapped his hand away to point at the heart himself. 'Not all the processes are missing. We can also tick off finding a girl you fancy because you clearly did that. And there is love as well because you love her! You said so.'

Griff shook his head. 'I did and I do—but it is irrelevant in this premise because that didn't happen on this diagram. That happened ages ago.' He drew a wiggly line backwards from the first box and off the paper. 'I cannot pinpoint exactly when I fell in love with the minx because it crept up on me long before I was aware of it—but it was probably back when we were children when I didn't have the good sense to understand it or avoid it. Not that it makes any difference anyway, because she doesn't love me in return, she loves him, and I'm damned if I know how to make her swap allegiances.'

'Yes, you do!' Piers whacked the diagram with such force two of the now empty champagne flutes toppled over. 'It is right here in black and white!' His index finger tapped box five. 'Wooing is the answer. It's the only missing box.'

'He's right.' Luke slapped the table too, earning him several glares and a few audible tut-tuts from the other diners. 'You are just going to have to court your wife until she forgets her fop and loves you back.'

Griff stared at the diagram and then at his newest, wisest best friends in the entire world. 'And how do I do that? When I am me and she is she and never the twain shall meet?'

'Well,' said Luke as Piers gestured for more champagne, 'why don't we make a list...?'

Chapter Twenty

The Marquess of T. was presented with a bill for ten pounds, six shillings and fourpence this morning, after the pleasure boat he stole and capsized on the Serpentine last night sank without a trace. When asked for an explanation of this outrageous behaviour by the park warden on duty, his tipsy lake-soaked companions, Lord E. and Mr P., stated that they were merely celebrating the birth of the future Lord T. and had perhaps taken the tradition of wetting the baby's head a step too far by thoroughly wetting their own as well...

Whispers from Behind the Fan
—August 1815

Griff's dark head was bent heavily over a diagram, his hand splayed in his rumpled hair and his expression so perplexed Charity could practically hear the cogs of his mind spinning as he worked through whatever problem currently consumed him so.

In deference to both the late summer heat and his

usual casual attire when working, his coat hung on the back of his chair so he could don it at a moment's notice if the need arose. Piled high on one corner of his desk was the stack of books on every aspect of child rearing from pregnancy to teaching your offspring to read. She couldn't help but smile at the leather bookmarks and scraps of paper which protruded neatly from the pages, noting his determined progress in each mighty tome because he absolutely had to understand the mechanics of everything.

As if he sensed her he looked up, smiled somewhat gingerly then hastily slipped the drawing beneath a pile of others.

'Good morning.'

'Surely you mean good afternoon?' She glanced pointedly at the no-nonsense wooden clock ticking on the mantel. 'You had a late night. I hear Luke and Piers turned up out of the blue and then led you astray.' He nodded and that seemed to pain him. 'What time did you get back?'

It had been the first evening when Griff hadn't been in the hallway to greet her upon her return from the theatre and she had missed him. She had given up waiting for his return and drifted off some time around midnight. When she had inevitably awoken ill a little before dawn and he hadn't come in to commiserate with her as he usually did, she had poked her head around their connecting door and found him sprawled face down, stark naked and dead to the world. To her shame, she had lingered over the splendid sight, enjoying the way the sunrise turned all that bare skin golden while casting intriguing shadows over the muscles which lay beneath it. He had a fine pair of shoulders, did Griffith Philpot, and lovely arms too. And his bottom…well that was quite distracting and had certainly taken her mind off her nausea for the minute or so she had gazed at it.

He smiled sheepishly. 'Two, I think, though I cannot be sure. My evil companions plied me with liquor and then things became a little hazy.'

'I am sure your bracing swim in the Serpentine sobered you up.'

'Ah…' He winced. 'You heard about that, did you?'

'I didn't hear about it, Griff—I *read* about it.' She thoroughly enjoyed whipping the newspaper from behind her back and snapping it open. '*You* are finally all over the gossip columns! All of them.' For effect, she cleared her throat and then read aloud her favourite sentence from the damning report. 'Mr P. from Bloomsbury became quite distraught when he realised he had mislaid a single boot at some point during his midnight swim and had to be physically restrained to prevent him wading back in to search for it.' She shot him her best impersonation of her mother's disapproving glare over the top of the paper.

'In my defence…' He huffed out a groan and rested his head on the table. 'I have no defence. It was an impetuous, reckless and stupid thing to do and I am truly sorry. If it is any consolation, I now have an entire battalion of invisible grenadier guards marching inside my cranium and my stomach has turned into a butter churn. And I loved those boots. They were Hoby's and cost a fortune. After six months of perseverance, I had finally broken them in, and they fitted like a glove.'

He looked so mortified, and so tragic, Charity resisted the temptation to sit upon his desk and stroke his hair. 'Piers is in a worse state apparently and had to sit through Faith's blistering lecture while hugging a bucket in his lap and Hope sent Luke straight to the doghouse the moment he returned because he in his drunken state fell over his own feet, broke the dressing table stool and woke the baby. He was last seen snoring on a bench in his garden still clutching the bunch of yellow roses he had hacked out of my mother's garden, so he's in the doghouse with her too. I know all this, because she sent me a note this morning inviting me to resume my music lessons with her and Signor Fauci this afternoon.'

Griff lifted his head enough that he could glance at her mournfully. 'When you deliver your blistering lecture, can I ask you not to shout? Or at least have enough mercy to postpone the shouting for an hour or two until I feel better? I only went out in the first place because they had extended the hand of friendship and I thought it might aid family relations.'

'I shan't be shouting.' She smiled in sympathy. 'I shan't even be lecturing. Because it was good of you to try to heal the breach and I know what a bad and persuasive influence Luke can be. I am also quietly relieved to discover that you aren't quite as sensible as you have always led me to believe…and because I am more than guilty of the odd impetuous, reckless and regrettable impulse one time or two, I am in no position to judge. People in glass houses should never throw stones.' Then the smile turned wicked. 'Although that pious magnanimity doesn't mean I won't be gloating for quite some time at your outrageous drunken exploits. Who'd have thought I would ever see the day that Gruff Griff the Kite-Hogging Fun-Spoiler would be hauled over the coals by the authorities for theft and wanton destruction?'

'I think I was threatened with breach of the peace too.' He looked thoroughly sick to the gills and miserable. 'For singing at an ungodly volume on Piccadilly in the small hours before the unfortunate incident with the boat.' That conjured up a hilarious image.

'What were you singing?'

'For the life of me, I cannot remember but by the hoarseness in my throat I do not doubt it was at volume.'

'It sounds like you had a momentous night.'

'One that I am still paying for now.' He sat upright again and attempted a valiant smile despite his slightly grey pallor. 'But it was self-inflicted, and while I am supremely grateful you have seen fit to spare me a blistering lecture, I deserve no sympathy for the state I am in and shall stoically soldier through it. So enough about my stupidity, how are you feeling?'

'Oh, you know. It comes and goes. At the moment it is gone and I am grateful.'

'I am glad to hear it.'

The ever-present awkwardness began to descend again and before it settled fully Charity decided to end the conversation before it became stilted. 'Anyway… I only stopped by to tell you that I am off to my mother's now for that lesson in an attempt to further heal the chasm we created and then I am meeting Dorothy afterwards at the modiste's for the final fitting of her wedding gown.' She wanted to ask if she would see him later once she was done, but that felt too wifely.

'Why don't I drive you?' Before she could answer he rang the bell to summon Mrs Gibbons and then, no doubt, his shiny red curricle. As he stood, she watched him briefly waver against the effort of it before he blew out a very controlled breath and shrugged on his coat. 'We could have a spot of supper after all your visits and then I could take you to the theatre too. I might as well do something useful with the day as I think it's fairly safe to assume that I am in no fit state to get any meaningful work done.'

'Are you in a fit state to drive? You do look a little…fragile.'

'It will pass.' He adjusted his cuffs and squared his shoulders. 'And the fresh air will do me good.'

Despite Mrs Gibbons also questioning his intention, Griff would hear none of it and not ten minutes later he lifted Charity on to the perch and climbed up beside her.

It was the first time she had been in his curricle and with him beside her, the two-seater bench definitely erred on the cosy side. Her thighs, hips and upper arms pressed intimately against his, so close Charity could feel every corded muscle she had gazed so shamelessly upon this morning. She used some idle conversation to distract her from that delicious image as they set off.

'I am looking forward to getting back to lessons again. With everything, I haven't been able to see Signor Fauci in weeks…although I cannot say I am particularly looking forward to spending time with my mother. She is over-critical of my singing at the best of times without the added ammunition of being royally disappointed in me.'

'Why on earth would she criticise your singing?'

'Because she has been doing it for years. Because she thinks she always knows best and because she is my mother.'

'Ah…yes. There is that. Mothers are tricky.'

'That trickiness is multiplied when your mother is Roberta Brookes—who has apparently forgotten more about singing than I could possibly know. Who has an opinion on everything I do and who disapproves of some of the liberties I take in the cadenzas especially.'

'What's a cadenza?'

'It's a passage written into the music which the composer has left to the singer's interpretation. Usually at the end of an aria.'

'The final flourish?'

'Exactly. It's a chance to play. To impress the audience. Dear Mama is a purist and thinks I play around with those far too much. Whereas I think they were put there to do exactly that and that the amount I play with it should depend on each audience and situation. What brings the house down on one night might fall a little flat another, so I change things to anticipate their needs and to keep myself amused.'

'What does Signor Fauci think?'

'He has never said—largely because my mother is so infuriated by my continued rebellion on the subject that he likely cannot get a word in edgewise.' She shrugged, resigned to it after so many years of butting heads with her. 'While I trust her ear and her experience explicitly, and I appreciate that she means well and only wants the best of me, as I have become more experienced I also have my own ideas. Things which I think suit my style and my voice better.' The last thing she ever wanted to be was a pale imitation of her mother. 'Faith has similar battles with my father. She wants to paint her way and he thinks his is superior. It is one of the perils of working with family, I suppose.'

'It's always been the same with me and my father.' They were pressed closer as he turned a sharp left on to Russell Square, and he made no attempt to shuffle back the few inches he had shifted during the manoeuvre. 'But our working relationship has improved since we mostly work under different roofs. Perhaps you should consider that too going forward? Retain some lessons with your mother so that you benefit from some of her wisdom but tread your own path in the rest of them.'

His suggestion made sense. 'I suppose I could move some lessons to Signor Fauci's house but Bayswater is such an effort to get to.'

'Why don't you have them at our house?'

Our house. How lovely that sounded.

'Because our house has no pianoforte and my mother's music room has absolutely every conceivable thing that any musician would need already. Not to mention it is conveniently only around the corner.' And to prove that, they turned again into Bedford Place. 'Thank you for driving me...surprisingly, all the fresh air combined with the motion of this sporty gig hasn't made me half as nauseous as the carriage does.'

He drew the curricle to a gentle stop then hopped down. 'Surprisingly, thanks to all the fresh air, I only feel half as nauseous now as I did ten minutes ago, so I think it is fair to conclude that my sporty gig has quite restorative properties as well as making me look dashing.' He grinned as he held out his arms. 'Once more into the breach.'

'Are you braving my mother's wrath too? I wouldn't blame you if you wanted to escape as you're bound to get a blistering lecture from her for last night—among other things.'

'We are in this together, Wife.' His hands spanned her waist as he lifted her and didn't let go the second her feet hit the floor. 'And a blistering lecture will be worth it if I get to spend the day with you.'

Chapter Twenty-One

*It is rumoured that Mr and Mrs Grenville Philpot
of Bloomsbury will today lay on one of the most
lavish wedding celebrations the* ton *has ever seen,
after their daughter, heiress Miss Dorothy Philpot, marries the dashing cavalry officer Captain
William Sinclair...*

Whispers from Behind the Fan
—August 1815

If fate was having fun at their expense, then there was a
cruel irony that their first official public appearance as
man and wife was at the exact same church where they
had hastily taken their own vows only two weeks ago.
Except today, there was a wholly different atmosphere
in St George's and he couldn't help but be envious at
the air of excitement and joyousness at his sister's nuptials which had been sorely missing at his. His mother
wasn't crying for a start and when she inevitably did,
she would shed happy tears not disappointed tears of
shame—but at least she was speaking to him again.
In deference to the occasion, everyone was speaking

to him again, though a great many still did so through obviously gritted teeth.

The congregation fell silent as the organist began to play and every head turned to witness the arrival of the bride. Dottie looked beautiful and was beaming from ear to ear on his father's arm, but although it was her moment, Griff's eyes were automatically pulled to her bridesmaid who was doing her level best not to outshine the bride but managed to do so anyway without trying.

At least to him she did.

It was unorthodox to have a married woman as a bridesmaid, but as the arrangements were already made and she was his sister's oldest and dearest friend, Charity hadn't been replaced.

As she approached the altar, her eyes flicked to his and she smiled, her way of informing him that she was perfectly well so he really shouldn't fuss, even though they both knew that she wasn't. She had been ill half the night and most of the morning and no amount of peppermint tea or fresh air had helped alleviate those awful symptoms which seemed to plague her constantly. Not that any of that was the least bit visible now. For the sake of her friend and everyone else here present, she had strapped on her actor's mask exactly as she did for her audience every night, ensuring that nobody knew how much effort her performance took or that it was even an effort at all. Thank goodness her understudy was stepping on the stage in her stead tonight; after five back-to-back performances and today's inevitably long day, she needed some time off.

The ceremony was short and sweet. The love between the bride and groom shimmered off them in palpable waves. Overwhelmed, Captain Sinclair stumbled twice over his vows and practically slumped in relief as Dottie said hers, almost as if he couldn't quite believe that she hadn't had a change of heart at the very last moment. He was so beside himself with joy when the vicar declared them husband and wife, he did the unthinkable and kissed her in front of everyone. Then kissed her again as they passed under the arch of sabres from his comrades in his regiment.

His exuberance and delight at his good fortune soon became infectious, and as the newlywed couple were showered with summer petals while their carriage pulled away, several of the married couples were similarly swept away with the romance of it all. Griff's father kissed his mother. Augustus and Roberta Brookes held hands. Piers slipped his arm proprietorially around Faith's waist and tugged her close while Luke, who had never been one for propriety at the best of times, tugged Hope behind a wall and when they emerged some minutes later he looked quietly pleased with himself while she looked guiltily dishevelled. The only two people not overcome with the sudden need to be affectionate were Griff and Charity and that depressed him. Instead, they stood somewhat awkwardly together, focusing on the back of his sister's departing carriage and pretending they were oblivious to it all until it was time to head back to their own carriage.

'That was a nice service, wasn't it?'

Griff nodded, still too unsettled by their reality for comfort despite his best efforts to the contrary. 'It was exactly as a wedding should be.'

Her blue eyes clouded behind her cheerful façade for the rest of the congregation. 'Not like ours, you mean? Solemn and tense with nary a smile to be seen? What a drab day we had in comparison.'

'Oh, I don't know. I think we had better music. I've

always thought "The Lord is My Shepherd" is more of a funeral song so I have no earthly idea why Dottie chose something so dreary. At least our hymns were lively.'

'That is something, I suppose.' She sighed as Griff closed the door, the weight of the jovial mask slipping as she leaned heavily back on the seat.

The carriage springs bounced as the coachman climbed up on the perch and she winced then closed her eyes, a tactic she had taken to using to ease the sudden bouts of dizziness which mercilessly plagued her. Beneath the artfully applied subtle rouge and powder, she was pale and he knew that the motion of the carriage in the busy midday streets wouldn't do her any good. She was much better in his curricle but with half of London invited to this service and carriages queued up, there would have been nowhere to leave it so he had reluctantly brought the coach.

'What say you we walk?' He also knew that if he mentioned she looked ill, she would deny it and soldier on regardless and they still had the wedding breakfast to get through. Before she could answer he rapped on the roof and threw open the door, then held out his hand because with Charity, it was sometimes better to ask forgiveness than seek actual permission. 'It's a lovely day, the birds are singing and its only ten minutes to my mother's house on foot and likely half an hour cooped up in here.'

She stared at the clogged street ahead of them and nodded. 'A walk sounds delightful.' As he had given her no choice, and likely because she also knew the alternative would have dire consequences, she took his proffered hand and then his arm. To give her the chance to regain her equilibrium while saving face, he set a sedate pace in the direction of Bloomsbury Square enjoying the feel of her nestled against him and wishing he could wave a magic wand and banish the awful morning sickness for her once and for all.

They strolled in companionable silence for a bit. At least it seemed companionable to Griff. What Charity thought about it, he had no clue, but she had a faraway look in her eyes, the colour was returning to her cheeks and she appeared content to be outside in the fresh air after an hour in the church. As they turned into the park she was the first to break it.

'They adore one another, don't they?'

'They certainly seem to.' And he envied that.

Only a few days into his plan to make her fall in love with him, he had been taking it slow, reasoning that such things couldn't be rushed no matter what Luke had to say on the subject. But he had been an attentive and dependable presence since their wedding day, adjusting his working patterns so that he was around during the day when he could be with her while working in the late afternoons and evenings after he had dropped her off at the theatre. He had also made sure he was now the one picking her up at the end of the night. That was partly protective, partly because she fared better travelling at a sedate pace in his curricle with the roof open and partly so that they could ride beside one another beneath the moonlight. If the poets and great writers since time immemorial raved about the mystical and romantic powers of the stars, and Luke and Piers swore by them, he would be an idiot if he didn't use them to his advantage too.

Not that he had been brave enough to attempt any sort of seduction yet, nor did he think one would be welcome. She needed to be comfortable in his presence first, familiar with him and that sort of romantic gesture needed to come after they were friends again and he had charmed her entirely. The friends part of the plan was the one he felt the most comfortable executing, the romantic and charming part, not so much. He had never possessed that knack nor been particularly good at flirting either. And the thought of presenting her with random bunches of flowers or jewellery while he waxed lyrical about her beauty made his toes curl inside his boots. True charm couldn't be contrived—at least not by him. In that regard, he had more in common with his sister's cautious husband than he did Luke.

'Did you notice the way Captain Sinclair gazed at her as they took their vows?' Her expression was wistful, allowing him to see that she envied the newlyweds too. 'Or the way his voice caught as he said them?'

'Or Dottie's mile-wide grin after he grabbed her and kissed her.'

'For a shy and reticent man, that spontaneity was rather…heartening. It certainly showed how besotted he is.' Her smile was tinged with regret. 'But it makes me feel doubly bad for trying to steer Dorothy away from him for all those months.'

If his last week of subtle wooing had achieved anything, it was a new openness between them. They weren't quite as chummy as they had been at Appletreewick, but they were getting there and that was a start. 'You were only looking out for your friend and ensuring she didn't make a mistake by rushing into things.'

'No, I wasn't.' She paused mid-step and pulled a face. 'I was being selfish, Griff. I knew they were perfect for one another, right from the moment he returned last spring and they couldn't keep their eyes off one another, but I purposely tried to stall things because I wanted to keep Dorothy here in London. I am ashamed to admit that I didn't want to be the last of us girls to walk down the aisle.'

She risked peeking at him to gauge his reaction before she tried to shrug it off, only the bravado didn't reach her eyes which were totally wretched. 'That was me attempting to uphold my part of our bargain by being brutally honest with you—even though it is painful to admit to such shallowness and before you ask, I am not proud of myself for it. But after Faith then Hope fell in love and went and got married in quick succession…and then…' As her voice trailed off, embarrassed, and she couldn't meet his eye, they both knew she was alluding to Denby. That episode in her life and her lingering feelings for him hovered between them like a spectre, reminding them both that Griff was not her preferred choice of husband, but he was grateful nevertheless that she didn't mention his name. 'Well…let's just say I wasn't behaving entirely rationally at that time and my view of the world was a little skewed.'

'It doesn't matter now.' Though somehow it did. Hearing her admit it, seeing her remorse, feeling her guilt made him envious of her self-awareness too. It was a brave thing to do to admit that you were entirely wrong. Braver still to admit to the reasons behind it. Charity could talk about her tangled emotions. That he couldn't—yet—kept him awake at night. It was all well and good Piers encouraging him to bare his heart and Charity asking for it directly, but to bare it and see the remorse in her eyes that she didn't reciprocate was too terrifying a prospect. One he certainly wasn't ready for. 'All that matters is that Dottie and her Captain are happy.'

'I suppose you knew though, didn't you? Or suspected what I was up to? You've always despaired of my selfish streak. Always seen through it and me.'

'You make up for that single tiny flaw in other ways.'

'I have only a single flaw?' More bravado but he suddenly realised she cared about his good opinion far more than he realised. 'And there I thought I had so many.'

'Your occasional selfishness isn't your only flaw, of course.' He couldn't resist teasing her a little and copied her playful tone, wishing he could flirt but was still too wary to try. 'You have a casual relationship with time and care too much how your hair looks. And then, obviously, there is your rebellious streak and your selective deafness. Your penchant for theatrics...'

'And there is the Griff I know and love.' She rolled her eyes as she chuckled, unaware how the word love uttered in the same sentence as his name made his aching heart stutter and yearn for it to be true. 'I might have known your seemingly pretty compliment had a list of caveats attached to put me firmly back in my place. A leopard doesn't change its spots.'

It was a flippant comment, but he got the sense that she also believed it. That he only ever saw her flaws and not the myriad other attributes which made her wonderful.

'But you make up for all that by your kindness, Charity.' If he couldn't yet flirt and confess his love for her, in the spirit of upholding his part of their bargain he could at least tell her some of what he really felt.

'You are generous to a fault, with both your time, your talent and your charm.' He swallowed, instantly tense and uncomfortable but he soldiered on. 'You have the canny knack of putting everyone at their ease. You are a born diplomat who makes people feel important and welcome. You have the rare ability to ask exactly the right questions at exactly the right time, and then you listen to the answers with an interest I envy.' She smiled and the honest words came a little easier. 'You are steadfastly loyal. Incredibly witty and clever. Selflessly noble when the situation calls for it, as your spirited defence of me at our tense and painful wedding dinner proved. You are also fun to have around, resourceful. Ridiculously hard working.' He began to tick them all off on his fingers despite his unease at bearing his feelings for her. 'Intrepid. Fearless. Charming.'

There was no hint of sadness in her smile this time—but there was open-mouthed surprise which shamed him. For both their sakes he should never have waited this long. He should have said all this years ago because every word was true. 'Oh, yes—and you can sing a bit too.' He held up his finger and thumb an inch apart, using humour to cover how exposed his heartfelt confessional left him feeling.

Her expression was bemused, as if she couldn't quite believe what she was hearing and that shamed him too. 'My goodness—I am all aquiver at such praise.' She flapped a hand in front of her face as if it were all too much but he swore he saw tears swimming in her eyes. 'If you are not careful, Gruff Griff Philpot, I am in grave danger of believing that you actually *like* me.'

It was on the tip of his tongue to confess exactly how much before he stopped himself in the nick of time. Too much honesty might only serve to make things more awkward if he admitted to everything too soon and it wasn't as if he needed to hurry along his subtle courtship—thanks to the baby he had put in her womb and the ring he had put on her finger, they had eternity. 'Let's not get too carried away.' Slow and steady would win this race. Hopefully. If he could work through the problem properly and subtly fix all the broken parts to make their basic premise sound enough to build upon. Then find the courage to say the most momentous words his heart ached to say. 'I find you tolerable.'

'You are such a dreadful liar.' She grinned and snuggled against his arm. It played havoc with his senses. 'Admit it—you like me a great deal.'

Thankfully, two children ran across the path laughing, saving him from answering. One clutched a brightly coloured paper kite, providing the perfect distraction from the present by transporting them both instantly back to the past.

'That looks uncannily like the one you had in Brighton, doesn't it?' She nudged him with her elbow as they sauntered forward. 'The one you flatly refused to let me fly.'

He cringed and she laughed. 'Are you ever going to forgive me for that?'

'I suppose that depends on whether or not you are ever going to forgive me for breaking your original kite.'

'A quandary to be sure.' He nudged her back, a little overwhelmed. 'But you stomped on it, Charity. I had known you for less than an hour and you jumped on my precious kite in a fit of rage. A man doesn't get over something that traumatic quickly. In another decade perhaps, when enough water has gone under the bridge, I might be able to give it some consideration...' He waited for her to laugh but she sighed instead.

'You were ten, Griff. Tall, handsome, intriguing and commanding and I thought you so impressive. Have you any idea how overwhelming that is for a six-year-old girl who had never really known a boy before to be confronted by such a magnificent specimen?'

It was his turned to stare open-mouthed. 'Magnificent specimen?'

She shot him an imperious glance. 'I was six. It's a difficult age. Try not to judge me for my childish *tendre* or to interrupt while I am trying to make amends.'

A *tendre* was a good thing, surely? The urge to beam at the admission was overwhelming but he buried it. Or at least most of it. 'My apologies. Please continue.'

'When you entrusted me with your kite, I was so determined to impress you that when I couldn't make it fly, no matter how hard I tried, I was ashamed. So mortified I almost burst into tears right in front of you, but I knew that if I did you would think me a silly little baby or you would pity me—and I couldn't bear the thought of either. Therefore, I stomped on your kite instead. I am not proud of my childish response, especially as it only made the situation worse and you thought me not just a silly baby afterwards, but a silly, spoiled, annoying and irrational one too. And when I stormed off, I still cried. In fact, I was inconsolable for a week and if it's any consolation, I've always felt guilty about it. So much so, I've never touched a kite since or dared try to fly one.'

She stopped dead and spun him to face her, shoulders squared and chin lifted. Bold and fearless as always. 'Therefore, if I have never said it before, my apology for that day is long overdue. I am sorry, Griff, from the bottom of my heart, for breaking your precious kite. It was a mean and petty thing to do. Please forgive me.'

'Because six is a difficult age?' She nodded and Griff blew out a breath, pretending to ponder it rather than haul her into his arms and kiss her, which was what he really wanted to do. 'Or because I am tall, handsome, intriguing *and* commanding?'

Her hands went immediately to her hips. 'I just profusely apologised for a decades' old crime in an impassioned monologue and that is all you heard?'

'I confess, I heard nothing at all after the shock at being called a *magnificent specimen.*' He wrapped her arm around his, enjoying her mock consternation and the gradual thawing of relations as the first part of his meticulously drawn plan seemed to be working. 'If you are not careful, Mrs Philpot, I am in grave danger of believing that you *like* me too.'

Chapter Twenty-Two

Charity awoke with his arm wrapped possessively around her waist and the unsettling feel of his big body spooning hers again. Only this time, she was staunchly under the covers and he was part clothed on top of them. She also had no earthly clue how they came to be so intimately entwined.

The absolute last thing she remembered after her horrendous middle of the night bout of nausea was Griff tucking her back into bed and stroking her hair while he continued to explain all the intricacies and benefits of Watt's parallel motion. Because for some inexplicable reason, his soothing deep voice murmuring unfathomable technicalities and mathematical equations seemed to send her back to sleep better than any sleeping draught ever could. She had a vague memory of last night's instalment having something to do with the precise linkage of pistons but certainly nothing beyond that. Nothing which would explain why they were apparently snuggled together—unless he had sent himself to sleep too with his purposely soporific delivery and then they had inadvertently drifted together like magnets.

He cuddled her closer as he shifted position, burying

his nose in her hair, then immediately stilled. Categoric proof that he had suddenly awoken too.

She felt each of his muscles relax simultaneously as if he had willed them to do so. 'How are you feeling this morning?' His breath was warm against her ear and created a flurry of goose pimples down her neck.

'All right... I think.' But she hadn't moved yet. Aside from the fact she was rather enjoying the unexpected pleasure of being held in his embrace, moving first thing, especially at any speed, was always problematic nowadays. 'That'll teach me to eat dessert. I knew that sliver of tart was a bad idea. I should have stopped at the toast you foisted upon me.'

Sudden nerves made her tongue loose. They had arrived home from Dorothy's wedding celebrations late and because he had thought she looked pale he had insisted she eat something. Then, she had lingered in the kitchen while they shared a slice of pie, using the food as an excuse to enjoy his company just a bit longer after such a lovely day.

'My stomach can handle toast but clearly apple tart is my new nemesis, and I shall have to add it to the ever-growing list of poisons which can no longer pass my lips thanks to our ornery demon child and his evil whims. Perhaps we should name him Lucifer?'

He laughed. A deep, unsettling, intimate rumble which sent ripples of awareness down her spine and into all four of her limbs. Then his hand slid to her belly and sent more nerve endings bouncing in several inappropriate places. 'I thought you were adamant we were having a girl.'

As her body couldn't be trusted with him so close, she twisted to face him making sure she put a good foot of distance between them as she did so. But even that wasn't enough to settle things because he was sinfully rumpled in just his shirt and breeches. His sleepy dark eyes were hooded as he smiled at her. His square jaw dark with morning stubble, the soft linen moulded to the muscles in his arms where he had propped himself on to one elbow and stretched taut across his broad shoulders exposing a tantalising V of golden skin at his undone collar. But his gaze was filled with happiness he made no attempt to disguise.

'Girl, boy—whichever it is, it's a menace.' It was a battle to keep her eyes on his face. They were keen to wander and ogle because they remembered only too well what was hidden under that linen. And beneath those breeches. The memory caused a flood of heat to her chest.

'And it's all my fault. I know.' He wound one finger through a tendril of her hair smiling as he tugged it. 'But it will be over soon… I promise.'

'You do realise that you have been promising much the same for the entire duration of our marriage.' All sixteen days of it. 'And you've persistently failed to come good on it.'

She sat, needing still more distance because this new incarnation of Griff was so intoxicating and unsettling, gathering the covers around her like a shield even though he had an intimate knowledge of what was under her nightgown too. For a moment, she thought he noticed her discomfort because he frowned slightly before it was replaced with a smile.

'How about I make it up to you with some breakfast in bed?' He quirked one dark eyebrow, making him even more rakish and appealing. 'Can I tempt you with some insipid weak tea and dry, tasteless toast perhaps?

I happen to know that in the absence of plain, boiled potatoes, it's our demon child's favourite repast.'

She was tempted indeed, but not by the food. The urge to touch him was overwhelming. 'That sounds perfect.'

'I know.' He leaned forward and kissed the tip of her nose, an affectionate, familiar and doubtless friendly gesture which shouldn't have caused her stupid pulse to quicken in quite the way that it did. But there had been a lot of affectionate gestures in the last week, all equally unexpected, fleeting and out of the blue, and each of them had played havoc with her nerves and her emotions because she had no clue what they meant.

Was Griff being nice and trying to put her at her ease or was he pretending to be nice because he felt beholden to be so? Or were the emotions he was finally allowing her to see real and did he care a little? More than a little? 'When a man has been married as long as I have, he knows these things.'

She nodded and to her intense relief, he hauled himself off her bed and padded barefoot out of her door. Alone, she slumped back on to the pillows, which smelled too much like him for comfort, and as she hugged one, she splayed her hand on the patch of mattress which still carried his warmth. Then guiltily snatched it back as the door opened again. 'Mrs Gibbons is on the case and says she'll have it up to us in a trice.'

Us!

Before she could query that statement, or argue against it, he settled himself back on the bed beside her, throwing a pillow against the headboard to lean against, stretching his long legs and crossing his feet comfortably at the ankles. 'How do you fancy a trip out today?'

'With you?' Because that sounded delightful.

'Of course, with me. It's another lovely day and with autumn soon upon us, we should take advantage of the weather and the fact that it is blessedly Sunday and you have the entire day off. We could pack a picnic and take the curricle somewhere green and pleasant. I can't promise anything as pretty as the Dales but Richmond Park is always lovely.'

'I haven't been there in ages.'

He grinned just as Mrs Gibbons tapped the door. As she came in, her gaze took in the dishevelled state of the bed and the pair of them still upon it and smiled knowingly. 'Dry toast and peppermint tea as requested.'

Griff jumped up, relieved her of the tray and pretended to sniff it with pleasure. 'The breakfast of champions.'

'Will that be all, sir?'

'Actually, no...' He placed the tray beside Charity in the space he had vacated and then solicitously handed her her tea. 'While my wife feasts, I need to talk to you about a picnic because we are off on an adventure.'

'You've certainly picked the perfect day for it.' Mrs Gibbons put the final pin in Charity's hair and beamed at her reflection in the mirror. 'Don't you look as pretty as a picture?'

'Thank you.' Her housekeeper didn't have Lily's deft touch, but she did a reasonable job. 'It's much better than I could have done.' Griff had insisted she hire a lady's maid, but the new girl didn't start for another week.

'I put plenty of hairpins in it seeing as you are off in the curricle. We don't want the wind turning it into a bird's nest the moment you set off.' Then she raised her eyebrows. 'Not that the master will notice, of course.

Besotted men rarely notice their lady's flaws.' If only. 'He was as giddy as a schoolboy this morning when he left.'

'He's gone?' This was news to Charity. 'Where?'

'He said he had to pick up something from his parents' house around the corner so I doubt he'll be long. And he's eager to steal you away by yourself...' After a pointed glance at the still messy bed, Mrs Gibbons raised her eyebrows again. 'Clearly he cannot get enough of you.'

It felt wrong to humiliate him by admitting that they had never used either of the beds in this house for the sort of activities the housekeeper assumed they were indulging in. 'Sundays are my only full day off. That is probably why he seems so keen.'

'Oh, it's not just that. It's everything. The way he looks at you when he thinks nobody is watching. The way he eagerly awaits your return when you are at the theatre. The minutes never go fast enough for him and he inevitably leaves to fetch you much sooner than he needs to because he simply cannot wait. His pride when you are on his arm. The way he attends to you when you are feeling ill and refuses to allow me to assist. The vast amount of money he has spent on the instruments for your new music room alone tells me—'

'What new music room?'

Mrs Gibbons instantly froze and blinked at her. 'You mean he hasn't told you?' When Charity shook her head, touched beyond measure, the older woman covered her mouth with her hand, her expression distraught. 'He never said it was a surprise but now I've ruined it!'

'I shan't tell him if you don't.' She couldn't hide her grin or her delight. Griff had bought her instruments.

How lovely was that? But poor Mrs Gibbons was still mortified.

'Why did he not tell me it was a secret?' She wrung her hands and looked ready to burst into tears. 'Unless he assumed that I would never betray his confidence and that makes me feel even worse.'

Charity took her hands. 'He should have told you not to say anything, but likely didn't because he is a creature of habit who never tells anyone anything—and hasn't considered that the household dynamics have recently shifted and you now have both a master and mistress.'

'Still…'

'I am an actress, Mrs Gibbons, and if I say so myself, a rather good one and you have my word that he will never know you let slip his secret. I shall be as surprised and overawed when he tells me as I am now.'

'But I feel awful.'

'Then don't. The household dynamics *have* shifted and we girls must always stick together. I should like very much that you trust me as implicitly as I already trust you.'

The older woman finally smiled. 'Mr Philpot has often bragged to me of your acting skills. Why only the other night he lamented about your Figaro mucking up his lines again in the first act and your quick thinking and comic timing having to save him. Tuesday, wasn't it? It must be frustrating having to save his bacon again and again.'

Charity nodded, using every bit of that talent to cover this new and even more shocking surprise. That Griff had watched her from the audience this week and not mentioned it, and by the sounds of it had done so more than once if he was able to pinpoint the hapless Figaro's many errors so precisely. 'My Figaro likes a tipple, Mrs Gibbons.'

'Frequent and often too by the sounds of it. I know Mr Philpot was staggered they engaged him for this second run when he made so many similar mistakes in the first—but then, as he always says, the audience aren't there to see Figaro, they are there to see you. Having seen you as Susanna, I do not doubt that for a second.'

'I didn't know you had seen me perform, Mrs Gibbons?'

'Oh, I have seen you twice, Mrs Philpot. Your husband bought me and my daughter tickets for my birthday when it first opened at New Year's and then I got to go again in April when he had an urgent business meeting and couldn't use his ticket that night.'

Griff had gone to see her in April? Before their fateful trip to the north? She couldn't recall that.

The housekeeper handed her the bonnet which went with her cornflower-blue muslin, then primped with her curls some more after she put it on. 'But I have to confess while you still sounded magnificent, the view that second time wasn't as good. My own fault. I am too vain to wear my spectacles in public so from all the way up in the gods you were a bit of a blur.'

Oblivious of the significance of the bombshell she had just imparted, Mrs Gibbons began to put away the hairbrush and pins in the dressing table drawer. 'But Mr Philpot seems to prefer the gods for some reason and as it's his hard-earned money that purchases all those tickets in his desk drawer, it is not my place to question his choices.' Charity made a mental note to take a peek in that desk drawer at the earliest possible convenience. 'For he is generous to a fault all other times and spares no expense on those he loves.' She beamed again, somewhat sheepishly. 'Which you will doubtless see for yourself when all the instruments arrive.'

What a thoughtful and confusing man she had married. Who disapproved of her one minute and then sat high in the gods to covertly watch her the next. 'Which room has he picked for my music room?'

'Do you want me ruining all of the surprises?' At Charity's wicked grin she relented. 'The one opposite his study and facing the garden. Aside from the view and my suspicion that he desperately wanted you close by, he needed somewhere with a high ceiling for the pianoforte he has ordered. It is coming all the way from Vienna apparently, and is so tall it's been named after some strange exotic animal. One he claims can eat the leaves from the very top of the trees on the plains of Africa no less.'

'A giraffe perchance?'

'That's it! A giraffe piano. I thought at the time it was a funny name.'

That meant Griff hadn't just bought her a pianoforte, he had bought her the very best—a Seuffert Giraffenflügel which even her mother, who had literally everything musical ever invented, did not yet have because it was so expensive.

'But after he had done hours of research and consulted with a flamboyant little Italian chap who came to visit one evening, Mr Philpot decreed you could have no other.'

'Was the flamboyant little Italian chap called Signor Fauci by any chance?' He really had gone to a touching amount of trouble and not said a single word about it. How typically tight-lipped of Griff.

'He was. Do you know him?'

'Signor Fauci is my singing teacher.'

The older woman instantly scoffed. 'You don't need a singing teacher.'

'You are the second person to say that in as many weeks.' And while she was on the subject of things said more than once in such a short space of time. 'Mrs Gibbons, can I ask you exactly how Griff looks at me when he thinks nobody is watching?'

The housekeeper's face softened. 'Like a man hopelessly in love.'

It was her turn to scoff, even though her heart leapt at the thought. 'You are mistaken, Mrs Gibbons. You forget, we had to marry.'

'Perhaps…but I suspect it would have happened even without a baby anyway, don't you? For I also see the way you look at him too.'

Before Charity had time to formulate a denial, they heard his boots on the stairs, casting those insightful words into stone and giving her some serious food for thought. Was it really possible that some of her overwhelming feelings for Griff were reciprocated? She certainly hoped so.

Chapter Twenty-Three

'Ta-da!' Griff opened the picnic basket with an exaggerated flourish and enjoyed Charity's expression as she warily peeked at the contents then burst out laughing.

'Boiled potatoes and dry toast?'

'A bland banquet that not even our demon child could take issue with.'

'But what about the cake? The Prince of Darkness hates cake.'

'It's ginger. An ingredient which I am reliably informed is used extensively by mariners to ward off seasickness. They swear by it and never leave port without it, so I figured it was worth a try.'

She broke a corner off with her fingers and sniffed it before popping it into her mouth. Then sighed in pleasure at the taste. 'If it means I can eat cake again, then I am prepared to try anything—but know that I shall blame you entirely if it doesn't and I live to regret it.'

Before she could break off a second piece, he whipped the cake away. 'Dessert traditionally comes after dinner and you need to keep your strength up. Therefore, it's proper food first and then cake.' He took out the plates and while she continued to laugh, made a great show of serving her up a single potato, a slice of similarly boiled chicken and one triangle of toast. 'Your first course, *madame*—and I think you'll agree, what an insipid feast for the eyes it is! *Bon appétit.*'

'You're a tyrant, Gruff Griff the Fun-Spoiler. Have I ever told you that?' She feigned irritation but he swore he saw some affection in her eyes as she stared at the sorry meal and then took an unenthusiastic bite out of the potato. 'Do you think I will ever be able to eat anything that isn't white or beige ever again, Griff? I so miss fruit and sauces. And cheese and pudding. And chocolate.' With a huff she popped the second half of the potato into her mouth.

'Dr Macdonald said you should feel better by the sixteenth week.'

'Then I only have…hmm…' She chewed thoughtfully, brows furrowed. 'You are the mathematician so you can do the calculations because I need a light at the end of the tunnel to look forward to.' Then she grinned. 'We made our demon child on the night of the fourth of June or some time in the small hours of the fifth…' The casual but unexpected reminder of that night instantly conjured images of them writhing on the sheets for hours. 'And today is the twenty-eighth of August, so that is…'

Griff tried to banish the erotic sights, sounds and vivid memories of Charity in the throes of passion that fateful night to focus on the simple mathematical problem. 'Well there are thirty days in June…minus five leaves twenty-five. Plus the thirty-one for July and the twenty-eight so far in August. That's um…eighty… um…' Why wouldn't his brain work? Probably because the sun was picking out the flecks of shimmering gold in her hair. Her pretty blue dress was emphasising the deep azure in her eyes. The warm breeze had even picked up her perfume and wafted the heady scent of jasmine ruthlessly beneath his nose to distract him further. The same fragrance he had smelled when his lips had explored her neck while his body had been buried deep inside hers. As his throat dried with spontaneous lust at that, he forced out a cough in case his answer came out strangled. 'Eighty-four days.'

'And what is that in weeks?' She clicked her fingers just like she had that fateful night before she had kissed him, and he had lost his head. 'Come on, Griff! I thought you were supposed to be a genius. What is eighty-four divided by seven?'

'Eleven? No...' His addled brain struggled further with the simple bit of division. 'Twelve. It's definitely twelve weeks to the day.' The day all his wildest fantasies had come true.

'Has it really been three months?' Charity was talking about the length of her pregnancy but all Griff could now think about in his inappropriate and fevered state was what an age it had been since he had last had her. How many nights he had lain awake craving her. How torturous it was to be married to her, to be able to gaze upon her every single day across the breakfast table or know she was in her bed only a few scant feet from his and not be able to touch her in the way he yearned to. The way he had always yearned to. Even this morning, as he had awoken with her cradled in his arms, he had had to leave the bedchamber immediately in case she saw the overwhelming evidence of his rampant desire standing proud in his straining breeches. 'Only another month of torture to go then.'

Torture was exactly what it was.

Could he go another month without her after this morning? Another week? Another blasted hour?

'I bought you a present.' He blurted out the words and then scrambled to his feet to fetch it, needing some space to calm himself down. 'Wait there.'

He dashed back to the curricle and took his time unpacking the dusty box he had hastily retrieved from his parents' attic, using it to remind himself that his wooing of his wife was a steady hike and not a sprint. Slow and steady would win the race, not a ham-fisted, ill-timed and premature declaration caused by a surfeit of pent-up lust!

He willed his body to deflate and his pulse to return to normal, then took a deep breath before he emerged from behind his conveyance. 'Close your eyes and hold out your hands!'

She did as he asked, her lovely smile bewitching him all over again as he placed his forgotten toy in her outstretched fingers. She opened them then gasped, her lips parted as she gently traced the faded silk with the merest tip of one finger.

'It's your kite...' Her eyes lifted, questioning as she offered him a perplexed smile. 'The one you took to Brighton.'

'The very one...the kite I petulantly refused to let you fly despite the twenty pretty shells you brought me when you were six and I was a magnificent specimen of ten.' He stared at his feet as they shuffled on the grass, second-guessing himself for his impulsive gesture which had seemed like such a good idea this morning but now only served to make him feel daft. And what the blazes had possessed him to repeat the words *magnificent specimen*? What a blithering idiot he truly was.

He kicked an imaginary stone, feeling ten again and hopelessly tongue-tied. 'After your confession yesterday that you had never touched another kite since, I figured it was long past time for me to make amends for my childish behaviour seventeen years ago too. It was in my parents' attic, doing nothing and I thought you might want to give it an airing.'

'Aren't you afraid I might break it?' She ran her finger reverently down the thin wooden spine. 'It looks rather fragile.'

'I don't care if you break it. I never should have. It's an old kite—not a priceless artefact.' He held out his hand. 'Come on. The conditions are perfect.'

'I have no clue how to fly a kite, Griff.'

'Then I'll teach you.'

He hauled her up and tugged her well away from the trees and on to some raised ground to demonstrate the basics. 'Turn your back to the wind and hold the kite thus.' As he held it out, the long, ribboned tail cracked and flapped in anticipation. 'When it catches the wind, let it go and very slowly let out the string, always keeping the line tight.' As it lifted into the air, he gently tugged on the string at intervals to encourage the kite to soar higher, enjoying her childish smile of wonder at the sight.

After a few minutes, he reeled it back and handed it to her. 'Your turn.'

The tip of her tongue poked out as she concentrated, mimicking his movements, but no sooner had she got it airborne, than it plummeted to the ground. 'Grrr... I still cannot do it.'

'Yes, you can. If at first you don't succeed...'

She glared at him with narrowed eyes but held the kite out again. This time, as it caught the wind, Griff came to stand behind her, wrapping his hands around hers. 'Don't tug it too hard or let the string go too slack. You have to tease it…give it some freedom…that's it… then give it a nudge to remind it that you are in charge.'

As it soared higher, the upper winds caught it and she leaned back against his body as her arms took the weight and he risked letting go of her hands. As withdrawing completely while she was so consumed would likely result in her falling backwards, he rested his palms on her hips while enjoyed her expression of wonder.

'It's flying, Griff!'

'I know.'

'This was such a lovely idea. The perfect way to spend a Sunday.' She twisted her head to grin at him and just like that, something strange and wonderful happened.

The emotion overwhelmed him and he let her see it.

Their eyes locked.

The air shifted.

And simultaneously, in that charged and joyous moment, they both closed the remaining distance between their mouths as if it was the most natural thing in the world to do.

Chapter Twenty-Four

I t was a tender kiss.

Soft and full of meaning and neither she nor Griff were in a hurry for it to end. They both paused briefly as his precious kite hit the ground behind them with an ominous thud, but then his lips whispered over hers again as he laughed and the kite was forgotten. All that mattered was the honesty of the moment and the hidden mutual affection it revealed.

While there was desire, this kiss wasn't about heat or passion, although she felt them. Nor was it an explosion of lust so fierce it consumed them. It was gentle and curious, as if they were both experiencing the sensation of one another properly for the first time. His hands rested lightly on her hips. Hers on his shoulders. Everywhere else, their bodies barely touched, yet Charity still felt him everywhere. From the flickers of need kindling between her legs to the rapid, excited beating of her heart, every reaction was for him. For them, this special moment of understanding and nothing else.

At the exact second when it would have been perfectly acceptable to deepen the kiss and allow the restrained lust to bubble over as it had with such ardent fervour as before, they mutually broke apart. Only an inch or two as they stared at one another in wonder and bemusement—because it was wonderful as well as confusing. Charity had never been so overwhelmed by a simple kiss in her life.

Wordlessly, he led her back to the blanket, and they kissed again. Then they ate cake and laughed and held hands as they lamented the state of his kite. He tried to fix it and gave up. They exchanged more kisses, some were brief, some lingered but none went further than the first. They packed away their picnic. Took a slow, meandering ride around the park and down to the river. Strolled along the Thames for an hour arm in arm stealing more chaste kisses along the way when the need arose and the coast was clear, and again all the way home where they ate a companionable dinner and talked about nothing in particular for another hour afterwards.

At no juncture did either of them question what any of it meant or where it was going. They didn't talk about their feelings or the past or their future in case they burst the magical bubble that surrounded them. They simply went with the flow and revelled in the present until they were all alone in their drawing room after they had bid an intrigued and delighted Mrs Gibbons goodnight.

The door clicked shut and they stared at one another from opposite ends of the sofa, the atmosphere now charged with uncertainty alongside the anticipation. 'I suppose this is the part of the evening where things inevitably get awkward?' Charity took a sip of peppermint tea to calm her sudden nerves.

'Only if we allow them to.' But by the way the fingers of his left hand were rhythmically tapping his crossed knee, he felt as suddenly gauche as she. They stilled as he caught her watching them and he laughed as he winced. 'All right… I'll be brave and actually be the one to say it for a change. It's been a lovely day. Unexpected…and encouraging for our marriage. But I have no expectations of anything more yet, or at all, if that is what is worrying you. I am quite content just to be in your company and know that right at this moment you are just as happy to be in mine.'

'That's really all?' Her silly heart yearned for a declaration of some sort or a hint which confirmed some of Faith's, Hope's and Mrs Gibbons' romantic suspicions.

He stared at his knee again, then exhaled. 'I cannot deny that I wouldn't say no to a kiss goodnight…once the evening is done. If you are agreeable, that is.'

As much as her nerves appreciated his gentlemanly restraint, her body didn't. 'And what if I wanted a kiss now too, Griff?' Of its own accord, her gaze dropped to his mouth as her lips tingled before she forced it back to meet his.

He swallowed. 'Then I wouldn't say no to that either.' But as his gaze heated, he made no move to take advantage of her invitation.

Before her bravery disintegrated completely, Charity shuffled closer then hesitated when he remained fixed to the spot, refusing to move a single muscle. 'At least meet me halfway, you wretch. Don't make me think this is all one-sided.' Because it didn't feel like it was. He hadn't confessed any sort of feelings for her, yet there was something in his eyes, an intensity she hadn't seen in them before that suggested he felt it too.

'I can't.' As he shook his head, his index finger wound itself into one of her curls and the gold flecks in his dark irises turned instantly molten. 'After all the delights of today, I don't trust myself not to overstep the line.'

'We are married. I didn't think there was a line?'

'Then I shall give you fair warning, Charity, if I kiss you now then one kiss won't be enough.'

Sometimes, once in a blue moon, Griff said the love-liest things without even realising he had said them. 'Your warning is duly noted.' She pressed her lips to his and was immediately engulfed in his strength as he hauled her into his lap.

This kiss was decadent and unrestrained. Long and deep and unmistakably carnal. His hardness pressed insistently against her hip as his tongue finally tangled with hers, making her moan into his mouth as her arms coiled around his neck.

While her fingers explored his chest and shoulders beneath his coat, his found and removed every pin in her hair until it all fell in a tousled curtain. Then his palms slid possessively down her thighs, dipped under her skirt and petticoats to smooth back up her stockings until they found the bare flesh at the top and paused. 'Say the word and I'll stop. I don't want to do anything that you are uncomfortable with.'

She smiled against his mouth as she kissed him again. 'That is duly noted too.' Then in case he had any other ridiculous notions of being gentlemanly, she nipped his ear with her teeth then nibbled a lazy trail down his neck while she undid his cravat and slowly pulled it away to discard it on the floor. Because he was right about one thing—a kiss wasn't going to be any-where near enough tonight.

She kicked off her shoes and snuggled closer, enjoy-ing the irregular beat of his heart beneath her palms, then sighed as he peeled away first one of her stockings and then the other. 'I adore your skin. It's like warm silk.' His lips lingered on her jaw until a million goose pimples exploded on her flesh. 'The memory of it has haunted me since our first time.'

It was the first real acknowledgement he had ever made of the way he felt about her and she hugged the words to her heart as he rained open-mouthed kisses down her throat and collarbone, then across the tops of her breasts above her bodice. 'The memory of you that night has haunted me too...' His hand cupped one breast, his thumb gently grazing the outline of her puckered nipple through the thin muslin of her dress until she moaned and arched against him.

'Your curves...your passion...' He kissed her mouth again as he filled his big hand with her bare bottom beneath her skirts. 'Your trust in me...'

Exactly as it had that first time, the strength of her desire for him shocked her and made her bolder. With clumsy fingers, she undid his waistcoat and burrowed beneath his shirt to rake her nails over his back, the barrier of their clothes now a dreadful inconvenience when her skin craved the feel of his from head to toe. Impatiently, she wrestled with the buttons of his falls and he stilled and stared down at her, his breathing gloriously laboured, and his questioning eyes darkened with desire. 'You don't have to do that...we don't have to do that. This is more than enough.'

'Not for me, it isn't.' Charity wanted all of him. Wanted to give all of her to him again and more. She wound her arms around his neck and tugged him back to her mouth, then lost herself in his kiss until he wrenched his mouth away.

The rampant desire in his gaze was unmistakable. 'Should we continue this upstairs?'

She nodded and he stood, staring down at the mess she had made of his clothing as if he couldn't quite believe it, then he smiled and held out his hand.

Neither spoke as they climbed the stairs but they repeatedly stopped so that they could kiss some more until they finally reached the landing where he hesitated, looking awkward and unsure, rumpled and utterly gorgeous as he stared at the two bedchamber doors. 'Which would you prefer?'

'Yours...' She grasped the handle and turned it quickly as the nerves also got the better of her. 'I have never ventured inside this room before, so it feels fitting tonight that I do.'

This was new and unchartered territory for both of them. They might have already experienced carnal knowledge of one another that fateful night in Sheffield, but that had been purely carnal. An unstoppable and unexpected physical maelstrom borne out of anger and hurt. A raging tempest of exploding passion and confused, fraught and long-bottled emotions which had nothing to do with affection.

This was different. It was anticipated. Premeditated. A defining moment in their long relationship which would alter everything completely. A consensual and reasoned decision to move to the higher plane beyond the physical. The enormous but essential step which took them away from their childhood and the fraught years of early adulthood and on to the unfamiliar path which might just make their marriage work.

It was undeniably a step in the right direction, but it was daunting none the less. The sheer weight of what they were about to do hung heavy in the air, making them both more nervous and conscious of one another in a way they had never been before. When she welcomed him into her body it would mean something. Perhaps not love—yet—for him at least. She accepted that such a momentous thing could not be rushed no matter how much her heart willed his to keep pace with hers. But the acknowledgement of mutual affection and blossoming trust which they desperately needed if they were ever going to fix the unfixable.

He waited for her to enter and he followed her inside. As if she had anticipated an evening of seduction, Mrs Gibbons had already turned down the bed on both sides. Her robe lay on top of his on the chair in the corner. A single lamp flickered on the nightstand in the gentle breeze from the open window. The room smelled of Griff. His subtle, spicy cologne. The soft citrus of his shaving soap. Charity took it all in, running her fingertips over his razor and brushes on the dressing table. Items so intimate to him yet up until this precise moment, completely alien to her.

The door clicked shut behind her and she turned to find him still leaning on the frame, respectfully giving her space even though she didn't want it but clearly desperate for her to close it.

Her body tingled with awareness as she walked towards him. Excitement warred with trepidation and made her limbs heavy. Expectant warmth pooled between her legs and heightened her senses. Her breasts ached for his touch. 'As we never had a wedding night, I suppose this is it?' Her pulse quickened at the prospect of all that was to come.

'Only if you want it to be. We don't have to...' She pressed a finger to his lips.

'I am not here under any duress, Griff. I do not feel pressured or obligated. I came of my own free will.' She smiled as her fingertips traced his mouth, enjoying the way his eyes darkened. The way his chest rose and fell as he fought to control his breathing, to disguise his arousal. All for her. 'I know already that you will stop in a heartbeat if I change my mind. I know that you will not hurt me, that you would rather die than do so. That you don't have any expectations or rules or ulterior motives either. And I also know that you are as anxious about tonight as I am because this is a momentous step. But I also know it is the right one. For us and for our future together.' She stroked his cheek to memorise every aspect of his rapt expression. His hunger, his yearning, his iron-clad resolve to always do the right thing. 'Now, for pity's sake, kiss me. Because I want you so badly tonight that it hurts.'

As if she had just given him the earth, he opened his arms and she gladly walked into them, revelling in the unleashed passion of his kiss. Revelling in him. Them. This unexpected and magical moment.

They took their time undressing one another, looking their fill and consigning all the details of each other's bodies to memory in a way they hadn't had the patience with before. Initially she was timid about baring everything, but he wouldn't allow that. He gazed upon every aspect of her nakedness in awed wonder, skimming his hand over the flesh his eyes had just raked as if he had never seen anything so lovely. He told her that she was the most beautiful woman in the world and in that second, as his rampant body twitched impatiently against her stomach and his heart hammered against her palm, she believed him.

They held hands when they finally wandered to the bed and as she slipped under the covers he slid in beside her, propping himself on one elbow so that he could fully explore every curve with his fingers, letting every ounce of his appreciation for her body and her show. Then, when he finally fused his mouth to hers, she sighed against it, pulling him on top of her because she needed to feel his weight.

For the longest time all they did was kiss and touch. A delightful, honest and enlightening prelude as they became familiar with this new and unforeseen phase of their seventeen-year acquaintance. Charity wanted to tell him how she felt, how she had always felt in the deepest recesses of her heart. How much their new closeness meant to her. More than anything, she wanted to hear those poignant words from him too but in their absence he showed her all those things in the heartfelt timbre of his kisses and his intense affection in each and every touch.

When they eventually allowed the impatient lust to consume them, that too came with more closeness. It became about both giving as well as receiving, luxuriating in the other's pleasure while allowing themselves to be vulnerable too. He worshipped her breasts, laving them until she arched against him. He moved lower and kissed her intimately until she bucked and writhed in torment, then held her close after she lay boneless and blinded by the stars he had put in her eyes until the passion built again.

This time it was Charity who undid him, repaying the favour by ignoring his protestations and taking him into her mouth, then boldly loving every throbbing inch of him until his clenched hands twisted in the sheet and his big body strained for release. But he flatly refused to let go that way and on a growl he rolled her beneath him, laced her fingers in his and stared deep into her eyes as he gently eased himself inside.

After that words were superfluous as pleasure took

over and they drowned in the sublime sensations of being joined. There was no anger this time. No hurt or battle. No haste or race to the finish line. They took their time, eking out every caress, every sigh, every poignant thrust until she lost sight of which part was her and which was him but understood that this was always meant to be. Her and him. Him and her. The sense of rightness was all-consuming. And when he came and her body pulsed in ecstasy around his, he cried her name in exultation as she cried his and they tumbled overwhelmed but perfectly entwined into the bright oblivion together.

Chapter Twenty-Five

'Have some mercy and cover yourself over, woman!' Then Griff was rushing around the room like a man possessed towelling the residual shaving soap from his skin as he rifled in his closet for a fresh shirt. They had had quite the night. Thanks to the hours of delicious lovemaking, a short, exhausted sleep following a brief interlude of the dreaded morning sickness, Griff had overslept. But as he had had to have her again neither of them had paid particular attention to the clock. 'I am already hideously late and if you are not careful I will miss the entire blasted meeting and that will be all your fault.' He stared at her and then stared heavenwards as if praying for strength. 'In the name of all that is holy, use that damn blanket, Charity, I am struggling to concentrate!'

Enjoying his discomfort, she stretched her arms above her head and smiled her most seductive smile as his eyes greedily drank in her nudity from the end of the bed. She had been reticent about baring everything, but now that she had seen just how much her body undid him, all shame for being so scandalously wanton went out of the window. 'Would being late be so bad?' She stroked his thigh with her foot, the impressive evidence of the effect she was having on him visible as another erection strained against his breeches. 'Doctor MacDonald did warn you that a pregnant wife could become libidinous and that unfortunate state of affairs is entirely your fault so it stands to reason you should have to pay for it in kind.'

'I cannot say I recall that being *all* my fault.'

'Of course, it was your fault—you lost your head at the most critical moment, forgot to be sensible for a change and planted a baby in my belly.' Feeling like a siren tempting a sailor to the rocks, she ran her fingers through her hair and then trailed them over her bosom.

'You are killing me.' He snatched up her robe and tossed it over her. 'And so will my father if I abandon him to the investors alone. This is potentially a big contract. Huge. For two new state-of-the-art coal mines in Glamorganshire that basically need everything and I have to be there to explain my designs because my father can't.' To her delight, he seemed devastated by this inconvenience. 'But I will happily pay tenfold for my carelessness this afternoon once the meeting is done.'

'I have a rehearsal this afternoon, so I won't be home until tonight.' She pouted and rolled on her side, ensuring the silk robe slipped to her waist and knowing full well he adored what a little gravity did to her breasts. 'Are you really going to make me wait that long?'

His eyes travelled up her body, obviously tempted and then he wrenched them away as he shrugged on his shirt and then his waistcoat. 'I shall be outside the theatre waiting for you on the dot of ten ready to ravish you. Don't be late or I won't be responsible for my actions.'

'And if I am?' Because they both knew she would be as a point of principle now.

He snapped open a starched cravat and wound it around his neck. 'Then I shall have to break down the stage door, fling you over my shoulder and then I'll have my wicked way with you on your dressing room floor.' He grabbed his coat and bent to brand her mouth with a thoroughly decadent kiss, then as he reluctantly pulled away there was an odd look on his face. An air of determination about him she hadn't seen before. 'Charity, last night was lovely…really special and I meant to say…what I wish I'd have said…' He winced at his clumsiness at articulating his emotions. 'What I've been meaning to say…' He swallowed, so awkward it made her smile and Griff laughed and shook his head. Then he stared earnestly into her eyes, then took her hand and stared at that as his fingers idly twirled the gold band on her wedding finger. 'You see, my darling Charity…'

Darling! How marvellous.

'The thing is…'

'Mr Philpot…' Mrs Gibbons's knuckles rapped on the door and he dropped her hand like a hot coal. 'Your curricle is outside and by my reckoning you are now a full forty minutes behind schedule.'

Wincing again he stood and smiled sheepishly in either relief or irritation at the interruption. 'I had better go.' He jerked a stiff thumb at the door but before he turned, she caught his sleeve.

'What have you been meaning to say, Griff?'

He smoothed a hand over her hair, his expression filled with yearning. 'Something much too important to attempt to articulate in a hurry and on the hoof.' Then he kissed her again with aching tenderness, his hands cupping her cheeks. 'I dare say they'll hold till tonight so that I can do them justice.'

That sounded as if he was finally going to admit that he had deep feelings for her if the heartfelt use of *darling* was any gauge—maybe even his love. The prospect made her heart swell against her ribs and choke her throat. A little overwhelmed thanks to the happy tears which suddenly pricked her eyes, she neatened his cravat knot and smoothed his lapels to cover it, feeling for the first time like his wife in every sense of the word. 'Then go and be brilliant.'

She watched him leave and then sank back against the pillows grinning for several minutes as she basked in the joy of it all, then hastily pulled the covers over her as Mrs Gibbons knocked on the door again.

'Mr Philpot insisted you should have your peppermint tea and toast in bed this morning because you need your rest.' The housekeeper shot her a knowing look as she deposited the tray on the nightstand. 'And I wanted to remind you that it is my half-day off if you need anything pressing.'

'Only some help with my hair, Mrs Gibbons, then I might visit one of my sisters or do some shopping, so you can leave earlier if you want. I know you are eager to spend time with your grandchildren.'

The older woman helped her get ready and then happily bolted out of the door. While Charity waited for the carriage, she couldn't resist wandering into Griff's study to see if there really were covert tickets to *Figaro* hidden in his drawer.

The top of his desk was a shambles, which was most unlike him. Clearly in his haste to find all the right drawings this morning he had rummaged through all his papers fast and hadn't had the time to put them all back in the labelled leather tubes he meticulously organised them in. All her fault and she wasn't the least bit repentant about it, but feeling wifely, she sat in his big leather chair and set about tidying it. Thanks to Griff's penchant for order, it wasn't an onerous task. The name of each project was written in the top left-hand corner of each enormous sheet of parchment and each page was numbered so she made short work of putting them all in the proper cases.

As she rolled up the last set of plans for the Philpot Two-Cylinder Mine Ventilation Pump Version No. 13 she spotted her name on the corner of a sheet hidden beneath his blotting pad. She retrieved it and laid it flat on the desktop and then blinked in surprise at the title written in Griff's precise, sloping handwriting—*How to Fix the Unfixable.*

More staggering still was the diagram filled with boxes and arrows which all circled and linked to a giant heart in the centre which was emblazoned with their names and flanked by two chubby hand-drawn Cupids wielding bows.

In typical Griff fashion, each box was numbered and contained a specific set of instructions. Some were very detailed, some sparse. In one—*Make Charity Aware You Exist*—was a list. Pick her up from the theatre; insist on eating meals together; use every opportunity to offer her your arm; be the first face she sees in the morning and the last at night; attend every social function she wishes to attend without complaining.

In the box marked *Foolproof Ways to Woo a Woman* he had crossed out leave her love notes, pick her flowers and carve your initials on a tree and left in sit together under the stars and take a long drive in the countryside.

Under *Grand Gestures* was only one thing written in capital letters: MUSIC ROOM.

But the box which utterly disarmed her and made her heart melt like butter was the one labelled *Ways to Make the Most Beautiful and Sought-After Woman in the World Fall Hopelessly in Love with Gruff Griff the Fun-Spoiler* because that was completely empty save the three tiny pen marks which suggested he had pondered that conundrum long and hard and hadn't the faintest clue how to proceed. It also told her that he had no earthly clue that he really didn't need to ponder that conundrum at all because she had already fallen hopelessly in love with him. That momentous event had happened at approximately half past three on a blustery Wednesday morning in Bloomsbury Square seventeen long years ago.

She stroked her index finger around the heart and the cherubs which told her he cared. What a daft pair they were. And what a lot of time they had wasted hiding what they truly felt. Tonight, she would cast aside her stubborn pride and risk baring her soul to encourage him to do the same.

'Mrs Philpot?' The maid poked her head around the door. 'You have a caller. A gentleman.'

'Do I?'

'A Lord Denby. Are you home?'

'Good heavens, no!' What on earth could he possibly want? Unless… She groaned out loud. 'Actually, I will see him.' Because if he had come for what she suspected he had, she would enjoy sending him packing with a flea in his ear and would let him know in no uncertain terms that while he might have scant regard for the vows he had taken, she had meant every single one of hers.

* * *

Griff couldn't wait to get home. Every minute of his interminable meeting with the investors had felt like an hour and he practically sprinted out of the office the second they signed the contracts in the hope that he might catch his lovely new wife well before she left for the theatre this afternoon. Usually, he would have hung around with his father to toast their good fortune, but today he had much better things to celebrate and all of them with Charity.

Last night had been astounding and not just because she had welcomed him into her lush body. There had been an unmistakable connection between them that hadn't been there before. It was impossible to quantify or explain what had occurred in his bed beyond a profound meeting of souls, which would have been a wholly unsatisfactory classification as far as his academic brain was concerned if it hadn't been the absolute truth. It had hit him like a steam-powered loom shuttle the second he hauled her into his lap and had left him reeling since, although why the blazes he hadn't told her all that at the optimum time last night was a mystery.

At the time, as always, not vocalising his feelings was habit. Self-preservation. The morbid fear of her rejection, which was ridiculous when she had given herself to him so freely and completely. There had been affection in her eyes as well as desire and he was kicking himself for not seizing the moment and making the single grand gesture which ultimately meant the most.

But enough was enough! He couldn't wait a second more to tell her that he loved her. That he had always loved her and always would. She was his everything and he couldn't be more delighted to be shackled to her for all eternity.

He pulled up his curricle with a screech outside his house and sprinted up the steps, suddenly wishing he had a huge bouquet of flowers to surprise her with.

The maid opened the door and he barged past grinning at his great good fortune. 'Where is my wife?' He fully intended to kiss her until she was breathless first then confess all.

'She went out a couple of hours ago, sir.' Instantly he deflated. 'But she left you a note.'

He found it propped against the ormolu clock Dottie had bought them as a wedding gift and impatiently tore open the seal.

My Darling Husband,
   I very much enjoyed your outstanding performance last night—so much so I must insist upon an encore later and perhaps an early matinee tomorrow?
   Passionate regards
   Your wife
P.S. I was particularly impressed with your costume, Griff. Naked suits you.

He laughed at the saucy note and then sniffed it because the minx had doused it with her seductive jasmine perfume too—purely to torture him. It had worked. He was already as stiff as a board and would likely remain in that state until she put him out of his misery later.

With a soppy grin on his face, he read it again as he backed towards the sofa, congratulating himself at his good fortune to have a wife who made no secret that she adored his touch. And who was he to disappoint her? If she wanted an encore, it would be his pleasure to give her one. Or two. Or five if he didn't die before-hand, but what a magnificent way to go. Buried deep inside Charity as she writhed in ecstasy as he told her that he loved her.

Picturing it, Griff flung himself on to the sofa and then scrambled back to his feet clutching his backside as he yelped in pain. 'What the blazes!'

Carefully, he extracted the barb which had pierced his poor buttock by a good half an inch, then stared at it in agony. Because on top of the thick silver pin was an emerald the size of a quail's egg and it certainly wasn't his.

Chapter Twenty-Six

It was barely one minute past ten when Charity burst out of the stage door, but instead of finding Griff sat there waiting in his curricle as she had expected, he had sent the carriage. She tried not to feel disappointed, knowing he must have a good reason else he wouldn't have let her down and climbed into the carriage clutching the red-ribbon-tied box she had bought expressly for him from the scandalous modiste's around the corner of Covent Garden who specialised in nightgowns and undergarments that left little to the imagination.

In the absence of Mrs Gibbons, when she arrived home she let herself in with her key. The hallway was dark but a thin shaft of light spilled from beneath the door to Griff's study so she shrugged out of her coat and headed there with her little gift for him, convinced he had orchestrated the completely empty house in order to give them more privacy for the carnal delights of the night ahead. She pushed open his door and to her complete surprise, found him sat at his desk working. 'I thought you were picking me up? I was promised a ravishing on the dot of ten.'

'I couldn't. I have too much to do.' He didn't even

bother looking up. That was her first inkling that something was wrong.

'Griff?' She walked towards him, depositing her box on the corner of his desk before she sat beside it. 'What's the matter?'

'We got the contract today and now there are a million things to do on the back of it.'

'Congratulations. But surely it doesn't all need doing right this minute?' She touched his arm and felt every muscle stiffen. 'It's late. Come to bed.'

He shook his head. 'I have too much on my mind, I couldn't possibly sleep.'

'Who said anything about sleep?' She smiled seductively as she stroked his arm. All bravado but she was floundering again and didn't know why. 'I bought you a gift...why don't you open it? I guarantee it will banish all thoughts of work immediately.'

His eyes snapped up, cold and unreadable and he sat back, severing the contact. 'I have to work tonight, Charity.'

It was a curt rejection and it cut like a knife. 'I see the disdainful and disapproving Griff of old has returned with a vengeance. What hideous crime have I committed this time to be so callously treated?' Had her flirty note offended him? Did he think such a wanton display of intent suddenly unseemly when he certainly hadn't had any objections about her forthrightness last night or this morning?

'Not everything is about you, Charity.'

Her temper snapped and she sent his precious papers flying with an angry sweep of her hand then stormed to the door. 'Go to hell, Griffith Philpot!'

'You're too late, Charity Philpot, for I am already there!' Something whizzed through the air and hit the wall in front of her before it bounced back on to the floor at her feet. 'I should imagine your precious Lord Denby is missing his most prized bauble and must be frantic as to its whereabouts. Although I cannot imagine how he came to lose it in *our* drawing room?'

Feeling sick to her stomach at the implication she bent and picked it up, then stared back at him as bland as bland could be even though he had just shattered all her foolish hopes for them and their marriage into smithereens. 'He must indeed be frantic. Thank goodness you found it. I shall make sure I return it to him first thing.' And with that she turned on her heel.

'Don't you think you owe me some sort of explanation?'

'Why would I waste my time defending myself when you have already found me guilty? And why should I even have to defend myself in the first place?'

'Because you invited Denby into this house!' His chair toppled over as he surged to his feet. 'Blasted Denby of all people! Here! Under my roof.'

'It was our roof a moment ago.'

'Don't you dare be flippant with me!'

'And don't you dare jump to ridiculous conclusions! Or blow hot and cold again when you promised me faithfully that you wouldn't!'

'How can I not when he is the one that got away? The one you've always really wanted! The superior peer you would have chosen if you'd had a choice! So I shall ask you again, what was *Lord* Denby conveniently doing in this house on *our* housekeeper's only day off?'

'I'd have thought that obvious.' She wouldn't cry in front of him. Wouldn't give him that satisfaction of knowing how much his cruel words wounded. Let him think what he wanted because he would anyway. 'He came here intent on seduction and, being the sort who is so free and easy with her favours that I have kissed significantly more men than a proper young lady ever should, I let him.' That was the answer he clearly expected because no matter what she did, how hard she tried, he would always think the worst.

'Be serious, Charity!'

'I am being serious. There is no point denying it.' She shrugged, doing her best impression of a guilty woman unapologetic even though she was dying inside. 'We made passionate love on the sofa first and then, for good measure, we did it again in your bed. We went at it like hammer and tongs for hours as I am sure the remaining servants will confirm thanks to all the noise we were making.' Furious, she flung open the door. 'And there I was thinking that you were an outstanding lover...but then I had nothing to compare that first experience with—but my goodness...' She flapped a hand in front of her face as if she were hot. 'What a fool I was to save myself for you when Lord Denby was truly magnificent.'

Then she slammed the door. Apparently not just on Griff, but on all the foolish dreams she had woven around him.

Griff stood paralysed and mortified for ages, his breath sawing in and out until his brain finally began to function again for the first time in hours. Then the remorse was overwhelming. Why had he done that? Said those awful things? After last night, after this morning, after everything had changed for the better, why had he attacked first instead of thinking?

Because attack had always been his default position when his feelings for her overwhelmed him and he couldn't express them as he wanted to. Except now he could express them that way, and the only reason he hadn't was blind fear and irrational jealousy. Years and years of it all stored up and never properly vented and it had all exploded like his power loom leaving senseless carnage in its wake.

Shaking and queasy he noticed the gift she had bought him and immediately felt even worse. She had brought him a present and he had behaved like an imbecile. A lovesick, unreasonable and irrational cretin. Exactly as he always did wherever Charity was concerned.

He undid the red ribbon and pulled out the flimsiest, gauziest, most scandalous garment he had ever seen. Her costume for their encore, selected on purpose to drive him insane with lust. Him, not blasted Denby. The man she had undeniably saved herself for no matter how many others she might have kissed beforehand. And he had thrown it in her face.

On leaden feet he climbed the stairs, ready to beg and plead for forgiveness, to spill his guts and pray for her mercy, only to discover that like everything he should have done, it was far too little and much too late. For on the nightstand next to his bed was her wedding ring and the maddening, passionate, fearless woman of his dreams was gone.

In times of crisis, the Brookes family rallied united against the world, and the instant she had stepped through her parents' front door the call had gone out irrespective of the late hour. Now, several hours later and feeling empty, bereft and devastated that Griff had made absolutely no effort to make any amends, Charity was surrounded by all of them. All trying to make her feel better and fix her unfixable broken heart.

'You married an I-M-B-E-C-I-L-E.' Her mother clasped her to her bosom and stroked her hair as the clock in the hallway struck four. 'And you are well shot of him. How dare he accuse you of such nonsense!'

'I've a good mind to go punch the blighter on the nose again!' Her father was pacing, smacking his fist in his palm like a prize fighter about to go into the ring. 'No man makes one of my daughters cry and escapes the consequences!'

'Why are men so stupid?' Hands on her hips, Faith railed at Piers.

'Because they are all blithering idiots who think they know everything, that's why!' Hope jabbed an angry finger at Luke. 'Irrespective of what their eyes, ears and basic common sense tell them to the contrary!'

'Can I remind you that in this instance, Piers and I haven't actually done anything wrong?' As Luke defended himself, the unmistakable sounds of a curricle rattled along the cobbles outside the window and they all froze.

'Charity!' Griff's voice echoed in the silence. He hammered on the door and her father stalked towards it. 'I am going to kill him!' Like lightning, Piers and Luke followed ready to either assist or hold him back.

'I need to urgently speak to my wife.'

'She doesn't want to speak to you. You made her cry! You broke my poor daughter's heart!'

'I know. I've come to explain and to beg for her forgiveness and I will raise merry hell if anyone tries to stop me.'

Before a scuffle broke out between all the menfolk, Charity called out, 'I will hear him out, Papa, and then he can go.' It seemed only right to end their sham of a marriage face to face.

With her sisters and her mother standing guard behind her back, and her brothers-in-law and her father standing behind him ready to evict him at a moment's notice, Griff walked warily into the room looking every bit as wretched as she felt. 'I would prefer to do this in private.' He swallowed painfully when she refused to budge from the chair she was sat in then shrugged resigned. 'I think it goes without saying that I behaved like a blithering idiot tonight and that my overreaction was as indefensible as it was uncalled for but...'

He raked an agitated hand through his dark hair and swallowed hard again. 'Sometimes, things need to explode to be able to accept how badly wrong they are and how shoddily they were put together in the first place.' Was that an admission that he too felt they needed to call time on their relationship? 'I've been labouring for weeks over the fact that our basic premise is all wrong. We've cobbled together a marriage on little more than a wing and a prayer and so many missing essential components, but I thought I could fix it regardless if I worked out how to slot in everything that was missing. I was wrong. I would have come here sooner to tell you that, but I decided to give the puzzle one last go and stripped it back to the place it first went wrong in the hope I could rebuild it from there and it turned out I had to go back quite a way.'

He took a cautious step forward and tried to smile. 'Seventeen years in fact to that fateful first day when you burst into my life and I fell head over heels in love with you.' Behind her, Faith sighed as Hope squeezed her shoulder. 'I've been battling against that reality ever since.' Griff grimaced at her father. 'I tried to fight it, because our parents kept saying we were brother and sister, but while I had no problem accepting Faith and

Hope as such, I never felt that for you. Not once. Then as adulthood dawned and lust reared its head...' He winced at her mother looking so delightfully mortified she almost caved.

'Well let's just say I didn't handle that well at all and all my frustrations leaked out as anger and I tried to avoid you.' He noticed the slight tremor in his hands and instantly clasped them behind his back. 'I even went to Sheffield for four years to try to get over you but none of it worked, and when I came back, all these feelings I have for you...' He touched his heart and hers melted. 'They all got worse and so did my behaviour. I wish I'd told you how I felt before I left and then repeated it every day in all the years since and then perhaps I wouldn't have made the huge hash of things that I have. But instead, I buried it as I always do and hoped it might go away, drove myself mad with jealousy over blasted Denby until I could barely see straight let alone think straight and then kept lashing out at you like a wounded animal because you preferred him to me.'

'Griff...about that...' Before she could correct him he held up his palm.

'Let me finish, because I cannot fix this unless I am entirely honest with you and it's long past time that I was after tonight's spectacular display of complete stupidity. I just cannot keep bottling it up inside. All to no avail because I lacked the willpower to avoid you, no matter how hard I tried. I forced my way on to your trip north knowing full well I wanted you. I've watched you in *Figaro* forty-two times since January just so that I could gaze upon your face.'

'I told you I saw him!' Luke's outburst earned him a curt shush from his wife.

'And every single time you sing that final aria I am

hopelessly undone. Every time you smile at me, my
heart swells. Every touch makes it stutter. I married you
because I always wanted to, not because I had to. I want
you to know that solemn truth too. And after a long,
hard evaluation of all my pent-up, irrational hatred of
that dandied fop and his blasted emerald, I have come to
the conclusion that I couldn't care less how many men
you've kissed in the past, as long as you still deign to
kiss me in the future.'

Then he took her hand and stared deeply into her
eyes and she saw every one of his feelings as clear as
crystal. All the remorse. All the anguish. All the adoration. All the love she had always yearned for.

'Charity Grace Brookes, I realise I am unworthy
and that you could doubtless do better. I realise I am
a mere mister and will never be a duke, and I appreciate that I have been an unadulterated, unbearable and
insufferable gruff fun spoiler for seventeen long years
and that at best you find me tolerable. But it turns out
that I cannot live without you for even one second, so I
was wondering if you would take pity on me and give
me just one more chance to make our marriage work
and in return I solemnly swear that I will love you like
nobody else ever could for all eternity and that I *will*
never stop trying to make you fall in love with me back.'

She shook her head, overwhelmed. 'I am afraid you
are too late, Griffith Philpot…' She couldn't resist making him suffer a little bit more. Then she took pity on
him. 'For I am already there. You stole my heart and
took my breath away at the tender age of six and you
never gave either back.'

He laughed in relief as he hauled her into his arms as
the unfixable was fixed for ever in the space of a single heartbeat. Then they kissed, with such unfettered

and joyful abandon, that all the unseemly, complicated, forbidden and wonderful emotions they had both spent seventeen long years trying to hide from one another were finally laid unashamedly bare for everyone else in that crowded room to see.

In a strange turn of events, Gentle Reader, and for reasons best known to themselves, the fêted soprano Mrs Charity Philpot, née Brookes, married her husband of only one month, Mr Griffith Philpot, for the second time again yesterday in Bloomsbury just hours after she performed in The Marriage of Figaro *for the last time.*

In another break with convention, the bride wore a daring gown of bold scarlet silk, which she had apparently borrowed from her eldest sister, the like of which had never been seen beneath the hallowed spire of St George's before.

Also wearing red, her sisters, the Viscountess of Eastwood and the Marchioness of Thundersley, and her recently married best friend Mrs Sinclair acted as her bridesmaids.

Once the vows were said, Mrs Roberta Brookes delighted the congregation with a romantic medley of operatic arias while a dozen white doves flew above the congregation.

After the service two hundred people attended the lavish wedding celebrations where, I am told, the now twice-married Mr and Mrs Philpot waltzed together exclusively until midnight, when they left in his curricle.

I have it on the highest authority that the besotted young newlyweds are to honeymoon for the next month in the unlikely destination of Sheffield, while Mr Philpot rectifies a persistent problem with an exploding steam engine.

And if that wasn't enough gossip from our favourite regular scandals in Bloomsbury, it appears the boisterous celebrations continued well into the night, culminating in the ton's *favourite portraitist, Mr Augustus Brookes, being charged with a breach of the peace for causing a ruckus in his nightshirt in the middle of Bedford Place.*

Once his sons-in-law, the Viscount E. and the Marquess of T., had wrestled him into a pair of breeches, Mr B. was presented with a bill for eight pounds, four shillings and twopence, after all attempts to find the twelve turtle doves he had drunkenly pardoned and then freed from their crates failed.

Should anyone in the vicinity of Bloomsbury, or the streets thereabouts, happen to spot one of the missing birds, their furious owner has offered a significant reward for their safe return as he needs them all for another lavish society wedding tomorrow...

Whispers from Behind the Fan

—September 1815

* * * * *

*If you enjoyed this story, be sure to read
the first two books in Virginia Heath's
The Talk of the Beau Monde miniseries*

The Viscount's Unconventional Lady
The Marquess Next Door

And why not check out her other great reads

Lillian and the Irresistible Duke
Redeeming the Reclusive Earl
The Scoundrel's Bartered Bride
"Invitation to the Duke's Ball" *in
Christmas Cinderellas*